The
Broken
Elephant

For Fran

The
Broken
Elephant

Hope you
enjoy the
book!

Paul Francis

Paul
Francis

BREWIN BOOKS

BREWIN BOOKS
19 Enfield Ind. Estate,
Redditch,
Worcestershire,
B97 6BY
www.brewinbooks.com

Published by Brewin Books 2019

A CIP catalogue record for this book is available
from the British Library.

ISBN: 978-1-85858-706-6

Cover art by Lucy Dennison.

Printed and bound in Great Britain
by Severn, Gloucester.

1

The US government sent me his war medals. I keep them in a picture frame over the mantelpiece. I see them every day. Sometimes, people ask me why I have them and I say – please, sit down, would you like a cup of tea? Let me tell you how it happened...

Bangkok. Thailand. 1969

Al was in trouble. A whole heap of trouble. If I'd known how much, maybe I wouldn't have taken the job. But I needed money and I was scouting for work when we stumbled into one another at a party in the British Embassy.

'*All British residents invited to a birthday celebration for the Queen,*' the advert in the Bangkok paper said so I spruced myself up as much as possible in my low-rent digs and thought I would stand in for her Majesty, who was engaged elsewhere that evening.

Silk shirts, evening dresses and tropical suits swarmed around me as I tried to blend in, unkempt hair flopping onto the collar of an off-white jacket over denims and sandals. They were the only clothes I had. My suitcase disappeared somewhere in Malaya, slipped off the top of the Land Rover I travelled in with my friends. They went home, I stayed on. More to see, more to do.

"Matthew Benson, I'm a lawyer, pleased to meet you," I said to anyone who drifted into my orbit. "Hello, name's Benson, yes, really, I'm a lawyer."

I got polite smiles, one or two supplementary questions before people hurried away. No work offers. A pop group started to play in another of the grand rooms. I was standing alone, smiling pathetically, and about to give up when a hand grabbed my arm. I shrank away from the unexpected physical contact, expecting to find the bouncers had finally decided to throw me out. It was a man in chinos, khaki shirt, greased hair, as out of place as me. It was Al.

"You're a lawyer, right?" he said. "You speak English?"

"Yes, indeed. I am English."

"Sure as hell, ain't no guarantee, boy. Been talking to some of these guys, I could not understand a word they was saying."

I surveyed the braying masses. If not for the stifling heat, we could have been back home at one of my dad's poshest golf club events.

"No," I said. "I can understand that."

"I just said I couldn't understand it."

"I meant, I could understand you couldn't understand."

Al tightened his grip.

"You shittin' me?"

"What? No, of course not."

"I need a lawyer."

It could have been the mention of possible employment that stopped me moving away. Or perhaps the vice-like hold on my wrist. He leaned in even closer. I recoiled, worried he might have taken offence again.

"Court martial."

"My speciality," I said, poker-faced. "You're military?"

That explained why he kept glancing around. There were plenty of American soldiers in Bangkok and they did that a lot. They learned it in Vietnam. Their first instinct was to watch out for anything that could kill them.

"Yeah, I'm a goddam soldier, what, you think I work for the British Embassy looking like this, asshole? Now listen, you speak English, you're a lawyer. I need a lawyer, right?"

I realised later that 'asshole' could sometimes be a term of endearment as far as Al was concerned. Sometimes. He released his grip on my arm and pressed a card into my hand.

"Noon tomorrow," he said.

"What if I'm busy?"

"You ain't busy."

I looked at the card. The printed name was crossed out. Scrawled over in capital letters, in red ink: AL MOREAU. An address, in Banglamphu district, roughly crossed out, and another address in Chinatown, crossed out. I turned it over. A third address written on, Betty's Go Go Bar, Petchaburi Road.

"I might be interested," I said. "What's the case?"

But he was nowhere to be seen. I looked round for another drink; the waiter brought a tray. I took a glass of champagne, the waiter bowed and smiled. I had a job. Why not? I didn't know it would be one that would stay with me forever.

"Cheers, old boy," I said to myself.

The band was playing *Puppet on a String*. I went in to listen.

2

Doing my best to avoid the heavyweight punch in the face of midday sun, I ducked in and out under awnings where traders huddled, their goods piled onto the pavements, clothes, fruit, vegetables, handicrafts. Businessmen scurried by, women carried baskets on bendy bamboo poles across their shoulders. Children played, rattling cyclists breathed in clouds of exhaust smoke belched out by old Fords and VW Beetles. An Army truck growled along the dusty road, carrying fresh-faced boys desperate for fun into the city's outstretched arms. The air buzzed, like it never did in England.

Petchaburi Road was a long twisty strip of concrete with hundreds of cafes, bars and nightclubs. I scanned the vertical neon signs hanging out over the street until I spotted Betty's Go Go Bar, its entrance doors pock-marked with beetle infestation. Or possibly, and rather worryingly, bullet holes. A window ran the length of the establishment, the lower half frosted glass like an old pub, obscuring the interior.

An informal setting for a legal meeting but definitely better than my slum. I thought I would only be there this one time. How wrong I was. Outside, several young Thai girls wearing very little were sitting on tiny plastic chairs, a couple of men smoking and chatting, eating.

"Morning, ladies," I said. "Gentlemen."

The men grunted and nodded. The girls looked up from filing their nails. One spoke to me in Thai, like a songbird clearing its throat. The others giggled. I tried not to blush. I pushed open the door and at first I could see no-one in the gloom.

"Over here," a voice said.

Blinking to adjust my eyes, I made out a figure sitting on one of the stools at the corner of a long bar. The air was cooler indoors and I shivered a little as I weaved between the folding card tables and light wooden chairs. At the other end of the room, a stage came into focus, musical instruments idling, a drum kit, guitars, amplifiers. A few more girls sat around, casually holding hand-drawn numbered cards. One was dancing half-heartedly to a tinny *Good Vibrations*. A few men were scattered around the tables, drinking. I took my place next to Al.

"Mr Moreau," I said. "Not sure you got my name. Matthew Benson."

I held out a hand for him to shake. He didn't.

"Sergeant," he said. "It's Sergeant Moreau."

A Thai barman appeared, bowing and smiling.

"What'll it be?" he said in a heavily-inflected accent.

"Well," I said. "It's a little early but what I would really like is a nice pint of best bitter. Do you have any on draught?"

He smiled uncomprehendingly.

"Jesus, Mary and Joseph," Al said. "Whisky."

"Whisky," the bartender said, alighting on a familiar word. "Coming right up."

He slid me a tumbler and half-filled it with a watery sludge.

"Cheers," I said, raising the glass. It smelled foul. Al threw back his head and downed his drink in one. I knew a challenge when I saw one. This was a man's world. I guzzled down the searing liquid without pause. It burned my throat like chilli sauce. I dissolved in a spluttering fit. The barman looked worried as he wiped glasses with a dirty Souvenir of Bangkok towel.

"What the hell d'you do that for?" Al said.

"You did it first," I said, eyes streaming.

"Yeah, right," Al said. "But mine was tea."

I leaned on the bar, gasping.

"I don't drink that shit," Al said.

"Very sensible."

I took deep gulps of the air, Lucky Strike smoky from the night before, an aftertaste of strong perfume and weak beer.

"I ain't got long, I got somewhere I got to be," Al said, seemingly unconcerned by my continued suffering. He always had somewhere else he had got to be. "They want me busted bad. Military lawyer wants me to plead guilty."

I looked at him reflected in the streaky mirror of polished metal behind the optics. He was maybe in his mid-thirties, about ten years older than me, his face lined and leathered.

"You listening? Law says I can hire a civilian if I can afford it. I can afford it. Need one speaks English."

He ran his stony gaze over me, weighing me up. I thought I detected hope there, tempered by a slight doubt.

"I guess you're the only one in town," he said.

The whisky turned back around and crept into my temples. I nodded but the movement hurt.

"For a lawyer, you don't say much."

I pointed at my throat, which had constricted to the point I was capable only of croaking.

"Need a top guy," he said.

I pointed to myself with enthusiasm, wheezed, "Me."

He continued his disconcerting perusal.

"What's with the hippy clothes?"

"Suit. Cleaners. Bathroom?"

He nodded towards an uninviting dark corner. I fell off the stool and headed past the stage. The tired girls followed my staggering progress with amusement. The restroom was like the one in my apartment block, unhygienic toilet, broken glass on the flooded floor, grimy washbasin. I splashed brown water on my face, dared to drink a little of it, and examined myself in what remained of the mirror. Okay, Benson, you are the super slick civilian lawyer he needs to hire. With a law degree. Fully qualified. Well prepared to tackle the US army's judicial system. This couldn't be hard. I thought it best not to tell Al the truth. He would be my first ever client. This would be my first ever case.

Trying to appear as efficient and hard-ball as possible, I strode back into the bar and looked around. A guitar chord rang out, startled me. The band was setting up. No sign of Al. Panic. My only meal ticket, already gone. He must have seen through my disguise, spotted my callowness, fired me before I had even started. I hurried back to question the smiling waiter, who politely indicated on the sticky bar a large brown envelope with my empty glass on top. Inside, documents with legal headings – one looked like a charge sheet – but, best of all, money. A pile of Thai banknotes. Al was employing me.

"Didn't happen to say where he was going, I suppose?" I asked the bartender.

"Whisky," he said. "Coming right up."

3

"Throw the elephant. Goddam it, throw that elephant!"

The inevitable punch of heat stopped me in my tracks as I stepped out of the relative cool of the bar. No sign of Al but two young crew-cut Western men were sprinting in my direction.

"They're gaining on us," the man in front said over his shoulder. "For Chrissakes, lose the elephant."

Behind them, in pursuit, a middle-aged man and two Thai police officers, shouting what must have been the equivalent of "stop, thief". I moved aside, clutching my precious envelope, and the leading pair hurtled past. I could see why the first man was so insistent – his companion was considerably encumbered by a sizeable wooden elephant clutched under his arm. He finally heeded the advice and hurled his elephant recklessly around a corner. There was a short cry of pain.

"Sorry," he shouted and carried on running. The police and the man, presumably a shopkeeper chasing stolen goods, passed by. I joined a small crowd of interested locals peering into the alley where a young woman in shorts was on the ground, clutching her knee. There was much chatter but little in the way of actual assistance. I stepped forward.

"I say, are you all right?"

She looked up at me and smiled and right there, in a pop song missed heartbeat, I had another compelling reason to stay in the city.

"I guess so," she said. "Jeez, I did not see that coming."

She had a soft American accent, her brown hair was tied back in a headscarf with a floral print. Open-mouthed, I held out my hand. She took it, hauling herself to her feet.

"Thanks. I think I'll be fine."

She let go but then wobbled as she put weight on her damaged leg and fell against me.

"Ow," she said. "Poor thing."

"I'm sure you'll be okay," I said, wondering why she was talking in the third person and trying not to peer too obviously at her knee. "It's just a bruise."

She laughed, lightly, beautifully.

"I meant the elephant, silly."

The carved statue was indeed a sorry state as it lay trunkless in the litter and dust. The shopkeeper returned and, horrified, scooped it up. I conceived a grand gesture. I was, after all, suddenly a bit flush.

"How much?" I said, indicating the body he had in one hand and the trunk in the other.

"You buy?" he said, delighted. I fished around in the envelope, trying to count the notes by touch while keeping them concealed. I pulled out a handful I estimated might cover the cost. The shopkeeper's face lit up. He grabbed them, thrust the components of the elephant at me and made good his escape without the usual haggling. I suspected my payment may have been a little over the odds.

"But it's broken," she said. "What are you going to do with it?"

"Mend it," I said. "And then I'll give it to you."

She leaned on my shoulder with both hands, injured leg on tiptoe, looking straight at me. With those eyes.

"Yeah?" she said. "What if I don't want it?"

4

I loaded her gently into the back seat of a cab. A delightful fleeting encounter destined to be gone in the blink of a traffic indicator. I searched for the words to prolong it. Smitten, I couldn't find any but dopily flapped my lips. I watched helplessly as the driver prepared to whisk her away to whichever enchanted castle was her usual residence. She wound down her window.

"So when can I get my elephant?" she said.

I ran alongside the cab for a few paces, dodging the rickshaws, holding onto the door despite the cabbie's protests, setting a time and place with her for the broken elephant transaction.

"What's your name?" I called, halting out of breath as the cab dodged into the heaving traffic. I barely heard it as she called back, borne on a sudden wispy fragrant breeze. *Loretta*.

I danced and skipped back to my digs, up the jumbly stairs through the ghost train corridor to my room. Even the smell of sewage and dogs and rotting flesh could not sour the moment. What a day. I started to compose a letter in my head, "Dear dad, I got a job. No, not working in a bar. As a lawyer, like I said I would." There's more. "I fell in love with the most wonderful girl." No, not that, possibly overstating the case after one brief exchange. "Dad, I'm sorry." I couldn't say that either. Because, hell, I wasn't.

I lay sweating on my iron-framed bed, packing what turned out to be the rather meagre remains of the cash into my rucksack and the elephant into a jute bag. I intended to carry all my belongings with me whenever I stepped gratefully outside this chamber of horrors. A mosquito buzzed against the torn curtains. I watched a cockroach sidle across the tattered rug and thought I heard whispered voices outside my door.

"*Farang.*"

Foreigner. Scary mumbling, indecipherable. A sound like the sharpening of a machete. On human bone, probably. The place was like my old halls of residence, only with architectural input from Salvador Dali. Life is safer when you're not on your own. My friends were gone. All I had were the cockroach and a little lizard who lived on a top corner of the cracked wall, his conversation limited when we strayed from the subject of eating flies. I shushed them both, listening out for further plotting. All quiet. Must have been my imagination. I dismissed the persistent fear for the moment. Time to get to work.

"Okay, everyone, first item on the agenda," I said to my room mates. "A court martial. This is going to look so good on the old curriculum vitae for Benson, Cockroach and Lizard."

Not a bad name for a law firm. I was chuckling as I skimmed the first page of Al's letter. A chap called Captain Travis McMichael, presumably the military lawyer, was inviting my client to a further meeting at the Justice Centre. There was to be an expedited court hearing under the US Code of Military Conduct, didn't know what that statute was, made a note to find out and to set up the meeting with McMichael. So far, so good. Then I read the charge sheets.

Sometimes, a cloud over the sun in South East Asia came as a relief. It eased one's senses. This was not that kind of cloud. With perhaps an element of wishful thinking, I had assumed Al was up for some minor misdemeanour. A small fracas, perhaps, a punch-up, insubordination seemed likely. I could deal with that.

Then the charges fell. A monsoon. Al was a golly gosh hell's bells one-man tidal crime wave. Misappropriation of US government property, fraud, theft, illegal sale of an earth-moving vehicle, handling a stolen two-and-a-half-ton truck, currency manipulation in three countries, sale of electrical goods, all US government issue. Theft of a jeep, two jeeps, no, wait, five altogether. It was a surprise anything shipped out to Vietnam found its way to the front line past Al's grasping hands. The cockroach laughed. The lizard looked like he was about to hand in his notice.

"Dad, I got a job. Help me!"

5

"Not guilty," Al said.

He had appeared next to me at the bar in Betty's, lacking only a puff of magic smoke to herald his arrival.

"Possibly need a little more defence? For instance, on what grounds?"

He asked for a glass of tea. The barman, same guy as before, smiled and asked if I wanted a whisky. I ordered a Pepsi.

"Charges are bull," Al said.

"Right. As in, not credible?"

Hurrying over as quickly as I could with my bags, I had tried to start thinking like a crime lawyer, like my dad. I intended to advise Al that he should seriously consider a guilty plea at the earliest opportunity, save the court time and trouble, hope it would make a difference to the eventual sentence. We would be asking for mercy. I guessed that was something Al wasn't used to.

"Like I just said."

There were more customers in the dimly lit bar towards the evening, young Americans mostly, servicemen, in civilian clothes. A recording of some jazz was playing softly, the band members were on the stage, fiddling with instruments, a few girls got up to dance, prominently displaying their numbers. They seemed to be under the direction of an older woman draped in a silk kaftan.

"Who is Captain McMichael?"

Al snorted.

"He's an asshole."

"I rather thought he might be."

Al gave his "don't shit me, boy" look sideways.

"Army lawyer," he said. "Wanted me to plead guilty, take a deal."

This did not appear an altogether ill-advised move, in fact, it was uppermost in my mind, though clearly not in Al's.

"And the deal was?"

"Busted from sergeant E8 to E5, cuts my pension, four years home in Fort Leavenworth."

"Fort Leavenworth. Don't know it, nice place?"

"It's a prison."

Dumb move on my part. I really had to get to grips with the terminology.

"Ask you a couple questions," Al said. The woman in the kaftan came gliding towards us, smoking a black cigarette through a silver cigarette holder. Heads turned. Everybody watched her. It was impossible not to.

"Okay."

"You know what a fight is, boy?"

I hesitated. I had, of course, seen the occasional scrap, at school, once in the street. Al's level of fighting was some way beyond that. He did it for a living and if he was looking for a man to stand by his side, maybe that wasn't me. This was the moment when I could have said, no, Al, this is my first case, it's so far out of my league, it's on another planet, bye bye, but something in the tone of his voice stopped me, this tough man, with his sun blasted face and for a second, in his watchful eyes, a hint of vulnerability. He was, in his own way, pleading for my help because I was the only one he knew to get him out of the hole he had dug. Crazy.

"How's it going, baby?" he said, before I had chance to answer. I was a little taken aback but he wasn't talking to me, he was talking to the woman who had come up behind us and brushed her non-cigarette fingers lightly across his shoulders.

"Moreau," she said in a US-accented drawling Oriental voice that nearly melted the ice in my drink. "Introduce me?"

"My lawyer," Al said, touching her hand. "He's a friend of mine."

I took a slug of the Pepsi. Friend of mine. That was it; I couldn't walk away. One of the customers wolf-whistled and called out "Betty, honey." The woman smiled at me. I felt like the sun had dipped out of the sky and kissed me. She turned and floated across through the card tables towards the customers, like she was about to give a Papal blessing.

"Second thing is," Al said. "Why the hell are you carrying that elephant around?"

My bags were tucked by my feet for safe keeping.

"For a girl."

Al nodded, like he understood that was the only reason anybody ever needed.

"You see why I told him no?" Al said. "You see why I can't take the deal?"

"I suppose. Well, actually, quite frankly, I can't."

Al drained the last of his tea and carefully put down his glass, watching it all the way. There was a slight rattle from a shake in his hand as the glass hit the bar top.

"They kick me out, I got nothing."

He was looking at me but staring into his future and he couldn't see it, not without the sound of the marching boots, the raw smell of the olive drab uniform, the crack and zing of bullets, the shouts and cries of the men around him, his men, soldier men.

"Army is my life," he said, and looked away. "Boy."

6

After a night spent with the rucksack tucked under my pillow and my feet on the elephant bag, I took a cab to the grandly-named Justice Centre, a two-storey concrete block on the outskirts of the main city that failed to live up to its superhero comic book title. It was low profile, apart from the US flag flying from its roof and looked like it had been commandeered from some other enterprise, possibly a failed small business selling cheap kitchen equipment.

"Captain McMichael, please," I said to the young lieutenant at the front desk.

"Who shall I say is calling?" he said. In front of him, he had a line of small balls of screwed up paper he had been lobbing basketball style into a waste bin when I walked in. He seemed irritated by my interruption.

"I'm a lawyer," I said.

A look of disbelief crossed his face as he surveyed my crumpled white jacket and jeans, my sandals, the rucksack I carried instead of a briefcase, a bag with an elephant sticking out of the top. I really had to buy some new clothes.

"You're a lawyer?"

"Yes."

The soldier shrugged, picked up a phone.

"Captain McMichael? Guy here to see you, Sir. Says he's a lawyer.

No, I don't think he's selling anything, no, wait, Sir, he's selling second-hand wooden elephants."

I leaned forward.

"Tell him I'm representing Al Moreau."

"Says he's representing a guy called Moreau?" There was a pause. The lieutenant put the phone down.

"Go on through that door there. Captain McMichael will meet you."

He leaned back in his chair. I left my bags with him and I was tempted for a second to pick up one of the balls of paper and shoot it into the bin. I had not opened the batting and fielded at slip for the school Second Eleven for nothing. But I didn't. I might have missed. He went back to his game as I pushed through swing doors into a corridor where a man in a crisp smart uniform, probably late twenties, neat hair, shoulders back, was waiting, carrying a file of papers. He seemed flustered, busy, he looked at me uncertainly.

"Can I help you?" he said.

"Matthew Benson," I said. "I'm representing Sergeant Moreau."

"You're representing him? At what?"

"In the trial."

McMichael hesitated, looking me up and down, then showed me through into a stuffy small office with filing cabinets and a desk with two chairs.

"We have US Army lawyers. Right here, in this building, a lot of them. Are you a US Army lawyer?"

"Sergeant Moreau has a right to counsel. It's in your Constitution."

I had been dredging up all I could remember from my law degree, I couldn't remember the amendment number and I was already winging it a little.

"You're telling me what's in the US Constitution?"

"Only what you should know already."

I had decided to play this on the front foot, to go right after it. I didn't know what McMichael was like, except in Al's undoubtedly jaundiced view, so I wanted to show him I would take no nonsense from the start.

"It's a military case. It's a general court martial," he said.

"Exactly, it's an adversarial process. Sergeant Moreau is innocent…"

At this, he made a kind of choking sound and seemed to be struggling for breath. He waved his hand for me to continue as he recovered himself.

"…until proven guilty and he has engaged me because he is entitled to be represented by anyone of his choice, including a civilian lawyer."

At least, that's what Al had told me. I had no idea if he was right or not and I wished I felt as confident as I sounded. At least I was still in the room. I had not been shown the door, though it had stayed open and I had attracted puzzled glances from several uniformed men as they hurried past. I had ignored them, concentrated on McMichael.

"I was working this case, Mr Benson, I didn't know Moreau had hired another lawyer though he did indicate he was unhappy with my professional assessment."

To put it mildly, probably. McMichael checked his papers.

"There's a plea hearing set for Thursday this week. Eleven am. I'm going to have to check this out. Talk to the judicial body first, I guess. Maybe the Pentagon."

He spoke quickly, leaving no room for interruption. The Pentagon. He had sent down his fastest ball. I sighed impatiently, shrugged it off.

"How long will that take? I have other urgent appointments."

I was due to meet Loretta. Also, I didn't want to stay in that building a second longer than I had to in case someone called my bluff.

"And the prosecutors. I'll have to run this past them," he said.

"Perhaps you could give me their names? I always like to know who I'm dealing with."

"Blaine Soames is in chief, Todd Raniero is second chair. Both also US Army Captains. You want to write those names down?"

He could see me fishing in my pockets for the pen I hadn't got and held out his Army issue biro.

"Paper?" he said, tearing a page from his notebook.

"Thank you. I seem to have left everything in my other suit."

He nodded, watched me write, took his pen back.

"This is an unusual scenario we have here, Mr Benson. Where can I reach you?"

This was something I had not considered. There was only one place I could think of.

"You can reach me here." As matter-of-factly as I could, I took Al's card out of my pocket and showed it to him. "There's a telephone number on there."

He waited with his pen poised and then looked at me with a raised eyebrow as if he was now thinking this was some big joke.

"Betty's Go Go Bar? That's your office?"

"Temporary. A correspondence address."

"Betty's Go Go Bar," he repeated slowly and deliberately as he wrote it down and then stood up, indicating the interview was over.

"If I don't hear from you, I'll see you in court with Sergeant Moreau," I said.

"Let's not get ahead of ourselves here. That's got to be checked out."

"At the Pentagon?"

"It's a situation I have not come across before. I don't have the authority to make a decision."

"If you must," I said, sighing, as if this was all becoming a minor nuisance. "I can see no obstacle. I take it the courtroom is somewhere attached to this building?"

It didn't seem like a bad guess and he nodded, still uncertain of what he could say to this intruder into his neat circle of lawyers.

"Good day," I said. I didn't look back, I was smiling inside, I had been good, I had been damn good, and I pushed back through the swing doors. The Lieutenant sprang upright until he saw it was just me and then he went back to lobbing paper balls into the basket while I regained my belongings.

I picked one of the paper balls up as I passed his desk and flipped it sideways; for a second I could see the batsman struggling to gain the crease, if it hit the wickets, he was run out, St Bertram's would win the game on a sunny late afternoon with the green fields stretching down to the river and the whole school watching. The paper ball arced towards the bin. It hit the rim. It rolled around. It dropped into the centre. The Lieutenant whooped. I walked on, clenched my fist and punched the sky.

7

The flower market near the river bridge was the only place I could think of in a hurry, which on reflection had not been a great idea. There was hardly room to breathe and I struggled with my bags through the crowds, trying to get close to the river, the Chao Phraya, the winding backbone of the city. Stalls screamed with colour, all kinds of blooms, floral scents hung in the air.

"You're the prettiest flower in the market," I mumbled, practising. No, stupid. And cheesy, for goodness sake. I reached the bridge, jumped up a few steps to get a better angle but I couldn't see her. She probably had better things to do. Long-tailed boats sailed by. I peered across the sea of faces. There were other foreigners, young men mostly, wide-eyed, being shown around by girls, this was a popular stop on the trail of sights.

"Fixed it yet?" There she was, a few steps below me. She was wearing the headscarf, sunglasses this time.

"You came," I said.

"Hi."

"Hello. You're the…" I stopped myself just in time. "How's the knee?"

"It's fine," she said. "I put some arnica on it."

She kicked out her leg to show me, almost tripped a woman carrying two enormous baskets loaded with flowers and reached forward quickly to apologise. The woman smiled and carried on and Loretta put a hand to her mouth and laughed.

"Let's go this way," she said, weaving through the crowd, pointing at the stalls, making comments I couldn't hear above the chatter, courteously fending off hustlers and traders. I stumbled inelegantly in her wake like a humble and devoted porter, trying not to clip too many people with the elephant. In a lull, I heard her say something about dating, not sure what it was.

"I don't think I've ever been on a date," I said, hurrying to get alongside to join in the conversation with my fatuous remark. She stopped. I bumped into her.

"You've never been out with a girl?"

"Well, yes, of course, numerous times, but we don't call it a date in England."

"Is that so? This is your first date?"

"I suppose it is."

"Then it will be my first date, too," she said. "Like being in fifth grade."

She made her eyes big and put a finger coyly to the dimple in her chin and made like she was nervous.

"Hey, Scooter, you wanna go on a date?" she said in a high-pitched voice and she laughed, and we carried on walking. "I gotta tell you, Scooter, I don't make out on a first date. Not that kind of girl."

"Disappointing," I said. "Free love and all that."

"Not at my store, baby."

My repartee had swiftly run out, along with my breath.

"Perhaps we could have a cup of tea instead?"

"That sounds like a charming idea, old boy."

We sat down at a tea stall, awkwardly on brightly coloured plastic chairs that were much too small. The waiter hurried over and took our order for two iced ginger teas. We watched the wooden boats tightly packed on this stretch of the river off shoot, the rooftops of the small houses and the shops angling down above the water's edge. Flat bottomed boats carrying colourful spices punted by, the aroma wafting up from the filthy water. I bought a single damask rose from the basket of a passing tradesman and presented it to Loretta with a deep bow.

"Why, thank you, Scooter. Most gracious," she said.

She told me she was a nurse. I think I had been hoping she was a tourist, a traveller like me but not so. Her life was quite different.

"A US Army nurse." She gave a mock salute with more than a little irony in it. "Sah!"

She twirled the flower absent-mindedly between her fingers, a shadow falling across her face like a flock of B52 bombers had blocked out the sun. She looked around, scanning faces in the crowds. She did that a lot, out of nowhere, all of a sudden. I didn't wonder about it just then. Perhaps I should have.

"It was…I wanted to but I didn't, kind of," she said, shaking her head so the sunglasses slipped down her nose. She pushed them back. "Not fair. I shouldn't have come. Not ready, I'm sorry."

She got up to leave, accidentally tipping over the tiny chair. The waiter dashed across and fussed over putting it upright. She held out the flower to give it back to me.

"Wait," I said, trying to think of a persuasive argument to make her stay. I pointed to the elephant, head sticking out of the bag. "If you go, what happens to him?"

If she had gone then, I knew it would be for good. I didn't want that. I wanted another hour, another minute even. Another second.

"Elephant blackmail," she said. "That's a low trick."

"I can stoop lower."

"Yeah?"

"Yeah."

She hesitated, then sat down again, almost toppling off the chair. I reached out to stop her falling and so did the waiter, hovering nearby, clearly worried she was incapable of staying seated on his child sized furniture.

"Okay, Scooter," she said. "But get this, I'm not staying for you, I'm staying for him."

She waved the rose towards the elephant. I nodded in agreement. As a distraction from whatever was troubling her, I told her a little about what I was doing there, about the case, about Al, fellow American. She expressed a keen interest.

"I would never have guessed that. You're a lawyer, Jeez."

"Thanks."

"I mean, I didn't think you were, like, a professional. Just a guy. Not military, just a guy."

"Some bum?"

"Right, exactly. An English bum."

"I think I need new clothes."

She checked out my stained and crumpled attire.

"You need new clothes."

We found a stall hung with all kinds of vestments where the eager gap-toothed trader waved us into the relative cool under his awning.

"You're kinda tall," Loretta said, rifling through the jackets. "Get the biggest size they got here, okay, how about this one?"

It was linen, off-white. Loretta rummaged through the trousers and produced a matching pair.

"Perfect," she said.

"Does he have a changing room?"

"What do you think?"

"Then how do I know if they fit?"

"Try them on here, don't worry, I'll turn around and close my eyes."

Loretta turned her back and made a show of putting her hand over her sunglasses. I shuffled into a darker corner, eased off my sandals and stepped out of my trousers.

"No peeking," I said.

"Uh-huh, believe me, I would not want to do that, Scooter."

The new ones were light, a little baggy perhaps but comfortable. Loretta turned around and nodded approvingly so I delved into my rucksack in search of the required payment. We haggled, Loretta had a grip on this, unlike me, and she insisted the guy throw in some soft brown shoes with the price. I gave him some notes. He looked at them and held out his hand again.

"Not enough," Loretta said.

"I have more, wait." I stuck my hand into the rucksack but I couldn't locate the remaining notes among my few belongings.

"Here," Loretta said.

She handed over the rest and the trader smiled and bowed as we left.

"Really, that's too kind. It's embarrassing. I have the money."

"Sure. And a new suit. And shoes."

There was a brief eddy in the crowds and she turned to look at me, straightening the lapels of my jacket.

"You owe me," she said. "Cash."

She tapped me on the nose with the flower.

"And a fully fixed elephant."

She smiled and took off her sunglasses.

"You're paying, Scooter," she said. "Next time."

8

Al's interest in motor vehicles of all kinds, mostly stolen, had given me an idea and I was to meet him at the small garage where we had all tearfully abandoned Mary Jane, the Land Rover that had been our home for four months, my friends now back home, Pete, Alfie, Mike and me. The Riders on the Storm, we had christened ourselves, though Riders on a Light Shower might have been more accurate. My hastily conceived plan was two-fold – Al could help me with the sale and I could get him in a quiet place long enough to discuss the case. We needed a strategy and we didn't have much time, in fact, we had no time. The hearing was scheduled for next day.

The garage was a small corrugated iron workshop on the edge of dusty waste ground, home to a few scrap cars. My heart leapt for the second time that day – there was my second love, Mary Jane, resting serenely if a little forlornly among her fellow retirees. We had slept in her, quarrelled in her, sung in her. I had all my things with me. I could just get back into my beauty and drive. Keep the adventure going, flee this ridiculous job. Then Al instantly appeared, like a woodland sprite, albeit one with a chequered past. He gave Mary Jane the once-over, like he was assessing the value of a prize steer or whatever he would have done back where he came from.

"You drove here in this piece of crap?" he said, without compassion.

"That piece of crap is my beloved Mary Jane," I said.

She was a bit dented, admittedly, the worse for wear, scratches, the result of a near disaster in Germany, the windscreen had a crack but the cage bars on the top were intact except for the gap my suitcase had slipped through.

"You want me to find you a mug, right?"

"A discerning collector, I thought."

Al sauntered over to the workshop. I dropped my bags in the shade of a wall and sat on my rucksack, dreaming of my next date with Loretta and wondering how I could get Al to stand still. He came back, tossing the car keys from one hand to the other.

"Okay, garage guy just wants it off his lot. Giving the place a bad name and that's saying something," Al said, indicating the other broken-down inhabitants. "I know a lot of guys, see if anybody's fool enough to suck it up."

"That's very good of you. While we're here, I was hoping for a moment to talk about the court hearing? You do know it's tomorrow?"

"Yeah, I know."

"Then give me something I can work with."

"Sure," he said. "Later. Not now. I got somewhere I got to be."

I hurried after him with my bags.

"Why are you avoiding this?" I said but he had stopped listening already, pointing to Mary Jane's nearside wheel.

"What the hell?" he said.

Not wishing to draw attention to ourselves by painting the Land Rover in psychedelic Carnaby Street swirls and flowers, like some VW vans we had seen on the way, we had written "Freedom" in small letters in white paint and an arrow pointing forward just above the wheel arch. We had rather liked this understated expression of intent.

"That's a real polite revolution," Al said. "You know what freedom is?"

"I've studied it."

"You don't find freedom in a book, boy, you find freedom down the barrel of a gun. It's what those people in Vietnam are fighting for."

This was clearly a subject on which Al had first-hand knowledge. Nevertheless, I felt I had to defend my position. I was, after all, university-educated and had once taken part in a debate on the subject in Great Hall. And I watched TV.

"Which side?" I said.

"You crazy? Only one side fighting for freedom, boy."

I had the feeling he was going to ask me if I was a damned Commie, you a Commie, boy, you sure look like a Commie. Like that, like a parody of John Wayne. But he just shook his head in apparent despair and headed for the driver's door.

"You sure you don't want me to drive?" I said.

He stopped and looked at me as if I had just volunteered to lead a tank division into enemy territory.

"The wheel is on the right-hand side. It's a stick shift," I said.

"Yeah?" he said, opening the driver's door.

"Just thought it would be easier if I drove, that's all."

"Don't worry about it." He climbed in and started the engine. I threw my bags in the back and got into the passenger seat. It moulded itself around me in a familiar hug.

"You still carrying those bags around?" Al said, gunning the accelerator furiously.

"I don't want to leave them in my accommodation."

"Accommodation, huh? Big word. Me, I'm a small word guy."

Al skidded off the foreground, swerved expertly in and out of the dodgem traffic, driving one-handed on the wheel, leaning on the horn like everybody else when required and especially when it wasn't, the ever-present tooting background noise of South East Asia. Getting behind the wheel and spinning in the traffic maelstrom appeared to relax him.

"Duck," he shouted. I flinched and slunk down in my seat. Al laughed. "Shoot. Run. Find the little words are best, know what I'm saying?"

"Very funny," I said. "It is, however, quite a different line of work."

"Ain't that the truth. Tell you what we're gonna do here, take you to Betty's. Betty's got accomm-o-dation. Hey, man, what the hell kind of driving was that?"

He jammed on the brakes. The wipers rattled on the dirt and insect-smeared windscreen. If I moved in to Betty's, I would be living above the shop, so to speak. I couldn't get away. But at least I would know where I could find Al. And I would be safe. More or less. Though judging from the state of the downstairs toilets, Betty's dedication to cleanliness was not of the highest order. I was considering this and almost missed Al talking about the case.

"You wanna know what it was, here's what it was, ran me an Army motor pool," Al said. "Near Saigon. Ve-hicles in ve-hicles out, all kinds. I had a hundred guys."

Some facts, along with vehicles pronounced like it was two whole words. I chose not to correct him as he was in, for Al, full flow. Basic, perhaps, but it was a start. Al leaned on the horn and stuck his head through the open window, shouting something in Thai. The radio was still on a local station we had discovered on the approach to the city, playing mainly Western pop music. *Hey, Joe* came on.

"Hendrix, man," Al said.

"And what happened?"

Al sang to the radio. I joined in. Loved that song. Still do. Still play it now. I have my turntable still and my JVC 30 watts per channel amp and I put on the scratched album and listen to it rock.

"Gave me a rear job, assholes," Al said. "Lot of guys want rear jobs. Not me. Yeah, that's what happened. They took me off the front line."

Motive. Opportunity. We were getting somewhere but I couldn't see how he had gone from that to the scale of criminality alleged in the documents.

"That's all very well but how does that result in the charges?" I asked as we sped around a corner and I had to grip the door handle and there was Betty's bar ahead of us. Al pulled the Land Rover onto the side of the road, kicking up dirt and causing the group of men and girls to look up in alarm from their seats by the door. They saw it was Al, didn't seem surprised at his startling arrival and nodded and waved a general greeting, before going back to whatever they were doing. Waiting, eating, smoking.

"Talk to Betty, settle in," Al said. "Me, I'm going to dump this crock somewhere before anybody else sees me driving it. I know a lot of guys. See if I can get some dumb-ass to buy it."

I got out with my bags and stood in front of what could be my new home. Al leaned over.

"Nice suit."

He drove off.

9

My new rooms were palatial in comparison to my old place, though admittedly that wasn't difficult. They had a bathroom with a shower. A separate living space with Thai wall hangings. And a bedroom. A little noisy from the road incessantly grinding by and the music downstairs and the neon signs would still be flashing outside but this was luxury living and rather surprising given the condition of the rest of Betty's place. The proprietress herself had escorted me up one flight up the dingy back stairs and shown me around, waving away the question of rent.

"You take care of Moreau. Moreau takes care of me," was all she said, ignoring my protestations that I needed an indication in order to budget.

"Mister Matthew," she said simply, smiling, sprinkling my name with spices, tapping me on the cheek with her fingernails like she was petting a stray puppy. I decided not to pursue the vulgar question of money at that juncture, grateful merely to be in relative comfort, so much so that I swooned into a dreamless state, overslept and arrived a little breathlessly outside the courtroom the following day.

"Improperly dressed. Got a tie?" McMichael said.

I put my hand up to my open-necked shirt and realised I was short of this one vital piece of sartorial equipment.

"I'll get you a spare. You're not sitting next to me with no tie."

"Why would I be sitting next to you?"

"I've been in touch with the Pentagon. Military HQ in the States? Top brass?"

"Of course, I know what the Pentagon is," I said, though I had never expected my name to be reverberating around its corridors. "What's going on?"

"I'm still waiting to hear back definitively in the affirmative about your admissibility in this case. They want me to hold your hand."

"You're kidding me," I said. "The hearing is due to start."

"They insist on you having an Army lawyer alongside."

Al appeared next to me from nowhere. I hadn't seen him as I dashed out of Betty's and hailed a cab or I could have escorted him to court, made sure he got there. I needn't have worried, he was on time, smart in his dress uniform.

"What's this guy doing here?" he said, indicating McMichael.

"Morning, Sergeant," McMichael said.

"Morning," Al said. "Sir."

He managed to make it sound as if he had just scraped the word off his shoe.

"I'll get you your tie," McMichael said, turning back towards his office, sensing we might need a moment for an attorney client discussion.

"Army command wants him in with us," I said.

"It's a frame, goddammit. You know this is the asshole wants me to take a deal?"

It didn't bother him that McMichael was still in earshot. I hoped the tie would match my suit.

"I can handle it," I said to Al, omitting the fact that I had not been given clearance to participate. He was running his tongue nervously around his lips. In this arena, he was way out of his depth. Indoors, in the Justice Centre, this was not his normal area of operations. Suspicious of everyone, looking for someone to trust. McMichael returned and handed me my tie. A poorly chosen light blue. I decided not to complain.

"Benson is not a military man," he said to Al. "I will be second chair, co-counsel. I'm going to tell him what he needs to know. Okay?"

I edged towards the door. I wanted to go in ahead of the others. My stomach might have been churning but it was still a moment to savour. I took a deep breath and my first steps through the double doors of a real live court room. Ahead of us was a raised dais with an American eagle, the Great Seal of the United States, on the front of it, partially obscured by the court clerk, and to his side, a stenographer. Behind it, a huge Stars and Stripes was tacked to the wall.

We walked along a centre aisle through three rows of benches and McMichael steered us towards an empty desk to the left at the front. Across the aisle, the two prosecutors were already in place. They didn't turn around. The room was windowless. A wooden-bladed fan purred softly and ineffectually in the ceiling. A military policeman stood by the double doors we had come through, another by a door near the judge's dais, both carrying side arms. I sucked in some of the clammy air. I felt like I was going into the headmaster's study to be beaten up by highly-trained prefects.

"Watch me. When I stand up, stand up. When I sit down, sit down," McMichael said.

"What's this?" I said. "Simon says? I do know when to stand up, thank you."

I heard a chair scrape back on the tiles and one of the prosecutors appeared in the aisle.

"Morning, Travis," he said to McMichael, who studiously ignored him. "Introduce me to your new friend?"

I stood and reached out to shake hands.

"Matthew Benson," I said.

"Todd Raniero." He had a sharp face and a sharper accent. "Captain Raniero."

The military always made sure everyone knew their rank, straight away, all the time. It didn't matter to me; I wasn't part of all that.

"A pleasure," I said.

The other man seated at the desk gave me a short wave and what seemed a genuine toothy smile.

"Captain Blaine Soames, Sir. Howdy."

His accent was softer, more Southern, I guessed, more like Loretta's. I returned the greeting. McMichael leaned over to me.

"Careful, Benson," he said. "They're pros. They'll try and get in your head."

They appeared initially like very nice chaps but I supposed that was the intention and took note of McMichael's warning. I ran a finger around the inside of my collar. It came out soaking wet. I was way beyond nervous now. These two guys were in their element; I was a flyweight who had just got into the ring with Cassius Clay. Raniero went back to his seat as the door to the side opened and a man in his fifties, grey hair, stout, a face like a mountainside, strode in, judge's robes flapping open over his uniform. McMichael groaned softly. The clerk announced the court was in session with Major Bill Jackson presiding.

"Well, gentlemen, what are we doing today?" the judge said. Soames got to his feet.

"Plea hearing, Sir," he said. "Sergeant Moreau is facing serious charges and the prosecution would wish for him to be arraigned, Sir."

The judge looked across to us. His eyes narrowed as he scanned from Al on the outside across to McMichael on the inside, skipping over me in the middle and then darting back. He indicated with a look that one of us should address him. McMichael nudged me.

"Stand up."

I swallowed hard and pushed myself to my feet.

"I appear for the defence," I said. McMichael tugged my sleeve.

"Your Honour. Or Judge. Call him something," he hissed.

"I appear for the defence, Your Honour Judge," I stuttered. Oh, Jesus. "We are ready to proceed."

"And you are?"

"Matthew Benson, your Judge." I squeezed my eyes shut, wishing at that moment to be whisked away on the back of a unicorn to some far-off land, never to return. Raniero made no real effort to stifle a laugh behind his hand.

"You are not an Army lawyer," the judge said. "You are not, as far as I can tell, even an American. What are you doing in my courtroom?"

"I have been instructed by my client to appear on his behalf in these proceedings. Judge."

"Can he do that?" The judge looked at Soames.

"The final verification is pending, Your Honour, but it seems so."

"What's wrong with Army lawyers?" the judge said. "They do a damn fine job. A damn fine job."

"I don't doubt it, Your Honour. My client considers a new attorney would best represent his interests and those of the court."

The judge stared at me. I stared right back. Right back, straight into his steel-hard unblinking eyes. No, these buggers were not going to intimidate me. I was there; I was going to take them all on. There was silence, apart from the occasional drip of sweat falling from my forehead onto the desk. Flies buzzed. One of the MPs shuffled his feet. The fan spun. The stenographer sat with his fingers poised over his little machine.

"Then let battle commence," the judge said.

10

McMichael and I sat back in the small office which seemed to be used for purposes that didn't easily fit into the general smooth running of the Justice Centre, like the confidential chat we were having. Jusmac, I had discovered they liked to call the building. They were fond of names like that, the US military. I was only surprised they hadn't called it Fighting Leopard Centre or something.

Throughout the hearing, Al had stood parade ground rigidly to attention, arms straight down at his sides, thumbs in line with the crease of his perfectly pressed trousers. I would have to ask him where he kept his laundry iron when we were back at Betty's. His eyes were straight ahead to the flag, looking over the top of the witness box, not at the judge, who watched him closely.

"Not guilty, Sir," he snapped out when each charge was read by the clerk. "Not guilty. Sir."

Then he had gone; he said he had some business to attend to, he had somewhere he had got to be and he would leave the legal stuff to me.

"Okay," McMichael said, flipping through a considerable pile of papers. "Here's the evidence they're going to rely on for the pre-trial hearing. My guess is they're hoping Moreau will plead guilty."

"And my guess is that he won't," I said.

"He hasn't seen the evidence yet."

"I doubt it will make any difference."

McMichael tapped his pen against his lips and considered the situation.

"If there's a trial, they will have to bring witnesses from Nam. We have a deal with Thailand to hold general court martials here to make it easier for that to happen. It's called a status of forces agreement."

He checked to see if I was following. I nodded as if I knew all that already. I didn't.

"Summary court martials are held in the field. Minor offences. That's not what we're dealing with here."

He got up, looked out in the corridor and closed the door before sitting on the edge of the desk and folding his arms.

"Moreau is one almighty bothersome cowboy," he said. "He's a highly decorated soldier and so far as I can tell they want to make an example of him, they want everybody to know no-one can get away with running the kind of black market operation he had going, Jesus Christ, you heard the charges."

He picked up one of the documents and waved it in the air.

"Look at this," he said, and flipped it towards me. "He shipped an earth-moving vehicle from his motor pool through a Hong Kong middleman and it was traced to Switzerland. Switzerland! How the hell did he do that? Don't know. But he did. You know how big those things are? And look at these – he signed for jeeps, they never saw combat, he had them painted white and he sold them on to mining companies in the Philippines."

I had a quick look before he snatched the paper away from me.

"And now he pleads not guilty and they have to bring in witnesses, somebody to give evidence against him and you know what? No-one will. He had a hundred guys in that motor pool under his command and not a single one will open their mouths to put him away."

"Why not?"

"Because they thought the sun shone out of his crooked ass. He's a great guy, he was keeping them off the front line, he was making them money. See this charge? Allowing girls on to a military site, that's a misdemeanour. Allowing the use of contraband substances on a military site. Drugs, another misdemeanour, not even a separate penalty. But it kind of shows what was going on. The place must have been like Vegas."

I got the feeling McMichael was secretly impressed. I know I was. Al was a criminal mastermind in his own niche way.

"If there's so much evidence, I'll need to see it as soon as possible."

"I can't do that." McMichael shook his head. "Not till I hear from the Pentagon."

"Then hurry it up. You're supposed to be on my side, don't forget. I didn't ask for you on this case and neither did Sergeant Moreau. You're here. Act like a lawyer."

I thought I might have gone a bit too far but at that moment the door opened and Raniero entered, grinning, carrying a huge pile of bound papers.

"What the hell do you want?" McMichael said. Raniero's face fell.

"Whoa, what's up?" he said. "I thought you might want this."

He dumped the papers down with a resounding thud that disturbed one or two of the flies that had been rummaging around on the desk. I could see a title on the front of the pile, which stood at least eighteen inches high. US Uniform Code of Military Justice. I think I had been expecting something a little less comprehensive, perhaps along the lines of the Highway Code booklet. But there it was, the tome I needed, and all the other documents. It looked more than a week's work to me.

"Little light reading for you, Benson. Enjoy," he stood and waited.

"Okay, Todd," McMichael said, scowling at the papers thoughtfully. "You've had your laugh, don't take this personally but beat it, you slimy ambulance chaser. You're interrupting a defence case conference."

Raniero held his hands up in mock surrender and backed towards the door, his smile fading.

"Only trying to help," he said.

"Mr Benson doesn't need your help," McMichael said. "He has mine."

11

Our second date. We were going to the pictures. A popular pastime in Bangkok; there were a number of picture houses showing Hollywood films, subtitled for the locals. So I took another shower with the intention of sluicing off the layer of sweat that gathered on me during every day and also because I could, because I had a shower in my rooms for the first time in months. The prospect of seeing Loretta again was exhilarating. I was singing to myself. *I Feel Free*. Cream song. I wrapped the towel around me, wondering if I could walk to the cinema or get a tuk-tuk or a cab or the tram, which would have been cheaper. We would get something to eat, too, maybe some street food from one of the stalls.

"Makin' yourself at home, boy?"

Al was sitting on the little two-seater settee, his feet up on the coffee table next to the elephant.

"What on earth?" I said, backing towards the bedroom, fumbling to cover myself with the towel. "Don't you knock?"

"I did. Guess you just didn't hear me. Elvis."

I gained the modesty of my bedroom, edging around the single bed that filled most of the space as I got dressed. I was sure I had locked the door.

"How did you get in? I mean, I know you got me the rooms but you don't live here."

Al didn't answer. I had a sudden concern that he was actually a co-tenant in my apartment and peered back around the door.

"Do you?"

He shook his head. That was a relief at least. As I returned to the living room to tie my shoes, I saw he was carrying an envelope. The kind of envelope he had previously packed with money.

"Goin' someplace?" he said.

"As a matter of fact, I was going to the cinema."

"Not working on my case then, huh?"

"How? You won't tell me anything."

"I told you plenty."

"You really haven't, actually. You've swerved my questions and all you did in court was plead not guilty, which is fine, that's your prerogative. And we can maintain that stance in the pre-trial but then we need a defence."

"None of my guys will testify?"

"As I understand it."

"Then I'm home free, right?"

He reflected on this, tapping the envelope against the table. He knew the case would rest on testimony in court but I had been thinking about it and I wasn't convinced; there must be more. They wouldn't have brought the case this far without something to fall back on. It might come down to Al taking the stand and I was increasingly uncertain as to the success of that strategy. His attitude was likely to blow up the whole thing.

"Up to a point," I said. "I don't think we can put Fort Leavenworth completely out of our minds just yet, mind you."

The mention of the prison stopped his restless tapping.

"Walls are no good for me, boy. I can't go to no jail."

I had, I admit, mentioned the prison deliberately to focus Al's mind. I didn't want him thinking he was out of the woods. However, I had underestimated the effect; I watched him calculate the options.

"You won't," I said, a little too firmly. "Not if I can help it."

At least he didn't laugh at me or anything like that, in fact, he seemed reassured.

"Fighting talk," he said.

"However, we will have to postpone this discussion," I said. "I'm going to be late."

I stood up as a hint. Al stayed where he was.

"Your girl. Where d'you meet her?"

I recounted the incident.

"Like just after you got to be my lawyer, that right?"

"Yes, what of it?"

He gave me his stare, the one that suggested I should already know the answer. I didn't.

"She's a nurse. She's been in Vietnam," I said.

"Nurse, huh?"

Al raised an eyebrow. I didn't know why; at that point, the questionable and undeserved reputation attached to nurses in Vietnam had yet to filter through to me. I checked my watch.

"Don't get me wrong, you may not be a bad looking guy or nothing, hell, I wouldn't know," Al said. "But it's what we like to call in the Army one hell of a goddam coincidence."

"That's not exclusively an Army expression, is it? Okay, say what you're thinking."

"Secret service."

I laughed.

"You think Loretta is secret service?"

"From what I hear, they was all over this investigation. CIA, too."

"The CIA?"

"Everywhere."

"Let me get this straight, you think Loretta is some honey trap? Infiltrating you through me?"

"You said it, boy."

"No, I didn't. You said it."

Al left the envelope on the table and got up.

"Best get ready," he said. "I'd like to meet her. I ain't been to the movies in a long time."

It dawned on me slowly what he was suggesting. It was not exactly the second date I had planned. I couldn't see a way to get out of it without being less than polite.

"Betty likes movies," he said. "Where at?"

"Alhambra." I was searching for a way to suggest I didn't want Al to be a gooseberry, almost told him the wrong cinema but I hadn't thought quickly enough on my feet.

"What's showing?"

"*The Graduate.*"

"Western?"

"I don't think so. It's about a kid who has an affair with an older woman."

He didn't seem impressed.

"Any horses in it?"

"I shouldn't think so."

"How about something else? Wait, I got it, Thai kick boxing?"

I flatly refused. The romance of the occasion would clearly have been marred.

"I'll go get Betty," he said. "See you there."

And he went out. I picked up the envelope. More money. He never handed it to me; we had no contract. He just left it but the delivery was up to him and this was proving lucrative work. I could maybe afford to get the elephant a professional nose job but in the meantime, I was left to reflect on the fact that he thought my paramour was working for the secret service and he would be bringing Betty to meet us at the pictures while he checked her out. I decided to take a cab so I could get there early. I wanted to warn Loretta we would be double dating.

12

The square was thronged with people, the traffic was non-stop, the tuk-tuks and the cabs with their lights on mainly ferrying people around to the bars and the hotels, the businessmen of the day giving way to the pleasure seekers of the night. I was immediately hounded by touts offering to get me tickets for the evening's performance. I waved them off, knowing that all they would do would be to buy a ticket from the box office and then charge me extra. I was onto their game.

"It's okay," Loretta said, laughing after I explained to her what was going on. She was a good sport. She had turned up, which was wonderful. "It'll be fun, I want to meet him."

"Why?" I said, before I could stop myself. I bit my lip. I was getting sucked into Al's suspicions.

"Honestly? I was kinda getting bored with just you, Scooter."

"He was so keen to see the picture," I said, choosing not to divulge the ulterior motive for Al's tagging along. "He wanted to take his girl to the movies. Just like me."

"Don't get ahead of yourself," she said. "Get in the queue."

"The queue? You mean, there's other boys?"

"No," she said. "I mean the queue to get the tickets."

She pointed over to the box office, a window near the foyer, where a line was forming.

"Maybe they won't show up," I said, hopefully, as right at that second, Al appeared with Betty hanging onto his arm, dressed in a tight blouse and mini skirt and knee high white boots like she had just stepped off the bus in the middle of London, straight out of a magazine picture for the Swinging Sixties.

"I hope we're not late, Mister Matthew," Betty said and the fluorescent lights on the buildings around us in the square glowed more brightly for a second as her voice drifted up to them. The glare exposed the lines on her face, she looked older, brittle.

"No, not at all," I said, trying to behave as if this was all perfectly normal. "Four tickets, right? I'll get them."

I introduced Loretta, who gave a small curtsey and looked sweet and charming and they all gave the little Thai greeting, hands together, head bowed so that was very jolly and I went to get the tickets, preparing to hold up four fingers in the dumb show that had served me well across other continents.

"Four," I said. "Many thanks."

The old woman behind the window selling tickets pointed to a sign offering a choice between Stalls and Circle. I hesitated. I had failed to ascertain any preference from my fellow cinemagoers. There was some shuffling in the queue behind me and a little muttering as I tried to make a choice while also looking back over my shoulder. I saw Al home in and start talking to Loretta straight away. I had to do my best to keep them away from one another, I didn't want her to get an inkling he thought she was going to stab him in the back, using me as the dagger. The woman jabbed her finger at the sign more urgently and I opted for the Stalls, though I regretted this choice as soon as I had made it. Under pressure, I found it hard to react. I knew it. My dad knew it, he had told me before about it, not to do with buying cinema tickets specifically, just with everything.

"Buddy, move it out," someone said in the queue behind.

"Terribly sorry," I said and took my tickets and moved back to the others. Betty was laughing and touching Loretta on the arm, she seemed happy to be out of the bar. I announced we would be seated in the Stalls and asked if that would be okay and nobody expressed any objection. We went into the bright lights and the chilly air conditioning of the foyer with its smell of popcorn and hot dogs and orange juice, a cavernous ceiling and crystal chandeliers hanging down, a carpeted staircase leading up to the circle, gold leaf decorating the walls. Betty and Loretta went to the Ladies room to powder their noses, as Loretta put it, chatting together like old friends, leaving Al and me standing awkwardly to the side near a poster of forthcoming attractions.

"You can't really think she's with the secret service? That's crazy, now you've seen her. Isn't it?" I said. Next week was to be *Doctor Zhivago*. The crowd dissembled around us.

"They ain't all hairy-assed gorillas, boy. All shapes and sizes, even a cute package like this one."

"A cute package?"

"Yeah."

"Betty's a cute package, too," I said, by way of simple reciprocation.

"No, she ain't, boy," Al said. "Betty's a goddam fine, handsome woman."

Betty and Loretta emerged arm in arm, like they were on the red carpet at a premiere. They were attracting looks from everyone as they went to the popcorn stand and they were with me. Me and Al. I got a warm feeling. Al was surveying the crowds, looking at the doorway as if he expected a platoon of enemy troops to come bursting in, like he always did. I nudged him to look round and appreciate our dates. He grabbed my wrist hard as soon as he felt my elbow and then quickly let it go and put his hands up.

"Instinct," he said.

I rubbed my wrist as we went into the auditorium. Not broken, at least. I made sure Al was sitting as far away from Loretta as possible, because I didn't want him going through her handbag when the lights went down, looking for clues to her spying credentials. Betty informed us that in Thai, the film title became *The Force of Unnatural Lust*, which didn't seem to be a literal translation unless their academic system was oddly calibrated. The audience was mostly groups of young Thai men out for a good time, already laughing. There were a few Westerners like us scattered around.

"Sit here?" I said and ushered Loretta in first, then dived in next to her with Betty on my other side and Al got in last, on the end of the row.

"What was he talking to you about?" I whispered to Loretta.

"Who?" she said. "Want some popcorn?"

"Al. Did he say anything? Outside? Nothing about, nothing about…anything?"

I realised I couldn't put the question without either alerting her that Al was on to her, assuming she was really working undercover, or, if she wasn't, tipping her off to his unfounded hypothesis. I just babbled a little and, not surprisingly, she looked at me as if I was a crackpot and I couldn't wait for the lights to go down. And when they did, a curious thing happened. Al shook. He jabbed back against the seat so hard the row moved. It was black dark for a second, no more, then the film flickered on and the beam of light from the projector shone across the auditorium, with dust floating in its rays. I could hear him breathing fast.

"It's okay, baby," Betty said quietly, stroking his arm, as if she was used to this. "It's okay."

In the opaque light from the projector, I could see Loretta snatching a glance across. Al took some deep breaths, wriggled a little in his seat, put his hand on Betty's to indicate he was fine. He looked around to make sure nobody had seen what had happened.

"Something wrong?" Loretta whispered to me.

"It's fine," I whispered back. We settled down. The audience laughed a lot, mostly in the wrong places or so it seemed to me.

Not to them, I gathered they had a different take on the morality. Loretta passed around the popcorn. She kept glancing across to Al. Maybe she was thinking her nursing skills would be useful. Maybe she was looking for some other signs of weakness. She didn't hold my hand, like I had hoped. We watched the film, the tired old soldier, the bar keeper, the secret service agent and me. It was very good.

*   *   *

The pavement and the streets were wet from recent rain, headlights rebounded up off the gutter puddles as we poured out with the chattering crowd.

"The movie was entertaining," Betty said graciously, though throughout she had been more concerned about Al and was only half watching.

"Are you okay, Sergeant?" Loretta said. It was night time. She put on her sunglasses. Al nodded but he still looked a little pale underneath his permanent sand-blasted tan.

"I have to get back to the bar," Betty said, stepping out into the roadway to hail a cab. Where there hadn't been any a second before, a whole line of them seemed to fly towards her like the start of a Grand Prix, iron filings to a magnet.

"Are you sure?" Loretta said. "Do you want to go on for a drink? Some food?"

"Thank you, no," Betty said. "I sincerely hope we meet again?"

This could have been the invitation agent Loretta was waiting for. She should have leapt in, offered to set up another arrangement, to do some more background work but she just echoed that she hoped this would happen and then Betty said something a little alarming.

"I hope before the five days are up?"

"Cab's waiting," Al said.

"Enjoy the movie, Sergeant?" Loretta said.

He shrugged.

"Wasn't no shooting in it," he said, and waved and he and Betty got into the cab and disappeared into the night.

"Weird," I said. "Al. In there."

"Happens a lot," Loretta said as we wandered through the streets past the men standing in doorways at the bars and restaurants, calling for customers. We shook our heads and smiled without looking at them, city street wise. "I wish I could have got to talk to him a little longer."

"Why?" I said quickly before I could stop myself.

"Am I sensing something here, Scooter?" Loretta said. "You want to know what Al was talking to me about. Now you want to know why I wanted to talk to him."

"No, perfectly fine."

"You sure? Not suffering with the heat?"

"I am good in the heat, thank you."

"Pardon me for asking, I'm sure," she said. "What is it then, I'm wondering, I'm thinking, maybe a little bit jealous? Is that it, Scooter? Afraid the big kid is going to steal your new toy?"

She hooked her arm in mine and laughed. I confess I felt a little uncomfortable at this line of questioning.

"He has Betty," I said, realising too late my mistake. Loretta pounced.

"And you think Betty is a much better catch, is that it? No way he would ditch the classy dame for some gutter kid like yours truly, that what you're saying?"

"Not what I meant at all, actually. In fact, he thought you were a cute package."

"He said that? Maybe my luck's in after all."

She spun me round in the street and stood in front of me and took off her sunglasses.

"You do know I'm only teasing, right, Scooter?"

At that moment all I wanted to do was kiss her. I didn't. I just laughed and nodded and said of course I do and we walked on. I imagined we were walking in the direction of her hotel but I didn't ask, I was happy to keep ambling through the crowds.

"Soldiers, they spend a lot of time in the dark. No sleep," she said.

"He had a flashback?"

"Maybe."

"I think I get it."

"You won't but that's okay. I like that you're a peacetime guy. A non-combatant."

We bought some food from a street vendor, I wasn't sure what it was, something fried in a kind of sloppy batter, a small animal or insect most likely, and I told Loretta about fish and chips, wrapped in newspapers, a nostalgic image that had me thinking of home.

"Sounds delicious," she said, nibbling the last of whatever it was from the wooden skewer it was cooked on. I had a question to ask but I couldn't face the answer. What Betty said had been running through my head but I was aware of the old lawyer's adage in court – never ask a question if you don't already know the answer. What I did know was that this would already be Day Three. Loretta was talking about hamburgers back home in Florida.

"Five days?" I said, interrupting, trying to keep the cry out of my voice.

"What?"

"Are you really only here for five days?"

"Don't ask me that, okay, Scooter?" She let go of my arm and walked on ahead of me.

"Wait." I caught up with her.

"That's what we get. Five days. In every eleven-month tour. Sometimes you can get a stand-by, sometimes you can get another couple of days but mostly it's five days, for most people. Rest and Recuperation, they call it. R and R."

She sounded angry, maybe not at me, maybe at the war. First time I had seen her angry. Petulant, yes, lovely, yes, angry, no.

"R and R?" I said. "Sounds like an amateur pirate."

She gave me a puzzled look and then laughed.

"I guess that's probably an English joke," she said.

A cagey answer. Maybe she was here for longer. If she was, then whoopee, if she wasn't, we only had two days left. A ten-storey block of chromium and concrete loomed ahead of us, not on its own, it had similar companions nearby, some even bigger. The Rajah hotel.

"What if I am only here five days?" she said. "Would that bother you?"

"No, honestly, I will be glad when you're gone," I said. "Yes, it would bother me. It would bother me so much."

I wanted her to be a secret service agent. I wanted her to snoop on me, I would do something suspicious, to keep her here, following me around. She ticked off a count on her fingers.

"Day one, we met, two, we bought a flower, three, we went to the movies. And we did this," she said, and kissed me quickly on the lips. "Four and five, who knows what will happen?"

She ran away, into the pool of light from the hotel foyer, and I stood on the pavement trembling and a cab drove by and splashed rainwater all over my trousers.

13

"The Pentagon got back to me," McMichael said as we met in the small office.

"You really checked me out with the Pentagon, Captain?" I didn't know what else to call him. He hadn't invited me to be familiar and address him as Travis.

"You don't believe me?" he said, opening a file. "Okay, hear this. Matthew Benson, St Bertram's school, whatever the hell kind of name for a school that is, left in the sixth form, I guess that's a kind of grade level, Durham University, 2.1 degree major in law, second subject history, how am I doing so far?"

I was dumbfounded. I couldn't actually believe someone had looked so closely into my background. It was more than a little unnerving.

"All righty, father a lawyer with his own practice in Worcestershire, that's in England, right? Criminal law speciality. Mother was a teacher, now retired. No siblings. Training year at a law firm in Birmingham, I'm guessing daddy's connections got you that job, right? Moving on, successfully completed training, fully qualified as a solicitor, didn't take another job."

He closed the file.

"Then let me guess, thought to yourself, hey, this is the Sixties, there's a big world out there, let's get on the road, am I right? I added that last part myself."

"That's correct," I said. "Not only is it correct, you made it sound predictable and dull and middle class, so thanks for that."

"Hey, don't knock it. We play the cards we're dealt, right?"

It had all changed when we bought the Land Rover, when I said to my dad I wasn't going to take up the place in his firm not right then, maybe not ever, who knew? McMichael had nailed that – this was the Sixties, we didn't have to do what we were supposed to do. That was what was mapped out for me and now instead here I was. The exuberance of the young had opened up a door and I had nudged it a little wider and now here I was with McMichael in a little office in Bangkok not sure what the hell I was doing.

"I guess you fought your way up to get to be a lawyer?" I said. "Is that why you're looking so smug?"

"God, no," he said. "I had all the help I wanted, same as you, middle class, same as you, but being a lawyer kept me off the front line in Vietnam. I do a longer tour but I don't get shot at, not regularly, anyway. See what I'm saying? We play the cards we're dealt."

"Yeah, very wise," I said. "Okay, I believe you."

"Now, you sign this."

"They gave me clearance?"

I had mixed feelings. I think part of me was hoping that I would be turned down, I could just go up to Al and say, I'm dreadfully sorry, they won't let me act on your behalf, good luck, goodbye, and get the next flight out before he could ask for his money back. Instead, McMichael was pushing a piece of paper towards me.

"Here. And here."

The form seemed to have been hastily assembled. I read it carefully, every line, like I had to do at work, wills and trusts and property deals. McMichael had expected me to do that, he would have done it himself, it's a kind of legal habit, I still do it today, when a form says have you read the terms and conditions, tick the box, I have always read them, word by word. He sat back and waited, arms folded. There was nothing incriminating. It was just a general release, giving me no comeback on the US government should anything go wrong. I signed it.

"You want to get some insurance," McMichael said. I knew he was right. This was serious now. If anything did go wrong and Al decided to sue me and it was found to be my fault, I could lose everything. I could buy insurance if I could find any from anywhere and I could afford it. Or I could gamble on my own skills in court. Which was not the best but probably the only option.

"I'll take that under advisement."

"Just saying," he said. "Just so you get the full picture, here, let me demonstrate. This is you."

He picked up a dead fly and placed it on the side of the desk.

"And there's the US government and military establishment and the CIA and the secret service and the Army of the Republic of Vietnam. Here."

He picked up a pile of folders and placed it on the opposite side.

"That's the evidence," he said, indicating the folders. "You can take them now."

I pulled the folders towards me and started to look through them, closely typed pages detailing all the felonies Al was alleged to have carried out. I would have to go through every single one in the finest detail. I would have to discuss them with Al. Some hope.

"You know why they're letting you take this job, don't you?"

"Okay, go on. I know you've got something you want to get off your chest, let's have it."

"Because you're the FNG."

This could have been a legal term; if so, not one I was familiar with, so I looked quizzically at my reluctant co-counsel.

"You don't know what it means? That's what the grunts call a rookie who gets sent out to their unit as a replacement, let's say, in the Iron Triangle, or someplace like that when one of their guys gets killed or injured. He's raw, he fires at nothing, he makes too much noise going through the jungle, they're afraid he's going to get everybody shot. He's a liability. And he's called that until he proves himself in a firefight."

I stood up and tucked the folders under my arm. I had not expected so many.

"I think I get the picture," I said.

He brought the flat of his hand crashing down onto another insect on the desk. He picked up the body and examined it and placed it next to the first one. I sighed heavily. I didn't need any more pressure.

"Okay, very graphic, I'll buy it, what's that?"

"That's my reputation," he said. "Right there, next to you. FNG. What's it stand for? Four-can New Guy. That's you. You got the job because they want to win. You're the rookie. You know what they think you're going to do?"

I headed for the door.

"Go on, tell me, you know what you want to."

"They think you're going to screw it up. No, wait, that's not quite right. I'll rephrase. They are absolutely certain you're going to screw it up."

14

So that's what I was, the FNG. I couldn't deny it. Al didn't know that. Or maybe he did. He was just so desperate, he had to take me on. He couldn't defend himself, he needed me. I went back out through the outer office where the same Lieutenant sprang upright on his chair until he saw it was just me. I waved briefly to him. He lobbed me a paper ball. I caught it and in the same movement hurled it straight into the bin from ten yards away, straight into the centre.

"Groovy," the Lieutenant said appreciatively and held out his hand for a high five, which I duly gave and carried on into the street where I saw Soames and Raniero. They were standing in the shade, looking as if they were being casual, Raniero was smoking a cigarette, as if they had just been taking the air and this was a coincidence. Raniero nudged Soames when he saw me coming.

"Gentlemen," I said, preparing to pass right by them. I was in no mood to discuss anything.

"Benson," Raniero said. "Didn't know you were here."

"I've collected my papers," I said. "I'll be seeing you in court next week."

"I heard. Looking forward to it."

"So am I, most sincerely. If there's any irregularity, you'll be hearing from me."

"There won't be," Raniero said, sliming around so he got in my way. Soames hung back even though he was nominally lead counsel.

He seemed embarrassed by Raniero. "One more thing. Some further evidence has come to light, isn't that right, Captain Soames?"

"There are procedural ways of presenting this, Todd," Soames said.

"I guess so," he said. "You want me to present this in a procedural way, Benson? Or don't you know what that is?"

"Present it in the proper way, Captain, whatever you have, I don't have time for any games."

I started to edge past him but he moved across and shoved a sheet of paper into my chest.

"Testimony," he said. "Add it to your folder. Add it to the evidence."

I took the paper from him and glanced at it. It was a witness statement. Raniero was leaning in right over me. If there had been bike sheds, I suspected he would have been offering me behind them for a fight.

"Get out of my face," I said.

Soames was pulling his arm.

"Okay, Todd, we've handed over the evidence, let's go."

"Raniero," someone called from the doorway. McMichael appeared. "What's going on?"

Raniero stood back a little, giving me some breathing space. He grinned lamely.

"I just gave your new friend some fresh evidence, Travis. I guess you'd better tell him what to do with it because he sure as hell doesn't look like he knows."

"What fresh evidence?" McMichael said.

"Witness testimony."

Raniero waited for a reaction. We weren't going to give him the satisfaction.

"Yeah, that's right, one of his guys turned on him at long last. It's all there, right there."

"Okay," I said, as calmly as I could as I saw the whole case crumbling before it even got started. "We'll assess the evidence. I actually don't see that it changes our position substantially."

I was trying to sound as if it didn't matter. It mattered. Raniero waggled his head from side to side and mimicked my accent.

"It doesn't change our position substantially, don't you know, old chap," he said, then reverted to his normal voice. "We think it does. We think that when you see that, you won't be bringing your English arguments into US courts without a guilty plea."

Raniero turned to McMichael.

"Our bet still on?" he said.

"What bet?" I said to McMichael. He shuffled his feet. "Have you been betting on us to lose? That's got to be unethical."

Soames entered the fray and we were there in a little group outside the building, voices raised, attracting puzzled looks from the passersby.

"That's enough," Soames said. "We're making fools of ourselves. People are watching."

"This dumb cluck will bet on anything," McMichael said, indicating Raniero.

"You bet him I wouldn't turn up, is that it? You bet him I won't have the guts to step into court?" I said.

"Christ's sake, calm down," McMichael said, pushing me away. Raniero and Soames started to go into the building, Soames with his head down, Raniero strutting.

"I'm fine," I said as McMichael ushered me away to a safe distance. "Fine."

"I was just on my way to get some smokes and I find you out here in the middle of a fist fight with the prosecution. I mean, I agree it's tempting to plant one in Raniero's kisser and believe me, no jury would convict you but try and keep it civil, for chrissake, man."

"I got it. I got this, it's okay."

It wasn't okay, really, my partner had just told me I was expected to lose and now the prosecution had given me something that meant a defeat was the most likely outcome.

"Okay, what's Raniero given you?"

"Witness statement." I showed him the paper, headed with the name of Private Tommy Saunders. He glanced at it briefly.

"Jesus," he said. "Not good. Take it and show it to Moreau, see if he knows this guy, see if he can think of anything."

He thrust the paper at me.

"This changes our position," I said. "Doesn't it?"

"It only changes from hell to damnation. Anything else happens, call me, I'm going to be busy back inside kicking Raniero's ass, just for fun."

I set off along the street and he called after me.

"By the way," he said. "If this case goes south, you owe me fifty bucks. I bet on us to win."

15

We spent the afternoon wandering around, Loretta and I, just seeing the sights. I dropped off my papers back at Betty's, told her I really needed to talk to Al as soon as I could. Loretta had a list of the things she wanted to see, to cram in as much as possible because it could be Day Four, though I didn't mention that. Being with me, it meant she wasn't harassed on all sides by stray men seeking a companion. I had become an unlikely bodyguard.

"Cool ride," Loretta said as we grabbed a tuk-tuk and beetled along in it to the usual cacophony of blaring horns and there was a hole in the canvas roof so a flap of it fell into my face and made Loretta laugh. The motorised rickshaw engine rattled and croaked, the driver shouted at cyclists and pedestrians, we got to the Wat Trai Mit, one of the Buddhist temples scattered liberally around the city with their sloping layered ski jump roofs, pointed corners and statues.

"Look at this, wow, Scooter, we don't have these in Florida."

We went inside where it was relatively dark and cool and Loretta chattered away like a schoolgirl on a field trip and we saw the statue of the Golden Buddha, the size of a two-storey house. Loretta said she was glad she had worn a sarong to cover her legs because she wouldn't have got in otherwise. She had on her headscarf and the sunglasses and she looked maybe a little bit like a secret service agent but my previous encounters with such a breed had been confined to watching *The Man From UNCLE* on TV so I didn't know.

"Boat ride?" I said as we found ourselves by the river.

"I'm bushed," she said. "Let's just watch."

A wizened old woman, bent under the weight of the baskets she carried on either end of a bamboo pole balanced across her shoulder, watched us as we sat outside a cafe.

"They come in mostly in helicopters," Loretta said, gazing out over the river, its surface almost completely covered by boats of one kind or another. "It's worst when there's massive casualties, we work shifts ten twelve hours, sometimes we have to decide who to treat first. It's called triage but it's really playing God. I guess I don't feel like God."

"You don't look like God. Doesn't he have a long white beard?"

"I think you're mixing him up with Santa Claus."

She smiled. Her mask had slipped a little. She wanted to talk about Vietnam. I hadn't asked her; she had just decided she wanted to tell me, I suppose as someone who had never been in a war, an outsider. My mind kept wandering back to the witness testimony I had been given and I had to try hard to leave it alone because Loretta was opening her heart.

"The trauma wards, young guys, nineteen, twenty, limbs blown away, you have to tell them when they wake up, tell them what's happened, because the doctors are too busy, how their face has been shattered, how they'll never walk again, or play baseball again or whatever they won't do again because they trod on a mine or they got shot or something."

The old woman was making her way towards us.

"You can't sleep. After a shift, sometimes, you go to the Officer's Club, that's all there is to do, listening out for the Hueys coming over, the helicopters. There might be a band playing. The officers hit on you, give you all their moves, you're a woman, you're a long way from home. You learn to switch it all off, block it all out. Death and dancing, that's what we do."

I reached over and took her hand. It seemed like the thing to do. She smiled at me. A tear ran down from behind her sunglasses. She wiped it away. This could not have been a cover story. Al was surely wrong.

"We all know what they think of us because we're women and we deal with bodies and they're men and they're the ones doing the dying. They think we're sluts, they think we can't hear, they think we don't know."

I shook my head sympathetically. How can you tell a woman you don't think she's a slut without implying that there could be a possibility and so a question based on a denial reinforces the assumption?

"I don't think you're a slut." I did it anyway. She laughed. I think my initial assessment was probably right. I should have kept quiet.

"That the best you could do?" she said. "Anyhow, you don't know me. I might be. I might be the biggest goddam ride in the whole of the Everglades."

"Would you like some more tea?" I said.

"I was a nurse back home in Tampa," she said. "You want to know why I joined up, Scooter? You want to be grown-ups for a little while?"

I nodded, though I didn't want to be a grown-up with Loretta, she was my playmate. I watched the old woman from the corner of my eye as she crooked a thin finger towards me and pointed to the birds I could now see were held in cages on the end of the bamboo poles.

"I'll tell you this one time," Loretta said. "Don't ask me about it again, okay?"

I almost protested that I wouldn't have time to do that. She was due to leave. I didn't think it was the right time to bring this minor difficulty up.

"We were due to be married, we had been together since we were 17, High School prom, you better believe it, straight out of a comic."

"I've seen it in the movies. Looks like fun."

The old woman started talking to us, gesturing to the birds.

"He joined up, the Kennedy thing, ask not what your country can do for you, ask what you can do for your country, all that, he believed in all that," Loretta said. "His tour was due to end, we had the place booked, the chapel, the reception hall. The whole shebang. He got killed two months before the wedding, maybe three, I don't know, his family never told me where exactly. South Vietnam, somewhere near the Cambodia border. I cried for months and months then I thought, I didn't want any other girl to go through what I went through, I was a nurse, I volunteered. How dumb was that? What did I think I could do? Save every kid?"

There was nothing I could say. The boats plodded by on the river, an occasional motorboat breaking through the constant din of traffic and shouting. The old woman held out her hand.

"What does she want?" I said.

"It's a Buddhist thing," Loretta said. "You give her money and she lets you set free one of the birds, look, there, inside the cages."

"What for?"

"They call it making merit. It brings good karma. Good luck."

And good business, probably, I thought, one thing about the Thai people, they were enterprising. Loretta took off her sunglasses and there she was, revealed, I was sure I knew her now. I gave the bird woman some notes, I don't know how much, but she seemed happy enough and she lifted the clasp of the big basket and gave us a bamboo cage each. The birds were squealing and chirruping frantically.

We walked over to the wall by the river, in a gap between the houses, perhaps because we thought they had a better chance of flying away if they weren't near the road. The old woman hurried after us so she could get her little cages back to fill with more birds.

"Good karma," Loretta said. "Say it. We sure as hell need it."

"Good karma," I said.

We held our cages to the air. The birds inside were about the size of sparrows, green and black. Together, we released the latches and they fluttered in the doorway and then flew up into the sky. We watched them darting back along the river, green black flashes, dipping over the boats laden with spices and vegetables until they were lost. The old woman took her cages back and bowed and went in search of more customers.

"Day Four," Loretta said. "You thought I was a slut."

"I didn't say that."

"And we set free the birds."

16

The band comprised a set of young musicians I think were Betty's relatives. They only knew five songs and to disguise any technical shortcomings, they played them very loud. I could hear them quite clearly in my rooms as I sat back on my settee and tried to assess the witness testimony from Private Tommy Saunders. It was damaging. Names, dates, details, orders given by Sergeant Moreau. This could potentially torpedo our entire defence, such as it was and there wasn't much to it in the first place; not guilty being only the starting point. I would have to glean some more from Al. *Mr Tambourine Man* was being slowly strangled to death downstairs.

I checked the watch I had bought from a guy in Poland. Genuine Rolex, only one pound ten shillings. No more work I could do without Al. I had asked Loretta to come back with me to Betty's because she said she wanted to see Betty again and I didn't want her to leave me. She wanted to go back to her hotel to freshen up and said she would come around later. Every second we were apart, I wondered if I had seen her for the last time.

The back stairs led me down to the door by the stage. The drummer was half a beat behind the bass player who was himself racing to keep up with the guitarist and the singer, dressed in leather trousers and with his hair done up in a Billy Fury quiff, was oblivious to any cue they were giving him, pursuing his own vocal frolics. The skimpily-dressed young bar girls didn't seem to notice, gyrating in a disorderly chorus line on the dance floor in front of them, their number cards attached to their wrists. A couple of them called to me.

"Mister Matthew."

"Evening, ladies," I said.

Betty was at the bar, sipping a Martini, and calling one of the girls over to her as she stood with a young Western man with a boyish face, about the same age as the patients Loretta had been telling me about. He had selected number eight. Like most of them – there were a fluctuating number usually between fifteen or twenty – she looked like she should have been sitting in a school assembly, taking her hymnbook from her blazer pocket to join in the singing. Instead, they were all dressed as if they were heading off to the lido for a spot of sunbathing and would be spending the day traipsing the bars and clubs and hotels of Bangkok with guys they didn't know. It wasn't my business, it was Betty's.

"They want a girlfriend," she had said when I asked her about it. "They want someone soft next to them. For a few days. They want to pretend."

The money that changed hands was a "bar fine" compensating the Mama-San who looked after the girls – Betty in this case – for taking them out of their place of work. It gave a more innocent gloss to the transaction; maybe that was how Betty got by, she could pretend she was running a dating agency. Whatever happened took place off the premises, her girls went back to the twenty-storey hotels occupied temporarily by their ever-changing boyfriends. Brothels were not exactly legal. Betty was very sniffy about the massage parlours. I think she felt they were giving her calling a bad name. Al was sitting at the bar in his usual place. It was crowded, I edged past a group of seven or eight men standing waiting to be served.

"Excuse me," I said. "Sorry, thank you."

They shifted a little, rather resentfully, I thought, and one or two of them gave me cold looks as I sat next to Al on the only other available stool. The barman, I had discovered, was Betty's cousin and his name was Preed. He came straight over as I waved to him. We had been formally introduced and I was an honoured guest in the house, so it seemed. There was some muttering among the group next to me who had been waiting much longer than me to be served.

"Mister Matthew," he said, smiling. "Whisky? Coming right up."

I shook my head and wished him a good evening and ordered a beer.

"How's it going?" Al said. "Busy?"

"I have some good news and some bad news," I said, trying to introduce a little levity into what I was about to say. "The good news is I have been cleared to take your case."

"That's the good news? Jesus, Mary and Joseph, the bad news is gonna be a real zinger," he said.

I couldn't tell if he was joking. I laughed anyway.

"Give me the bad news," he said.

"Private Tommy Saunders."

He sipped his tea and appearing to be considering the name, though I could tell from his initial reaction it was clearly familiar to him.

"Don't know him."

"The prosecution gave me his witness testimony."

I gathered from their talk that the group next to me were sailors and I had to lean closer to Al as they were nudging me uncomfortably. The boy who had been talking to Betty eagerly clutched his receipt. She gave them a slip of paper meant to guarantee they would bring the girls back unharmed and properly looked after. He held his chosen companion by the hand and walked back past the bar. One of the sailors stood in his way.

"What about it?" Al said.

"Well, it doesn't do us any favours," I said. "There's no use keeping secrets from me, I'm trying to help. Who is he?"

"One of my guys," he said. "Crazy. Poppies got him."

"Hey, where you going with my girl?" the sailor said to the boy who was trying to get past him, Number Eight in tow. Betty made a signal to Preed, who left the bar and hurried to the front doors. He came back in with the two men who hung around all day outside. They were bouncers, then. I had just thought they had nowhere else to go. They were not big men. They looked a little intimidated being inside. The band played *Shakin' All Over*, possibly the least accomplished of their repertoire. It was my favourite of theirs, even so.

"Private Saunders has a lot to say," I said.

"Does he now?"

"Out of my way, buddy." The boy knocked one of the sailors backwards so he fell into me. Number Eight looked alarmed and cast around for some support. The band played on. Maybe they were used to a restless audience.

"So sorry," I said to the sailor, who levered himself away and pushed the soldier. His friends got up from their table and came towards the bar. Ordinarily, at this point, if I had been in a pub back home, I would have slipped quietly away. But this was my bar. I knew the barman. By name. I had been to the cinema with the owner. Loretta was coming here to meet me. She was late.

"I looked after him," Al said. "I let him bring his girl on the site."

The two groups were now congealing around one another. The band segued into an approximate version of *Rock Around The Clock*. I moved to the side, clutching my beer. Al got up. There was some pushing and shoving among the two groups and I was jostled. One of the sailors sneered.

"You lookin' at, pussy boy?" he said, leaning closely into my face. It was not a question I could adequately answer. Also, he appeared to be drunk. Al tapped him on the shoulder. The sailor turned around. He was the taller of the two but he took one look at Al and backed away. It was extraordinary. It was like he had taken the lid off a simmering pot of rice. The two groups stopped squaring up to one another. Emboldened, the bouncers moved up behind Al, who didn't say a word but jerked his head towards the front door. He had identified the ringleader, picked him out straight away. The man knew that if anything started, he would be the first to take a hit and he didn't want that.

"Leave quietly," Al said. The sailor pulled himself up to a height far greater than Al's. He was reluctant to back down in front of his friends. Al was ready for this. "Don't pay for your drinks."

I had to admire his negotiating skills. He had given them a chance to save face – free drinks – and the choice was theirs. Get into a rumble with Al, which they could lose. Or take the cash offer. It was a good deal. They decided to take it and get out, though not without shoving past me roughly.

"Pussy boy," the leader said to me. "Be seeing you."

He didn't make this sound an attractive proposition. I gave him my hardest stare. He curled a lip. I don't think I was very convincing. I would need to work on that. The band played their remaining number before they would start the cycle again. It was the one they usually played last every night. Any band, all over Vietnam, so Loretta had told me, played it as the last song when they performed for the soldiers in the clubs, at dances, it carried with it a particular resonance. It meant a whole lot. The band had decided to play it early on this night, to defuse the tension, I guessed. As the first chords sounded, I realised one other thing. The time had come and gone. Loretta had not turned up. By The Animals.

We Got To Get Out Of This Place. Always brought the house down.

*   *   *

"Back in the world," Al said. "When I was a kid, we had these yellowjackets in the ground. You know what a yellowjacket is?"

US military always called it the world. This wasn't the world. Vietnam wasn't the world. America was the world.

"I don't," I said.

"You don't know what a yellowjacket is, boy?"

The bar returned to normal after the newly-averted trouble. The fresh-faced boy had left; one or two of his companions had taken the girls of their choice – numbers 12 and 16, actually, nice girls – and gone with him for moral support in case the sailors were hanging around outside. Betty had given Al a hug and whispered in his ear and anyone else would probably have gone bright red but not Al. The band was playing *Shakin' All Over*. Again.

"No, I don't know what a yellowjacket is, look, about this guy Saunders, what about him?"

Loretta was more than an hour late.

"It's an insect, it's a wasp, like a hornet. Big. Not as big as they get here, but big, thousands of them, we had some in our yard," Al said.

"That's very interesting," I said. "Normally, I am keen on entomology myself but there's a time and place."

"I'm talking," Al said. "I'm telling you this story about yellowjackets."

"Okay." I looked around to the door, shuffled on my stool so I could keep an eye on it. The bar was full. Preed had been joined by one of the older girls to serve the drinks. The band played *Rock Around the Clock* and Betty swanned around, smiling and greeting and keeping an eye on the smooth running of the establishment and refusing, as she always did, every request for a dance so I guessed I had time to listen to a story about insects. "Tell me."

74

"They nest underground. Near your house. We got them in Texas. You don't get them in England?"

So that's where he was from. Texas. I had wondered. Which state you were from seemed to be a big deal among the Americans we had met on the trip over. To the extent they would jovially call one another by the name of their home state. So if Loretta turned up – which was increasingly unlikely – I could have called her Florida. She probably would have found that amusing.

"No," I said. "We have hornets. And wasps. They're quite small. Did you know that sailor was just going to walk out?"

"Don't matter," he said. "He was leaving one way or the other."

Which I presumed meant either of his own volition or on the end of Al's boot.

"These yellowjackets, see, we didn't get them so much further north, where we lived before, my daddy and me but in Texas, yeah."

"Your daddy?"

"Yeah. We moved a lot. My daddy liked to keep moving. Fact is, he had to keep moving most of the time."

"What for?" I asked. It was either for work or because he was on the run from the law, I thought, though that might have been doing Al's family a disservice. I had no reason to imagine they were anything other than perfectly normal. It was just a hunch. Al took a sip of his drink. The band played *Mr Tambourine Man* in something that sounded like 11/8 time. I began to suspect that Al's drink on this occasion was a little more than tea.

"The yellowjackets?" I said.

"My daddy, he got these cans of kerosene and he poured them down into this hole, it was like a tunnel, it was like one of the tunnels the Vietcong use, they hide in there all the time, they come out and they go zap and they go back in again. You don't see them. But you could see these yellowjackets, man, flying all round, helluva sting if you got in the way."

Al was in an unusually expansive mood. It seemed as if the near-rumble with the sailors had energised him. I hoped to keep him talking, perhaps I could edge the subject around to something important, like the court case.

"Then he says to me, stand back, son, and he lit this match and he threw it into the hole and it just went up, like a flame shot from either end of the tunnel where these yellowjackets was living. I put my hands over my ears because there was this roar, this whoosh, like being close to an M30."

Al shook his head as he pictured the memory. Betty had joined us. She clapped her hands. She smiled at him.

"What happened, Moreau? What happened?" she said.

"These yellowjackets come flying out of the hole. On fire. Thousands of them. Flying, in flames. Dropping down dying. All over the yard. My daddy was laughing fit to bust."

The door opened. It wasn't Loretta.

"You know that fire? It kept on burning. We sat there and watched it, me and my daddy. Into the night. It was glowing. Smoke come out of it, man. I only got up when he told me to fetch him another beer."

Betty leaned against him, grateful for his assistance earlier, no doubt, but also because I think she just liked to hear him talk.

"Yeah," he said. "Wonder if they still get them there?"

"You don't know?" I asked.

"Hell, no. That was in 1953. I left the next day. I ain't seen my daddy since. Sonofabitch could have killed me throwing that match in the hole like that. For all I know, that fire's still burning."

Loretta was not going to come. We would not be dancing to *Shakin' All Over*. Not that night, maybe not ever.

17

"So sorry, sir," the uniformed clerk at the Rajah said, smiling apologetically. "We have no-one registered here under that name."

The day started early in Bangkok before the heat got too fierce so even though I had arrived first thing in the morning, there were plenty of people milling around in the surprisingly opulent foyer of the newly built hotel. Porters pushed cases and bags on gold painted trolleys. I scanned the crowds. It was popular with Westerners, clearly built to cater for the burgeoning new trade for visitors.

"She's been staying here," I said to the clerk. "Could you have another look for me, please? Loretta Maine."

The clerk obligingly skimmed through the register on his desk again but shook his head.

"Okay," I said. "Thank you."

I eased away from the reception counter and sat in one of the plush armchairs in the foyer, watching the people go by. A group of young men stumbled out, jostling, laughing, seeking entertainment. They could not afford to waste any of their valuable time. I thought I recognised one of the girls from Betty's as she came out, hanging onto the arm of a proud young man. It was. She looked surprised to see me and waved.

"Mister Matthew," she said. "How are you?"

She let go of the man's arm and walked over to me after planting a kiss on the side of his face.

"Hello," I said.

She seemed pleased to see me, though we had barely exchanged more than a smile and the most basic of greetings.

"Why are you here?" she said.

"I'm waiting for someone," I said. I couldn't explain who. Loretta had never been to Betty's so any explanation would swiftly be confusing. "Here soon."

She leaned closer to me.

"I have a nice boy this time," she said. "That's good, isn't it?"

"Yes," I said. "Very good."

"Will you tell Betty I have a nice boy this time?" she said. I nodded.

"I'll do that," I said.

"Enjoy your day, Mister Matthew," she said and went back over to her nice boy and she gave me one last wave as they left and I realised I didn't know her name.

"Wait," I turned around in the armchair but they had disappeared into the crowd. I sat back and made a list of the things that could have happened. Top of it was that Loretta didn't really exist at all and I had made her up in some quasi-religious stupor or something. Second, she really was a secret service agent and she had got the information she wanted and had lit out to report back to her spy bosses.

Third, she had been using a false name, either to me or at the hotel. Fourth – my list was growing too long and I had no way of cutting down the options – I had the wrong hotel, which was a possibility. I had only seen it in the dark. I got up, all set to continue my search and went out into the street. There were a dozen hotels like it within a few hundred yards. The hotel I was in had an enormous sign bearing its name. I couldn't have been mistaken. Besides, I couldn't go around every hotel in the city looking for Loretta, who might not even be called Loretta anyway.

I approached the clerk again, who gave the little formal bow as a greeting, which, I had discovered, was called a wai. The hotel was mostly full of men. There weren't too many Western women in the city so I was hoping to jog his memory.

"She's a little bit shorter than me," I said. "Brown hair? Wears a headscarf sometimes? Sunglasses? She always wears sunglasses."

He smiled politely and shook his head. Another clerk who had joined him looked over from the board holding the keys at the back of the desk. He said something in Thai to the clerk, whose face lit up.

"Ah!" he said. This looked promising. She was there! She was using a false name, for some reason, I didn't know or care why at that moment. "Yes, I remember."

The other clerk joined him and between them, they flicked through the register, going back a week. Going back more than five days. Chatting all the time.

"Pretty girl," the first clerk said in English.

"Yes," I said at the same time as the second clerk, who jabbed his finger at the page.

"Here," he said. And he turned the register around to show me the name.

"You sure?" I said. "You sure this is her?"

He nodded energetically and pointed to the name she had signed in under. Norma Jean Baker. I smiled. That was the kind of joke I would expect from her.

"Is she here?" I said. "Miss Baker. Is she here?"

The clerks rifled through the pages of the register again and they both looked disappointed, like they didn't want to let me down.

"No," the first clerk said.

"Do you know when she'll be back?"

The clerks held a short discussion then decided to come clean and tell me what had happened, bowing disconsolately before the first clerk spoke.

"She check out first thing this morning," he said.

I thanked them and walked out in a daze, kicking a piece of fruit along the gutter but it didn't go far before it split open. A pomegranate. The city was hitting its peak mid-morning cacophony around me but I didn't hear much of it, dodging automatically around the erratically ridden bicycles and the rickshaws and that might have been a Pontiac? Mike would have been straight onto that one, cars were his thing. He would possibly have got on well with Al, I thought and I missed them right then, my friends.

Mike was in love with Alfie. So was I, a little. But she was Pete's girl, she studied catering at the same teacher college where he was doing English. Catering suggested she would be more than capable of knocking up a decent meal at the roadside so she was in. We were stuck in a traffic jam in Italy and *You're Gonna Miss Me* by The 13th Floor Elevators came on some obscure radio station and Alfie slid out of the window and climbed onto Mary Jane's roof in her shorts and tie-dye shirt and her boots that had laces all the way up her calves and danced and people in the cars all around cheered. I missed those days. They weren't very long ago.

Pete and Alfie went back to get married I guess, start being teachers, have children, maybe she was already pregnant. Save up some money, maybe a couple of thousand pounds, buy a house. Mike had gone home because, well, he had had enough. He said break time was over, real life was waiting. I sat outside a café. Under an awning, it was shady. Inside, I could hear they were playing The Beatles. *Revolver*. A waiter came out and I ordered an iced tea.

It should have been the coolest thing in the world to do, sitting outside a café in a busy Bangkok street. That's why I stayed behind, that's the reason I was here, to breeze along insouciantly while I had the chance. But I had no money and instead I had a job and Al and I should have been working on the case. Al was busy. I wasn't due to meet McMichael. Anyway, I couldn't imagine either of them wanted to hear me sing the lament of the lost love of Loretta, which was, after all, no more than a foolish charade, my own misguided invention. A canvas-sided truck carrying servicemen went by, heading out to one of the airbases. They might have been going back to Vietnam but at least they weren't on their own, like me.

"You know what I'm thinking, Scooter?" That was what was missing, her beautiful soft voice. "I'm thinking you should have fixed my elephant."

18

"He is not here, Matthew," Betty said. Whenever she called me by name, my knees felt like they had been reduced to flannel. Everybody was leaving me. I was doomed to walk the earth alone.

"Where's he gone? Did he say?" It was mid-afternoon. The half dozen girls who would normally have been dancing were instead sitting on chairs chatting, filing their nails, because the band had turned up early to practise a new song that bore a vague resemblance to *Sunshine Of Your Love* by Cream.

"He said he would be gone a few days, he didn't say when he would be back."

"A few days? That's too long, what's he playing at?"

"He is playing at being Al Moreau."

Betty spread her hands wide and shrugged before gliding away, lit by the sun coming through the unfrosted top windows, patrolling her domain, pausing only for a customer to have the honour of lighting her cigarette.

I went upstairs to do some work, I wanted to look through the witness testimony, I was determined to have all my ducks in a row the next time I was able to talk to Al. I was surprised to find my door slightly ajar, though, as Al had demonstrated, there was something badly wrong with the lock. Maybe Al was in there. Maybe, hopefully, Loretta. I pushed the door open carefully. A man I didn't know was sitting on my settee, casually leafing through a six-week old copy of *Melody Maker* I had bought in a kiosk in France.

"Hello," I said.

"Hi." He was American. There was a pause. He continued to flick through the pages while I went further into the room, checking it was mine, yes, there were my things, the elephant stood on the chest of drawers where it should have been, trunk accusingly by its side.

"Can I help you?" I said. "Was there something you wanted?"

"No. I'm good," he said.

"Yeah, see, what I meant by that was, what are you doing in my room?"

He looked up, apparently puzzled.

"Buddy of Al's."

That explained a lot, particularly the lack of any communication. He stood and it was then I realised the right sleeve of his jacket hung limply and was pinned up halfway. He held out his left for me to shake, which I did, trying not to examine the area of his missing limb.

"Stan Bronsky," he said.

"Matthew Benson. A pleasure," I said. "Al's not here. In fact, this is not his room. If you don't mind me asking, how did you get in?"

"Opened the door. I still got one arm." He held up his left to demonstrate and grinned. He was probably a little younger than Al; it was hard to tell with veterans sometimes. His face was lined and pale, his hair was grey and hung in irregular long strands.

"No, I mean, it's supposed to be locked."

He shrugged, as if that had never made a difference to him. As if when he wanted to enter anyone's room, he did. He sat down again and discarded the music paper, selecting instead a worn old *Reader's Digest* condensed book version of *Moby Dick* which had mysteriously already been in the rooms.

"When Al and me, we shared a hooch together, at night we couldn't sleep, it's hard to sleep, I told him this story. As far as I could remember, anyway. It's about a shark, right?"

"More or less," I said.

"Yeah. Al liked it."

"He's not here."

"I don't mind waiting. Had a hard ride to get here."

He settled back onto the settee and closed his eyes. I took off my jacket. I didn't want to throw out a tired one-armed Army friend of Al's even though he was in my room and not Al's. I couldn't redirect him to his preferred destination, Al's room, because I didn't know where that was.

"I got a message for him. It's about Tommy Saunders," he said as he nodded off and his arm fell to his side, his head lolled and he was asleep before I could ask him what the message was, tell me, tell me, I need to know. He started to snore. I left him quietly and went downstairs with the intention of quizzing Betty about this new arrival.

"He told me he was a friend of Al's," she said, her voice curling towards the ceiling like the flames from a bonfire.

"Did Al know he was coming?"

"I don't think so. Al is not here."

"No."

"Where is he? This friend of Al's?"

"In my rooms," I said. "Asleep."

She considered this, smoking peacefully, though not in a way that suggested she thought he should have been elsewhere.

"He did look tired," she said.

I didn't want to leave him there for too long on his own and I thought that might be the extent of Betty's knowledge. Also, it was getting towards evening and she was busy as the bar was filling up so I went back upstairs and looked in cautiously. The settee was empty. I hurried across to check the money was still in the bottom of my rucksack. It was. A loud noise startled me and I swung round. It was coming from my bedroom and it sounded like someone had herded several catarrhal sheep in there but closer inspection revealed it was only Stan. He had kicked off his boots and was fast asleep on my nice soft bed.

*   *   *

"On my way back to Montana," Stan said as we sat outside the café next door the following morning. He had declined a shower after his extensive sleep on my bed which he had found, unapologetically, very refreshing. I, meanwhile, had spent a tortured night half on the settee with my feet resting on the elephant's back. The waiter brought us ginger tea and some sticky doughnuts with a smile. The sun had not yet got to roasting point and we squatted on small plastic chairs under an awning.

"Tommy Saunders?" I said.

"Poor bastard," he said, shuffling his tea cup around so the handle was to his left hand.

"He's a witness in Al's court martial."

Stan had the same kind of stare as Al; it went right past you at a short distance but it took in everything. They called it the thousand-yard stare, I discovered, because that's the range you look for, that's when you can first see the enemy approaching.

"Yeah. Tommy Saunders." He took a bite of the doughnut. "S'good."

"One of Al's men at the motor pool?"

"Yeah, I was there. I passed by on my way back to Montana, called in to see Al, I don't blame him for this." He indicated his missing right arm with a nod of the head. "They told me he was working as a liaison officer right here."

So that's what Al had been doing for so long in Bangkok. Not just awaiting trial but still in the Army, though not in a role he would have chosen.

"Just bein' friendly. We was buddies, Al had been in a lot longer than me, hell, Al has been in the Army forever but we spent a lot of time together, see, Al, you could trust Al, we shared a hooch mostly."

"Forgive me for asking," I said. "A hooch?"

"Place to sleep. You dig a hole, grab as many sandbags as you can find, pile them around, put your waterproof ponchos over the top, to keep out the rain but it don't keep out the rain, rains a lot in Nam. You sweat on the inside, get rained on outside. You're never dry."

The waiter brought us fish soup and rice.

"Sounds uncomfortable," I said.

"Yeah. This last time, we had been out a few days, in the jungle, looking for Charlie, Al knew the territory, hell, he had done it a hundred, thousand times, we set up a base to sleep, we knew Charlie – that's the bad guys – was near. So it was my job to set the claymores, that's these little anti-personnel mines we put around the perimeter."

He described the shape with his one good arm, a small curved box eight inches or so wide. He checked to see if I was still following. He kept looking at me. It was becoming unnerving.

"You wire it up, it fires off these steel balls in an arc, range of a hundred yards, you gotta see it to understand it but sometimes it fires at you if you don't get lucky. It was my turn on watch, but I knew Al wouldn't be sleeping, Al never slept, I heard a noise, see, they creep up at night and I guess I was half-asleep and I blew the mine. That's what happened to my arm. But Al was right there. If he hadn't pulled me aside, I would have been killed, I told him that enough times. But they blamed him."

"Who? The military?" I had paused with the spoon halfway to my mouth while I listened. Stan moved his soup bowl around to use the spoon with his left hand and slurped. He nodded.

"They didn't like Al much, he could be kinda difficult."

"Yes."

"Moved him right on back to the motor pool, said he had been out in the jungle too long. This soup is mighty fine."

"What did you do?"

"Stayed in Saigon a while after they let me out of the hospital."

I considered for a second asking him if he had been tended to by the most beautiful nurse in Vietnam. Also, I had the feeling he was trying to get me to open up about Al. I wished I could help him but I didn't really know anything.

"Al found me jobs to do. Al knew a lot of guys."

"Still does."

"Yeah. Sales. A little counterfeit money, black market, that kind of thing but I got tired, too many guys in these rackets now, see, you know the kind of thing Al was doing, right?"

"Not in detail," I said. "Certainly not with any proof."

"That so? Okay. The rackets ain't what they was, so I'm on my way back..."

"To Montana."

Stan looked surprised that I knew his destination.

"Right. Sure is a pity I missed Al but there's a Pan Am flight waiting for me."

He sat back, his soup bowl empty.

"Tommy Saunders?" I said as he appeared about to leave.

"Yeah, Tommy, see the guys Al was in with, not all of them is good guys."

"I imagine not."

"Some of them is guys the US government knows all about, some of them might even be guys working for the US government, hear what I'm saying?"

He gave me a conspiratorial wink and I tapped the side of my nose as if I understood. I didn't like Stan. He made me uneasy.

"Some of these guys that maybe is working for the US government, they had words with Tommy's girl, I heard at the motor pool, Tommy loves that girl. Tommy's girl maybe won't be so pretty if this all goes wrong, know what I'm saying?"

Stan raised himself up carefully, levering on the table with his left arm. I moved forward, intending to offer a helping hand but Stan's glare stopped me.

"I'm okay," he said. "So yeah, tell Al, sure am sorry to miss him but I'm on my way back to Montana."

He got up and leaned in as he passed, making no attempt to offer his half of the breakfast bill. He appeared to assume it was his reward. He grabbed my shoulder. The empty sleeve of his jacket swung across me. The tone of his voice changed. It was as cold as the rice.

"Al's a good soldier but he ain't too bright. You're a clever guy, you're a lawyer. Lot of guys want you to keep Al out of jail, hear what I'm saying? But also a lot of other guys want him in jail."

The fish soup had sunk to the bottom of my stomach like a depth charge. I didn't look around. Stan's arm had pinned me to my seat.

"If you lose this case, a lot of guys will not be pleased. But now, let's see, if you win this case, there's other guys ain't gonna be happy either. So you know where you're at, right, I mean, I'm just saying. You can't win if you win. You can't win if you lose."

He released my shoulder and patted it gently.

"So, yeah, you might want to think yourself, what am I doing here? Do I belong here? Do I need this? Huh?"

It was couched in a rather oblique way but I had the feeling Stan was warning me off.

"Just bein' friendly. On my way back to Montana. Tell Al I said hi."

He walked away. I turned and watched him vanish among the crowds. It was a curious way for a friend of Al's to talk. He had made it clear that no locked door was going to keep him out. Several things struck me from this rather baffling conversation, quite apart from the fact that I was shaking as I got the money out of my pocket. First, I hadn't told him at any point I was Al's lawyer. Second, he was on his way back to Montana but he had no luggage. Third. I didn't think he was just bein' friendly at all.

19

The cabs in Bangkok were festooned all over the front driving area with protection, to ward off any bad karma the passengers might bring in with them. Buddhist symbols, prayer flags and pictures of the Royal Family flew over the dashboard and hung off the rearview mirror. I felt like apologising to the cabbie I had employed to find the place because every symbol he had spread around would be having its work cut out to tackle the aura of bad luck hanging over me like a wet weekend.

I was on my way to see McMichael at a café of his choosing, away from the Justice Centre. He had called Betty's number from my card and wanted to meet but he hadn't told me why. The way this case was going, I wasn't expecting glad tidings. I gazed through the windows, composing in my head. Telegram to dad: "Send money for flight. Coming home." Western Union, thank you very much, ticket out.

"Mom and dad, it's good to be back, it was all fine, no, I came back because I missed you, not because I was under threat and about to lose my impossible first case, no money, living above a bar and the love of my life had vanished before I even got to know her. None of that, I just wanted to come back and spend the rest of my career drawing up restrictive covenants around a one bar electric fire in the back room of a solicitor's office. Count me in, dad, and I am happy that every day forever, you and I will both know I couldn't handle it. You and I will both know you had been right."

The cabbie was talking to me. Or maybe he was talking to the other drivers. There were plenty of other drivers to talk to, the city was one huge slightly shifting car park.

"You want to buy souvenir?" the cabbie asked.

"I have a souvenir, thank you. An elephant."

"Elephant no good. Jewellery. I take you to shop, my cousin, he has very fine jewellery. Diamonds."

"I'm not a tourist," I said. "I work here."

The cabbie seemed disappointed and shrugged and mumbled to himself.

"My wife picks wintergreen to sell in markets," he said, swerving to avoid a collision with a coach.

"That's fascinating."

"Make money. You know money drivers make? I rent car from Chinese man, pay gas, pay everything, repairs. Make no money. My wife picks wintergreen to sell in markets, make maybe ten baht a day, I make fifty maybe."

It didn't mean a lot to me as the currency was a mystery but I gathered it was a pittance.

"Pay rent, five hundred a month, six hundred a month."

"Yes, terrible." Dear dad, I don't want to be a cab driver in Bangkok.

"Work twelve hours a day."

"I can see your dilemma."

The driver nipped across a bridge crossing one of the little canals, klongs, they were called, heading for the side street where McMichael was sitting outside in a secluded and relatively cool side street. The cabbie approached him and turned to me with a big grin. I gave him what seemed an excessive tip, probably a day's wages. It just seemed like the right thing to do.

"You want souvenir? You want girl?"

Yes, I want a girl. But not just any girl, thank you. I shook my head.

"You want drugs? Plenty of drugs in Bangkok."

"No. What is this? A travelling market? Just drive the cab."

"My wife?"

"No, I don't want your wife."

"What is wrong with my wife?"

I got out quickly.

"Nothing wrong with my wife."

"I don't want your wife."

He made an angry gesture and drove off, tooting his horn, kicking up pebbles from the sliding tyres.

"Couple of things," McMichael said casually, after ordering us some iced tea. "Firstly, what do we know about this witness? And second, why are you playing around with the cabbie's wife?"

"What? I don't know the fellow's wife. She might be perfectly pleasant but I have never met the woman."

McMichael nodded sagely.

"Big mistake," he said. "They have a lot of relatives. Could go wrong real quick."

"Look, I have had nothing to do with the cab driver's wife, for goodness sake."

"Suit yourself. But if you want to talk about it, I'm here."

I sighed. It was a relatively mild day.

"Moreau not with you?" McMichael said.

"It appears he's out of town."

"What the hell is he doing out of town? The next hearing is in a couple of days."

"I don't know."

"Is he coming back? Is he in the wind?"

It hadn't occurred to me that Al would have vanished. I have no doubt he could have done it if he chose, slipped away into the jungle, got himself lost. No, he wasn't that kind of man. I doubted he had ever run from anything. Except school.

"He wouldn't know what to do without the Army. He needs it."

The waiter brought a teapot and two small cups and bowed and smiled. We flicked through McMichael's copy of the evidence. He had made more marks on the pages than I had.

"Why are we not meeting at the Justice Centre?"

"Change of scenery."

He hadn't looked at me; he was concentrating on going through the files. There was something amiss and as usual I was being kept in the dark. I had not had the best day and it wasn't even lunchtime.

"This testimony is going to be hard to rebut," he went on. "We don't have a counter witness, anyone to put up against him."

"What about the motor pool guys?"

"They won't testify against him. Not a single one of them. But they won't testify for him either. They're still in service, they don't want to rock the boat and end up lighting shit fires with mortars flying overhead. All we have is Moreau's denial."

"Shit fires?"

"It's what it sounds like. That's how they get rid of the human waste on a field base and it does smell as bad as you're thinking."

It also sounded a perfectly apt description of the kind of mess we were in.

"Soames and Raniero. We're meeting here because you want to keep away from them. Why?"

I had a theory, based on the things Al had told me. McMichael looked up from his folder. He was on the fourth page, scanning the notes about the digger that had been spirited away to the Philippines, allegedly.

"I get the feeling, there's more to this whole thing," he said. "I'm trying to find out what but all I know is those two are not the only ones pulling the strings. I don't want them to get an idea of what we're planning."

"What are we planning?"

"Beats me."

"Why should I trust you?" I said. "How do I know you're not going to go straight back and tell your buddies what I'm working on?"

"If you've got a plan, I'd like to hear it. You don't trust me, that's fine. I'm a lawyer, I'm used to that. But I don't like losing and like it or not, I'm on your team."

He poured us another tea from the pot. It was tasty, spiced.

"Sorry," I said. "I didn't sleep too well."

"Also, you might not believe it but I don't want to see an American soldier like Moreau end up in the hole. You know he was in Korea? Joined up when he was 17, got injured and that's how they found out he was too young. Won a Purple Heart. When he could, he joined right back up."

I hadn't known that. I would have to find out more about Al's exploits.

"Can we use that?" I asked.

"Might be our best defence, maybe some mitigation at least. Distinguished war veteran, he's been in Vietnam pretty much since the French packed up a few years ago and went home. I'll get you a copy of his records. He's a good soldier. He has more medals in his locker than anybody I've come across. The guy's a fighter. A good American."

McMichael seemed genuinely to appreciate Al's service despite their obvious differences. I thought I would have to ask Al to show me his medals one day. He must have them with him somewhere, he was a proud man. I decided to trust McMichael. I didn't have much choice; I needed his help. I told him about Bronsky's visit.

"Guy with one arm slept in your bed?"

"On top of the bed and anyway, that's not the point. Also, I wasn't in it."

McMichael seemed to find it amusing.

"You're a long way from home, aren't you, Benson?"

"What's that got to do with it? I'm not, repeat, not, backing out."

That was that. I had said it. Voiced my commitment, hoisted my colours to the flag, red, white and blue.

"I didn't think you would. Okay, listen, I'll check him out. Look at it this way, it gives you an incentive."

"Thanks," I said. "As a motivational tool, a veiled threat of violence does rate pretty high."

"Anything else happens, give me a call. Otherwise, I'll see you in court. With Moreau. If he shows up."

"He'll be there."

"That's the spirit."

He started to march off towards the main road, then stopped and turned.

"Stiff upper lip, old boy," he said and went away, laughing. In a good way. He was on my team. The waiter was in the doorway. For the second time in a few hours, I had been left to pick up the bill. My karma and my wallet were getting worse by the second.

20

The now familiar stool stayed resolutely empty next to me all evening. Occasionally, Betty would pass by on her way to charm another customer, flitting around like a business-minded Tinkerbell. She had not heard from Al. There was no Loretta. The band played *Rock Around The Clock*. Young men in their washed and neatly pressed civilian clothes sat at the tables and drank and watched the girls parade rhythmically in front of the stage. I sat sideways on, looking through the crowd in case any of the drinkers had grey straggly hair or were missing an arm but if Stan was in the building anywhere, he was probably already in my room. I held up a hand and Preed came over, smiling.

"Whisky?" he said. "Coming right up."

I shook my head.

"Beer," I said. "Thank you."

The blue smoke from Betty's cigarette hung in the dim lights like mist on a morning river. She came up next to me and tapped out some ash with a delicate flick of her finger, shrugged, and the silk of the kaftan shimmered on her shoulders.

"I have something to ask you, Mister Matthew," she said.

"As long as it's not too difficult."

"What do you see?"

Preed brought my beer and a Martini.

"Merci beaucoup," I said. "What do you mean, Betty? I see your bar. The stage, the band, girls, guys drinking."

She looked disappointed. I had not been in the mood for a test of my imaginative power but she clearly was in earnest.

"I'm sorry. What do you want me to see?" I said. She spread her arms expansively to take in the scene, the ash staying obediently on the end of her cigarette.

"A restaurant. Serving Thai food. To respectable customers. That's what I see, Mister Matthew. One day, there will be no war, these boys will be gone. I will be a legitimate businesswoman."

She laughed lightly, like a nightingale on hearing a particularly droll anecdote. She touched my arm, electric. The merest brush with Betty was like being hit with a cattle prod. I could see the dingy bar. I couldn't see the dream.

"There will be women in beautiful dresses, men in the most expensive suits, eating the finest food from the smartest tables."

"A proper band of musicians," I said, lightly, trying to share the vision. She frowned.

"What is wrong with this band?" she said. "They are my cousins." That explained a lot.

"Nothing," I said.

She leaned closer to me.

"You will not breathe a word to Moreau, will you? The time has not come," she whispered.

I couldn't see at that point the significance of keeping this unlikely possibility from Al but I was happy to concur if it meant something to Betty. Besides, Al and I were not on speaking terms, largely because he wasn't there. I found out later why it was important to her. It still makes me sad when I think about it now.

"Whatever you say."

She gazed across the bar, filling it with sophisticated chatter, glamorous bonhomie shading out the reality, the frantic and fearful desperation. I chose to change the subject.

"He's convinced Loretta is secret service," I said. "That she's snooping on him."

"Moreau is a crazy man."

"A crazy man."

She raised her glass and clinked it against mine.

"To Moreau being crazy," she said. We drank the toast.

"And Loretta? Where is she?"

"I was stupid enough to think she wanted me. Maybe it's me that's crazy."

"To you being crazy," Betty said. We clinked glasses and drank, though it wasn't a toast I thought was wholly applicable.

"Girls would want you, Mister Matthew."

"You think?"

"Kannika likes you. She told me so."

I recalled this kind of hushed intrigue filtering along the ranks of the benches set around the gym when we held a Saturday night dance with the local girls' school during summer term. One week it was at theirs, a couple of weeks later, it was at ours, so you could remember who was there and who looked interested and who didn't. They were young, they had their hair curling around their lightly made up pale faces in a modest modern style, sometimes with headbands, they wore cotton skirts below the knee and short socks and sensible shoes. I could do the waltz. The head thought learning it was socially advantageous.

Now the girls were dancing by the stage, shuffling in their sandals or high heels and evening wear of shiny halter-strapped tops and hot pants or mini-skirts, trying to catch the eye of some sex-starved soldier, displaying their number cards. Not any older than the ones in the school gym. Some of them not as old. I didn't know their names. I felt bad that I didn't know their names.

"Number seven," Betty said.

There was an ever-changing population, some of them found men, some gave up, went home, some simply disappeared, went somewhere else. I didn't ask too many questions. I wasn't there to judge how they made their money. They were all as thin as rakes, up from the country, supporting their families back home. It was like Al had said to me once, in this world, you got to take what you can, when you can, how you can. That's what freedom is all about. It ain't nothing more than survival, boy.

I stared across through the fug of smoke to a pretty girl, I recognised her, one of those who always seemed to find my presence a mildly entertaining diversion, I didn't know why. She looked older than the others with long dark hair cascading down her back and she was dancing as if she really thought the band was groovy. She caught me looking at her and waved and smiled. I waved back. It seemed like the politest thing to do.

"Because you are my friend, Mister Matthew, this one time, special offer," Betty said. "Five per cent discount."

I contemplated my beer glass. This sort of thing never happened in the school gym.

"That's very generous," I said.

Betty was watching me with amusement through the mirror. I was, in her eyes, just a red-blooded male and no different to any of the others.

"Loretta," she said. "Was that her name? Are you forgetting her already?"

The ultimate temptress wasn't going to let me get away easy.

"Look at Kannika, Mister Matthew. She will help you forget. Ten per cent discount."

I finished my beer and got up. Having Betty call me her friend was good enough for one evening.

"Number seven is not Loretta," I said. "And I have work to do."

Betty's mischievous laughter followed me out of the bar.

21

I wanted to catch up with McMichael, who was clearly way ahead in his preparation. And if he was, Raniero and Soames would be marshalling their formidable resources, flexing their muscles and strapping on the gloves ready for round one.

In my corner, meanwhile, I didn't even have the defendant. It was dark, the light in my room was dim, every so often a flash of neon from outside would illuminate some detail; records of incoming goods, vehicles arriving in Al's motor pool and then apparently vanishing into thin air. The documents were concentrated on a short period, summer, 1968. I sat on my settee, chewing gum, and I wished my partners Cockroach and Lizard were there. A small consolation for the absence of Loretta, I had to admit, but they would at least have been more animated than the elephant.

"You let me down, pal," I said to him, his trunkless tusked face staring glassily ahead.

I was using the trunk to trace my place on the pages when I spotted the clue. I sat up. I skimmed some of the papers, the copies of dockets, of order forms, of shipments, looking for one I could use as an example, to check against the rest.

"Wait a minute, old thing," I said to the elephant. There, July 17, 1968, signed in one two-and-a-half ton truck, pretty big, a six-wheeler, even Al couldn't have slipped that one up his jumper and gone out the back door. A docket from the mechanics, vehicle inspected. I put it on a pile by my side. July 20, 1968, vehicle moved on, headed for a unit in Tay Ninh, near the border with Cambodia. It had gone from the motor pool. And it had been signed out, not just by Al but with two other signatures, presumably the receiving officer, or maybe not, because the signatures appeared on other papers. And Al wasn't always the one signing them out. Or signing them in. I rifled through the papers, scanning the dockets, the order forms.

"FNG scores the winner," I said to the elephant. "Stays alive longer than the first week, oh, yes."

The band played *Mr Tambourine Man*. I was on the verge of getting up and sprinting across to the Justice Centre but McMichael would have left long ago and me running through the streets waving papers over my head shouting "I've got it" would have been preposterous. Tempting. But preposterous. I would do it in the morning. I picked up the elephant and gave it a hug and then took the chewing gum out of my mouth and plopped it on its head, jamming the trunk onto it and holding the two together. The trunk was curved and pointing in the air. The gum slipped a little but it held.

There was a knock at the door. Just as the day had got better, it could easily get worse. I dropped the papers, startled. After all that had been happening, I was on edge. I thought I had locked it, though if Bronsky had decided he wanted a bed for the night, that wouldn't have deterred him. I wasn't expecting any other visitors.

"Who is it?" I said, getting up and putting my ear to the door. A light shuffling of feet outside. It didn't sound like heavy boots, so maybe not Stan. There was no answer.

"Come on, I'm not opening the door until I know who it is," I said.

Another light knock. They weren't going away, whoever it was, and I couldn't sit there and ignore them so I decided to take a chance. I opened the door a crack and peered out into the darkness of the corridor, which stretched away behind her into emptiness.

She had on the sunglasses, the ones with the big round yellow frames. She was carrying a suitcase.

"Fixed it yet, Scooter?"

*　*　*

The elephant's trunk slid down as the chewing gum lost its stickiness and failed as an adhesive. We both watched as the trunk slowly dropped to the floor.

"Good job," she said.

"It was an experiment."

"You fixed it with, what's that? Doublemint?"

"Bazooka Joe. I like the comic strips."

"Maybe try something else next time, I don't know, say, glue, or something?"

"I will."

She sat on the settee with her hands clasped together, twirling her sunglasses by the earpiece, the suitcase in front of her, a small backpack containing the rest of her luggage leaning against it. She looked tired.

"Did you have something to eat? I could go and get us something?" I said but she shook her head.

"If I don't tell you why I'm here, can I stay?"

"I went to the hotel."

"Did you find me?"

"No. And I just missed Marilyn Monroe."

She smiled.

"I like to keep moving."

"Because of me? You knew I would look for you?"

"No. Well, partly, kind of but not the way you think. It's not always all about you, Scooter. Is it?"

"No. It's about you," I said. "Thanks for dropping by."

"I was just passing."

She came over and gave me a brief hug. It was wonderful.

"You're a good guy, Scooter. Don't let me hurt you."

Her head rested against my chest. I put my hand on her back. She tensed and pulled away.

"Make yourself at home. Mi casa es su casa as we say in good old Blighty."

"I will. Can I take a shower? I feel all kind of clammy, I walked a long way, then I got a tuk-tuk, it was so hot today. Is this the bathroom? And that's the bedroom?"

She walked around the rooms. It didn't take long.

"Nice place," she said, going into the bathroom with her small rucksack. "I saw Betty. Downstairs. She told me where you were. She said Al's not here? Do you mind putting my suitcase in the bedroom? I'll unpack when I'm through."

Unpack? Bedroom?

"Place is popping. Downstairs. Is it always like that?"

I took her suitcase, it was not big or heavy, and put it on the bed. The sound of splashing water and a squeal.

"Leave it running. It will get hot in a while," I shouted.

"Thanks for the warning."

I spread my papers out on the floor beneath the window and looked out down at the crowds in the street, then at the papers and shuffled them around a bit and I could hear Loretta splashing in my shower and if I was right and the more I looked, the more I thought I might be, the prosecution would need their star witness because without him – Loretta in the shower was a little distracting – I knew I would be able to take their case to pieces, rip it up, cast it to the four winds. I wanted Al back. Now, I didn't want to miss my day in court. I was padded up, I was on my way out of the pavilion and it was a batsman's wicket.

"Got any more towels?"

She poked her head through the doorway, face red from the

shower. The small towel I had been using was wrapped in a turban around her hair.

"That's all there is."

"What, this facecloth? Jeez, Scooter, what kind of concierge service you got in this place?"

She closed the door and I could hear her clattering around trying to dry herself on the inadequate towel. I got out some notepaper and a pen I had bought and made notes, trying to focus. My degree, as well as taking in the usual areas like tort and contract and equity had involved a separate module on advocacy, which I took. My education, despite what my father had to say on the subject, was not entirely wasted.

"This towel is not big enough, Scooter."

There were set patterns to cross-examination. Depending on the answers you got, which you should already know you were going to get from the testimony you had been given beforehand, you would follow a certain path.

"First thing tomorrow we go shopping," Loretta said.

Next question leading on to next question and I was writing this pathway down when I heard the bathroom door open and Loretta dashed across to the bedroom, partially wrapped in the small towel.

"Don't look," she said.

"Believe me, I would not want to do that," I said. I was lying. She laughed.

"I need my jimmy-jams."

I wiped sweat from my forehead, not entirely caused by the oppressive heat. So, for instance, Saunders would tell the court he had seen Al hold a meeting with a man from Singapore in his office at the motor pool. The next day, one of the jeeps was diverted out the back door. How did he know the two incidents were connected? Causation. Loretta came out of my bedroom dressed in silk pink pyjamas.

And then if Saunders said he knew the guy was concerned with the buying and selling of US government property, I would ask him how he could know that. And so on. Pretty straightforward really. I hadn't chosen the right time to concentrate. Loretta looked like she had always lived in my flat. There was a knock at the door. A look of panic crossed her face. She darted back into the bedroom.

"Don't answer it," she said. Another knock.

"Nobody knows you're here. Except Betty."

Even so, I eased the door open a crack before looking out. I was not expecting another visitor; the only one I wanted was already in my rooms. A young girl was outside. I recognised her as Number Seven. She smiled.

"Betty say to tell you fifteen per cent discount."

She turned quickly and ran back down the corridor.

"Tell Betty that's very funny," I said to her retreating back and went in and closed the door and turned to see Loretta peering from the bedroom.

"Who was it?"

"No-one."

"Sounded like a girl."

"No. No, it wasn't. Are you okay?"

Loretta had her arms folded. She looked pale. The knock at the door had frightened her. I didn't think it was just because she had heard another girl's voice. She was shaking. I wanted to go over to her and wrap my arms around her and tell her everything was going to be okay but I didn't. I couldn't say that with any certainty.

"I'm just plain exhausted, I guess," Loretta said. "It's been kind of a weird couple of days, so, yeah, I think maybe that's what I ought to do, what I'm going to go do, I'm going to go to bed. Goodnight."

She took it for granted that I would give up my room. I would, of course. She closed the door. For a second night, I looked at the settee and sighed.

22

Loretta was still in bed when I finally gave up on trying to sleep with my feet on the elephant. Sleep was over-rated. I couldn't think of a night in the last three months when I had got more than about four hours for one reason or another, usually because we had elected to set up camp in a place where the sun shone right into the tent at about four am or there were kids peering in through the flaps or animals or something. Or insomniac Alfie had got the kettle on. And then in my previous digs, simple terror had chased away the Sandman each night. And now because I couldn't get at my bed. On this occasion, I didn't mind. I would have laid on a bed of nails to be near Loretta. In fact, I woke up feeling like I had.

A discussion with Al was vital. The prosecution would be expecting us to go in with our hands up, to keel over in the face of this witness they had finally produced. The plea bargain was still on the table. In all honesty it might still be Al's best move. But at least I had a plan. All I needed was for him to turn up.

I went downstairs to cadge a pot of tea from Betty, or Preed or whoever was up, go out and get some pancakes maybe to take back to the room for breakfast. The big frosted window that stretched the length of the building and shielded the bar from passing eyes let in pale light diffused through the low-lying fog of cigarette smoke, its pattern lines changing with the shadows when a tram rattled past. The bar smelt stale, fusty, with a top note tang of alcohol.

I had a sense of peace. On the stage, the band's guitars lay propped up and idle, the drum kit at rest, and one of the girls was sleeping there curled up on a chair. The only sounds were her soft breath mingled with an occasional snore from a young Westerner who was also asleep, his head on his arms across a table like it was nap time.

I sat in the centre of the room, quietly, but the slight scrape of my chair disturbed him and he looked up, immediately awake, swivelling his head from side to side and then grimacing as last night's drinking hit him. I watched as he blinked and assessed his surroundings, realised he was safe, rubbed his eyes. He was just a kid.

"Hi," he said.

"A very good morning."

Betty came in, yawning. Her hair was wrapped in a kind of scarf, she was wearing a dressing gown that swept the floor. She smiled and waved and lit a cigarette and got herself a Martini glass from the shelf behind the bar to mix a drink.

"Sawatdee-kah," she said. The young man looked up at the sound of her voice, perhaps briefly thinking it was his mother calling him down for some Rice Krispies, having changed overnight into a Thai torch singer.

"Morning, Betty," I pointed to the stage where the girl was sleeping and put my finger to my lips, ssshh. Betty finished mixing her drink, took a sip. She took the tops off two bottles of Coca Cola, held them both expertly in between the fingers of her other hand, and walked across, dropping one off first next to the gaping soldier.

"On the house," she said, sitting at my table. In the early light, I could see the unconcealed lines wrinkling in her face.

"First one of the day, no olives," she said. "That's the secret, Mister Matthew."

"I'll remember that," I said. "Very amusing prank, by the way. I laughed a lot."

"You are very popular," she said, smiling. "You are a lucky man."

"Not quite as lucky as I might have been. Any news of Al?"

"No news."

"I want to talk to him."

"Ah, Mister Matthew, so do I. Very much."

The soldier swigged his Coke and coughed.

"I guess my buddies left, huh?" he said.

"Looks like it," I said.

"What day is this?"

"Could be Wednesday."

"Already? Jesus. Where the hell did that five days go, man?"

"You drank most of it," Betty said, not unkindly.

"Ain't that the truth?" He grinned at all he could remember of his R and R in Bangkok. "We go back today."

"Where to?" I said.

"Up country, I guess, maybe up near the DMZ, been there before, don't rightly know, they don't tell us nothing and then they say, hey, go in that jungle, go up that hill, there's some guys waiting for you there, waiting to blow your goddam head off, go look for them, find them, wipe them out."

Betty sipped her Martini and the life seeped back into her face.

"Best get going." The soldier got up and took exceeding care as he walked away from his chair, each step perfectly positioned. "You thinking I walk like this 'cos I've been drunk?"

We didn't reply. I was used by now to having US servicemen in my home. They lived on a trigger. It didn't pay to get too involved. This was nothing to do with us, the British. We had opted out.

"Hell, no, I walk like this the way I've been trained, I don't want to step on no booby traps, what they do, on the paths, they dig holes and they put sharp sticks in and cover them up for you to fall down."

When I was his age, I was cocooned in my safe world, cotton-woolled. I would never hear the whistle blow, be ordered over the top of the trench into a hail of machine gun fire.

"I seen a guy got his leg tore up, they put poison on the end of the sticks, man."

He trod carefully across the room, exaggerating each step as Betty and I watched. He was probably a bit drunk still.

"And there's mud, like this thick red clay, you can't pick your feet up. And mines, buried just under the topsoil, I know soil, I'm from Missouri. Your name Betty, right, ma'am?"

Betty nodded and yawned, covering her mouth.

"Bouncing Betty, you heard of that?"

"Yes," she said. "I get that a lot."

The soldier was undeterred.

"You tread on it, it comes spinning up into the air, I saw a guy, when it gets to about here, about to your middle, it goes boom, lets off these like ball bearings. Cut him in half. I didn't know him too well. So, yeah, I'm practising my walk."

He teetered towards us, arms out like he was on a tightrope.

"I got three months to go," he said, putting his empty Coke bottle on our table. "I'm pretty sure of one thing. I ain't never going home."

He shook himself awake.

"Better go find my buddies."

"Side door through there," Betty said, pointing past the stage.

"Thank you for the drink, ma'am. And for your hospitality. Real nice place you got here." He saluted. "I don't suppose I'll be seeing you again."

He turned and walked away, his boot steps echoing on the wooden floor. I wanted to stop him, to run after him, drag him to the floor and sit on his back until the war was over and he was not a child any more. The girl on the stage stirred. The soldier saluted her and left. She yawned and stretched. Betty sighed and said something in Thai, something Buddhist probably, some proverb, it sounded poetic. I asked for the translation.

"It means it's opening time," she said.

23

We spent the day idling in my rooms; I worked on some more preparation in case Al ever showed up again and Loretta skimmed through *Moby Dick*, occasionally getting up and walking across to the window, looking out and scanning the street earnestly for something or somebody. Wandering back to the settee, picking up the book again.

"You think the girls downstairs are happy, Scooter? The girls in the bar? They're awful young."

"Yeah, I noticed."

"You noticed the girls?"

"I noticed they were young."

She flicked through the book.

"Like the girl who came to your room last night?"

I put down my pen. She wasn't looking at me, she was pretending to be gripped by the adventures of Captain Ahab and his crew.

"That was a joke. From Betty. She knows I'm not interested."

"Not interested, huh? Not interested in girls?"

"Not interested in those girls."

"Must be scary, going to all those different hotel rooms with all those different men. I wouldn't want to do it."

"Nobody's asking you to." I looked through the notes again but they were blurring a little in front of my eyes.

"Would you pay for me, Scooter? How much?"

I gave up and sat back in my chair.

"Let's see, the going rate is ten dollars a night, at least that's what I've been paying for all these girls, that's where all my money's been going, you're right, discount for the week, so pound for pound, weighing it all up, for you? Thirty cents."

She threw the book across the room at me, laughing.

"I'm robbing myself but I know you need the money," I said, ducking as it flew past me and hit the window.

"Damn cheapskate."

And then I thought about it and I knew she was right and I turned a blind eye and everyone did the same because they were earning money and that was the way they did it and their families knew, they sent them, up from the villages because they could earn more in a day in the city than in a year planting rice. Looking after the pigs. Everybody does what they have to do.

"Let's go eat something," Loretta said.

We went out to a restaurant and we swapped stories about our home towns and we laughed and ate fish soup and rice, some pancakes. She wore her big round sunglasses and her headscarf and she took my arm as we crossed the roads and I didn't think she was a secret service agent any more, not for one minute.

"I'm going to find another hotel," she said. "There's a couple downtown, they don't look so bad."

I got a sinking feeling in my stomach not entirely attributable to the condition of the restaurant.

"Why?" I asked. "You can stay."

"That's real sweet of you, Scooter, but I can't."

We strolled past some curio shops. We had gone a little further afield, though I didn't want to stay out too long on the off chance I could get to talk to Al. We passed a shop selling pottery. Loretta stopped and looked in the window.

"Why not?"

"Because."

"If you go back to a hotel, I'll lose you again."

"Maybe you won't. Maybe you will. Maybe you'll want to."

We walked away from the shop.

"Besides," she said. "In your apartment, there's only one bed."

There are moments when you think you might have been pitched a long-hop just outside the off stump and it's waiting to be stroked away for four through the covers. You relish these moments, the split second when you know the ball is there to be hit. Loretta didn't seem to have noticed she had bowled one of these and was looking at some jewellery in a shop.

"I'm okay on the settee," I said.

And then you play the stroke and it's slightly mis-timed and the ball goes sailing past into the wicketkeeper's gloves. She looked at me, eased the sunglasses down her nose and peered over the top of them.

"You do know what you should have said there, right, Scooter?"

I nodded. I think I had gone bright red. She laughed and hugged my arm tighter. I bought her a bracelet, gold coloured with an intricate pattern.

"Payback for the suit," I said.

"You get a suit and I get a trinket? Because I'm a girl?"

"Because it looks pretty."

We went in through the side door at Betty's. The bar was filling up but I could see no sign of Al. Back in my rooms, I sat on the edge of the bed and then lay back. We had walked a long way. I closed my eyes. The tiredness washed over me.

"Okay, Action Man," Loretta said. "I guess I'll just go talk to Betty. Then maybe I'll think about packing."

"I'll be down in a minute," I said. "I think I'll rest a little."

I heard her go out and wondered what the hell I was supposed to do because I couldn't figure her, I didn't know what she wanted. When we were out, she would check everybody who passed by like she was looking for someone and now she wanted to leave but she didn't. Then she wanted to hide but she went to the bar. It was warm. Quiet. The band hadn't started to play. I dozed off and when I woke up it was dark.

"Loretta?" I said, stumbling into the living room. Her headscarf still lay across the elephant where she had discarded it and her suitcase was on the floor by the window. I splashed some water on my face and went out to look for her.

The band was playing a swing version of *Rock Around The Clock* with a hint of twelve-bar blues and some skiffle. The bar was full. I couldn't see Loretta, she wasn't with Betty, who was standing next to Preed, both looking a little anxious. The girls were dancing by the stage. They seemed nervous. Then I caught sight of some familiar figures. The group of sailors who had been in a couple of nights before, the ones Al had sent on their way. They were back, there were one or two more of them and they were staggering around, deliberately barging into some groups of soldiers. Loretta was right there in the middle of them, sitting by the bar, crowded in. The sailors muscled in around her, talking right into her face. She was trapped.

"Loretta," I called but she didn't hear me over the band and the general noise from all the men shouting. They were two and three deep at the bar, red-faced and swaying. Preed was working to serve them as fast as he could but he was flustered. The two bouncers who normally sat outside had come in to help but they couldn't keep up. I edged closer to Loretta.

"Excuse me," I said, shoving through, not wanting to upset too many people but my way to her was narrow and I knocked into some tables.

"Hey, watch it, Buster."

"Sorry," I said. It was the first time the bar had seemed an angry place. Maybe it should have been all the time; they should have been angry, these men, though not with each other and there was more jostling and Loretta saw me through the crowd and waved. The sailors nearest to her looked around.

"Well, if it ain't pussyboy," one said. My heart sank. It was the same big chap. He stood in my way.

"Excuse me," I said, trying to get through to Loretta.

"Hey, what's your hurry?" he said, barring my path. His friends clamoured around, laughing.

"Looks like the other guy ain't here, Larry," one of them said.

"Is that so?" Larry said. "Then this little lady here was just leaving with us, ain't that right, sister?"

Loretta shook her head.

"I'm not little and I wouldn't go anywhere with you even if you weren't the ugliest scumbag on this earth," she said in one of her enigmatic sentence structures. Larry tried to figure out quite what she meant. She was sitting on the stool where I normally sat, next to Al's, which was empty. She tried to move away.

"It's okay," she said, catching my eye.

"It's not okay," I said, still befuddled from my nap. "Larry, I hope you won't take this the wrong way but everyone is tired of your company. Please leave."

I reached across for Loretta's hand. She was looking at me in shock. So, I couldn't help but notice, was Larry.

"What the…?" he said, grabbing me by the front of my shirt. "Who do you think you're talking to, pussyboy?"

I knocked his hands away. He took a step back. His friends gave a chorus of encouragement. From the corner of my eye, I could see Preed and his comrades spilling beer as they watched. The band slid into *Shakin' All Over*. I had no choice. I could wait for Larry to hit me, which would almost certainly have resulted in some injury to my face or I could strike first and hope for the best. I took up a guard.

Larry spat on his hands and balled them into fists. He swung a right. To my surprise, I blocked it with my left forearm. The rest of the bar was watching. There were cheers and jeers. Loretta was moving away. I wanted to get to her. I swung with my right in an unpractised loop, half-closed my eyes and I didn't appear to hit anything but when I opened them fully, Larry was sinking to his knees, a look of pain on his face. I danced a little boxing step, jabbed with my left.

"Yeah, come on," I said.

But as he sank down, I could see someone else behind him. It was Al, whose fist was just returning from smacking him a sharp blow in the kidneys.

"Bar fight," someone shouted and I was swept up in a seething mass of bodies as the soldiers piled in and the sailors struck back and within an instant, the bar was turned into a brawl. I was still gaping at Al, who winked.

"Look after your gal, boy," he said, swinging another punch into the side of someone's head and sending them spinning. I dodged around him and stood in front of Loretta. A chair flew through the air and I stopped it from hitting her, pulling her behind me around the corner of the bar. The girls by the stage screamed. Bottles were flying. The band played. Someone hit me in the face. I swung another punch, I missed again, the man went down under a pile of bodies. I could see Al in the middle of all this, watchful, serene. Every move was targeted, every punch accurate and decisive. This was a man you would follow into battle. This was how he came alive.

Chairs and tables were crashing to the floor. The band dodged glasses thrown randomly around the room. Bedlam. I couldn't get Loretta out so I stood in front of her as a shield but when I looked around she had gone and she was standing next to me about to clout a soldier over the head with a chair.

A shot rang out and everybody stopped. Fists were poised in mid-air. Chairs hung suspended over people's heads and I realised why the furniture was so light. It broke easily. It could be replaced. Betty had a gun and was pointing it towards the ceiling. Preed and the two bouncers had ducked as she fired it. She took a drag from her black cigarette in the silver cigarette holder.

"Bar's closed," she said.

24

Taking advantage of an early night, the band had started to stumble around with the chords for a new song. There was lively chatter among the girls. Some of them appeared to welcome the time off and were preparing either to go home or have a night to themselves, several had followed the servicemen out into the street, still eager to make some money. Betty had let them go, to work on a freelance basis if they wanted. Al had made sure everyone else had left by standing in the centre of the room, balancing on the balls of his feet, fists clenched, the pose he would have struck had he ever been cast into a bronze statue. They had all gone, given him a wide berth.

"Sailors," Al said, shaking his head, taking a beer from off the bar.

Preed and the bouncers were counting the damaged chairs and tables, seeing which could be salvaged and which were destined for firewood. Betty was watching them, drink in hand. Loretta had dashed upstairs to fetch her Medevac first aid kit and was applying some stinging fluid onto the small cut and swelling I had just under my right eye. I winced.

"There, there. Be brave," she said. "You're going to have a shiner."

I could see Al watching her dab away expertly with the cotton wool, no doubt wondering if nursing skills were part of the armoury of a secret service agent. He put a hand around his jaw and worked his mouth from side to side. He had a couple of marks on his chin where some lucky punches had landed and a thin cut on his forehead. Loretta turned to him.

"That's a nasty one," she said, delving into the kit for some iodine and plasters. He backed away. "Hold still, this won't hurt."

He flinched.

"Now, just come on," she said. "You gotta be a brave boy for Loretta."

She stood with her plasters and her professional face and Al caved in meekly, letting her apply the ointment and stick a brown plaster across the wound.

"There now, that wasn't too bad, was it?"

"Guess not," he said.

"Let me see this." Loretta took his jaw between her fingers and worked it in and out and looked in his mouth to check for missing teeth. "Nothing broken. No loose teeth, I don't think, no, that's good. You'll live."

She smiled her nurse's about to go off a twelve-hour shift smile. Al swigged the beer.

"I go away for a couple of days and you got the whole damn US Navy staging fist fights in the bar, Slugger," he said.

"We're in court tomorrow morning."

"I'll take this upstairs," Loretta said. "It's late."

I had lost track of time, having nodded off in the afternoon. I had left Loretta downstairs in the bar on her own, surrounded by leering drunken sailors. What a boyfriend I was, if I was a boyfriend. For several hours, it appeared, when I checked the time. I was mortified. I slipped off the stool to hurry upstairs after her to apologise.

"Hey," Al said. I hesitated. I wasn't going to say thanks for saving me. Betty came up behind him and put her arms around his waist, one hand slipping past to put her Martini on the bar. She rested her head sideways on his back and smiled. Al shaped his finger into a pistol and pointed it at me, making a clicking sound with his teeth which made him wince.

"Good fight," he said.

The punch-up appeared to have made him wistful.

"Your girl has a jab like Liston," he said. I felt a little jealous. I was pathetically hoping he would also compliment me on my martial prowess. He didn't.

"Do it again tomorrow?" I said. "I mean in the courtroom, of course, not in the bar."

"Sure," Al said. It didn't seem the right time to ask him where he had been. I would either get no answer or one that was so long I would miss the moment to offer my grovelling apology to Loretta. I stepped over the debris and left him and Betty sitting there cuddling cosily, listening to the band at low volume trying to force their way into the opening chords of *Born to Be Wild*. Steppenwolf. The singer swung his microphone and caught it, pointed it at me, grinning. I acknowledged this with a wave and he went back to the song. I tried to convince myself it was a tribute to me. It probably wasn't. The adrenalin rush started to subside.

The bedroom door was closed. Loretta had gone to bed, probably still angry at me for abandoning her in the bar. Or just gone. It was quiet, apart from the chugging intro to the song leaking quietly up from downstairs. Her suitcase wasn't by the window. My first thought was that she had walked out on me because I had let her down so badly. If she had considered leaving anyway, this would have made up her mind.

I listened carefully. I could faintly hear movement from my bedroom so she had at least decided to wait until the morning before she left. It would give me a chance to explain. I didn't hold out much hope. There was nothing I could say. I picked up the court papers but I couldn't think straight. I sat back with my eyes closed, my head throbbing. I heard a light cough from the doorway of the bedroom.

"It's okay," I said, without opening my eyes. "I'm fine here. Look, I'm sorry I left you in the bar. I'm sorry I wasn't there. I'm sorry."

Another cough. I opened one eye. The neon lights were flashing through the window. Loretta was standing in shadow. She was leaning back, one foot on the door frame behind her, her knee bent, one hand behind her head, pushing up her hair.

"I'm looking for my hero," she said.

"Yeah, well, keep looking. Because there's just me." I closed my eyes again. "It's okay, you take the bed. I'm fine here, honestly."

"Ahem," she said. "For Christ's sake, Scooter, open your goddam eyes."

I opened them. I looked across the dark room. She was illuminated in her film star magazine pose by stripes of light through the window, flashing on and off, yellow, orange, electric blue. She was naked.

"Got thirty cents?" she said. She crooked her index finger and beckoned me, pushed herself from the door frame and went into the bedroom. I am not ashamed to say I leapt to my feet. I knocked over the elephant.

25

"What in glory's name happened to you two?"

McMichael was waiting outside the court room as Al and I arrived. We had driven across in the Land Rover, Al had yet to find a buyer, and he had parked it in a space reserved for prosecution lawyers, maybe by accident; knowing Al, maybe not.

"Nothing," I said.

"You had a disagreement?"

McMichael appeared to be mildly amused and I couldn't say I blamed him. Al still had the sticking plaster across the side of his forehead, a drying cut on his lip and a bruise on his chin. I was peering through a black and purple eye that Loretta's powder make-up had failed to disguise. Apart from that, we looked smart, Al was in his uniform, neatly starched. I had on my new suit and I felt on top of the world.

"Little accident," Al said. "Sir."

"Are we ready?" I said. "Anything we should know?"

McMichael shook his head. He had his papers in a folder. The hearing was due to start.

"Not from me," he said. "Any change in the position?"

He looked at me, doubtless hoping I was going to say that Al's intransigent stance concerning his guilt had finally been changed but I couldn't tell him that. I had asked him on the way but I had not been given a definitive answer.

"Leave it to me, boy," was all he had said, so I shrugged and opened the door for us to enter the same courtroom where Raniero and Soames were waiting with the same staff in attendance. Raniero looked round and nudged Soames as we approached.

"Well, blow me down, if it ain't Henry Cooper," he said in a mock English accent. "And if I'm not mistaken, Rocky Marciano. No, wait, it's Marlon Brando. Hey, I coulda been a contender."

"That's very funny, Raniero," I said. It had occurred to me that I was in the happy position of not having to call any of them Sir and I could tell that it rankled the prosecution. "What do you do for an encore?"

"Probably give you another black eye, Benson," he said, laughing. I needed to work on my comebacks. I had left him an opening and I didn't have a ready answer.

"Morning," Soames said, leaning across the aisle and talking over McMichael. "The deal is still on the table."

McMichael ignored him.

"Did you hear me?" he said.

"Sorry, Blaine," McMichael said. "I thought I had said go screw yourself out loud. Must have been just in my head."

The side door opened and Major Jackson strode in, storming up to the dais, hefting himself into his chair before we barely had time to stand up. He surveyed the room to see who was present, raising an eyebrow as he looked from my face to Al's.

"Boxing tournament is next door," he said. The clerk and the stenographer laughed as they were expected to. So did Soames as he got to his feet.

"That's very good, Sir," he said.

"Thank you, Captain Soames. I know. What do you have for me today?"

"Pre-trial review in the case of Sergeant Al Moreau, Sir. You will recall this case came before you last week when a number of not guilty pleas were entered."

"I'm familiar with the case. What's happening?"

"The prosecution has reviewed the case in the light of fresh witness testimony, Sir."

"Have you discussed this with the defence?"

"Yes, Sir."

If he was referring to the altercation outside the Justice Centre, I could not call that a discussion. I got to my feet, thinking I could score a point. McMichael looked down. Al had his arms folded. My hands were fluttering around on the papers in front of me.

"With all due respect, Major, the prosecution has not approached us with this testimony in any meaningful way," I said.

"Is that so, Mr..." He looked at his notes. "Benson?"

"We were not given full sight of this testimony until a couple of days ago. My client has been out of the area and we have been unable to assess its relevance as completely as we would have liked."

I saw Soames nod to Raniero, who started quickly scribbling a note. Probably nothing unusual in that but it put me off for a minute. I had said something wrong but I couldn't immediately figure out what it was.

"Sir, it is not the fault of the prosecution if the defendant has not been available," Soames said. "We served the testimony in good time for this hearing."

The Major turned his attention to me.

"What do you have to say to that, Mr Benson?"

The fan in the ceiling got louder as I searched for a reply.

"The defence has been given insufficient time to prepare."

"So you said."

"I only came into this case a few days ago."

Blunder. I knew right away Soames would be all over that and he was.

"Again, not the fault of the prosecution, Sir, the defence has experienced counsel as second chair and they were fully informed of the facts of this case in ample time. I urge the court to proceed."

The Major had shifted away from me and was looking at Soames. I had lost the opening exchange.

"I agree. What next?"

He was asking Soames. Not the clerk. Certainly not me. McMichael slipped a note across the desk.

"Sit down!!!" it said. I sat down. He leaned over to whisper.

"Put forward a motion to have the trial before a panel," he said.

"A what?"

"A panel of five."

"How come you're telling me this now?"

"You didn't know? Okay, ask for a recess. Quick."

I had been keeping an eye on the judge. He was looking at us. So were Soames and Raniero. I got to my feet.

"Could we please have a recess, judge?"

"On what grounds?" Soames said. "We've only just started the case. All we are waiting for is a plea. A recess is not good use of the court's time, Sir."

"It would allow my client a moment to consider his position which might be advantageous to the overall handling of this case."

"Sir, he has had plenty of time to think."

Soames was trampling me into the ground.

"You don't need a recess, Mr Benson. Let's get on," the judge said.

I leaned towards Al.

"You can have a panel or a single judge. What's it to be?"

McMichael joined in.

"Go for the panel, Moreau. Look at the odds. You have five members, it's a majority call. You have more chance, believe me."

Al shook his head.

"No panel," he said. "I want this guy."

"What? You think he's on your side?" McMichael asked.

Soames was back on his feet.

"Major, the court room is no place for a continuing case conference. It has to be time for the defendant to put in a guilty plea."

He sat down.

"You sure?" I said to Al.

"He's okay," Al said and I was back on my feet because I had also been listening to Soames and he had bowled one short.

"Judge, I would like to know why the prosecution is expecting a guilty plea. I don't think they can pre-empt the defendant's choice and I certainly don't think they should state it in court."

Soames had got a bit carried away. The Major smiled.

"He's got you there, Captain."

"I meant plea," Soames said, half rising and then deciding to stay in his place. "I apologise to the court."

"Nice," McMichael said.

Yeah, bring it on. I had clipped that one away through the leg side and it hurtled towards the boundary. The charges were put again. Al stood straight to attention as he had before.

"Not guilty," he said every time. A trial date was set for ten days time. I objected on the grounds that it was too soon, the defence hadn't been given time to prepare and so on but I knew I was going to get the experienced counsel argument back at me again and when that happened, I didn't pursue it further. The judge left. Raniero walked past us, pausing to get in a few parting shots.

"Man, that was amateur hour," he said to me. "Like back in the first week at Harvard Law School when all the real dum-dums got shot down. Bang, bang, bang. You're toast."

Harvard Law School? Their fast bowler had been to Harvard Law School?

"Yeah?" I said. "Well, I'm the toast with the most."

He stepped back.

"What the hell does that mean?"

I had still not got the hang of these side exchanges. It was harder than standing up in front of the judge.

"It means I'm pretty tasty, actually," I said.

"Leave it now, buddy," McMichael said. "You're sounding like a lunatic."

Soames gave Raniero a shove in the back and moved him on then winked at me and gave me a thumbs-up sign.

"I can see I'll have to watch myself," he said and walked off after Raniero.

"Bad cop, good cop. They do it all the time," McMichael said. "You did fine."

"Fine?" This was high praise indeed.

"Well, maybe not fine but okay. We're still standing."

Al tapped me on the shoulder.

"Ten days?" he said. "That's kinda quick. That's it, ten more days?"

He hadn't seemed worried while he was sitting there, as cool as you would have expected under fire. I wondered if it had only just occurred to him that the key was in the lock and the prison doors were waiting to let him in. Some doubt had crept in behind his not guilty shield.

"No, of course not," I said, because I was on a high, I had got through the first round and none of the blows hurt as much as the black eye. "We're going to win this case, Sergeant."

*   *   *

We drove back and left Mary Jane slumped forlornly against the side of an indoor market a couple of streets away from Betty's. Al assured me the vehicle would be okay, his mood having lightened considerably after we left the courtroom. He also told me he knew a guy who was interested in buying her. They just had to get the money together and then it would be all systems go.

It would be bye-bye, old girl. She had taken us as far as she could overland. Cambodia and Laos were off-limits, tons of bombs and chemicals raining down on them as the Americans tried to blast the Ho Chi Minh Trail, the supply line from North to South. They were the buffer between Thailand and Vietnam, the next dominoes to fall to Communism, in the eyes of the Americans.

"He slept in your bed, huh?"

On the way over, I had relayed to Al the troubling encounter with Bronsky, and he was picking up the conversation where we had left off.

"You seem to find this diverting?" I said.

"What?"

"The fact that he slept in my bed. I was on the settee, you know, and that is not really the point."

We walked on through the crowds. He didn't seem to be taking this too seriously. I had added my pessimistic interpretation of Bronsky's coded comments, and I had been waiting for Al to fill me in on some of the background details, his own take on the claymore blast, perhaps modest about his own heroics, something like that, a general overview of their relationship. None had been forthcoming.

"He mentioned that you and he were involved with some dangerous people," I said.

"World is full of them."

"And that they would be decidedly perturbed should you find yourself in prison?"

"I guess so."

"And he also suggested that if you were to stay out of jail, then others would be similarly cheesed off? Thus leaving us between the proverbial rock and hard place. He implied I would be held partly responsible."

"You're my lawyer, right?"

Sometimes, I wanted to grab Al and spin him round and shout into his face. We were approaching Betty's where doubtless he would resume his normal place at the bar and sit silently.

"Are you at all concerned about this?" I asked, skipping past a woman carrying two large baskets of vegetables on either end of a bamboo pole. Her strength was extraordinary. Al shrugged.

"He said he didn't blame you," I said. "You pulled him away from an exploding mine and he lost his arm in the blast."

"Mighty fine of him to say that."

"He said he was on his way back to Montana but he had no luggage. I think he's still here, I see him around every corner, goddammit, wait, talk to me, what about this guy? Also, a couple of other things while we're here, I want to show you some documents because I have a plan and where the hell were you the last few days?"

We passed the window of Betty's. Loretta was upstairs in my rooms. She had decided not to venture out, she preferred to be indoors. The two bouncers and several of the girls were sitting outside. They looked up from whatever it was they were doing, eating, sipping tea, smoking thin cigarettes and keeping in the shade. They greeted us.

"Why aren't you worried?" I asked as Al pushed open the front door. I followed him inside, nodding to my comrades in arms, and smiling at the girls, who laughed coyly behind their hands. I couldn't help but glance across to the stage as we walked in. Seven was there, the number displayed prominently on her arm for the benefit of half a dozen men who were sitting drinking. It was too early for the band. Recorded music played from the speakers. *I Can't Get No Satisfaction.* The Rolling Stones. She was dancing and she gave me a little wave. I smiled, without offering any encouragement. What a Lothario I was. I had a girlfriend. Mom and dad, she is a nurse. Al and I sat at the bar on our usual stools and Preed brought us a beer and a glass of tea.

"You want me to say I'm scared, is that what you want?" Al said. "Okay, I'm scared. How's that? It ain't new, boy."

He picked up the glass of tea. There it was again, the tremor in his hand. The glass shook slightly as he raised it to his lips. He tensed, stopped with it in mid-air and steadied it.

"I spent most of my life being scared," he said. "That's why I'm still alive."

I could see the value of this philosophy for a man whose sole function for twenty years had been to put himself in a position of peril. Being scared was a basic rule of existence for Al. Not, however, for me. In the words of Stan, win or lose, I would have to leave town as quickly as I could, though I really felt I should be regarded as the professional who had done his best and would be allowed to walk away unscathed, as lawyers do. Instead, I was right in the firing line, by Al's side. I was Doc Holliday to his Wyatt Earp. It was time to introduce my master plan.

"Who were the other two guys?" I asked.

"What other two guys?"

"The ones who signed the dockets."

"They were different guys, all the time different guys."

"Some of the names crop up more than others, believe me, I have been through every single one plenty of times. You see where I'm going with this? I can muddy the waters here, I can plant some doubt."

My intention was to cloud the case, throw as much at it as I could, suggest that Al was the innocent party here, he was the one being used by others in the motor pool. If I could get the others into court, it would be a day of glory. If I could introduce them, I had half a chance.

"Leave my guys out of this," Al said. "Don't bring up no names."

"What?"

He had kicked the legs out from under my platform. Let down my tyres.

"I don't want no more names for them to investigate, got me?"

"What about Tommy Saunders? He's right in the frame."

"Tommy don't mean no harm."

I was speechless. Exasperated, I got up to leave him on his stool before I said anything I would regret. I was on the point of quitting.

"You told me we was going to win," he said.

"Well, yes, I did but to do that, I have to have something concrete to build on."

He would give me nothing and yet he still appeared to have absolute faith in my ability to win the case.

"Lemme see," he said. "There is one thing maybe you oughta know."

A possibility. He might be throwing me a scrap I could work with. It was not to be. It was just something even more unsettling.

"And that is?" I asked.

"I don't know any guy called Stan Bronsky."

26

"Let's you and me go away for the weekend," Loretta said. "Get out of the city."

"Where to?"

"There's plenty of places, the coast. The two of us."

"How?"

"We could drive."

No more was needed. Mary Jane back on the road. A diversion. I was keen to get away, I needed time to think and the thought of spending a little holiday with Loretta was enticing; I didn't know she had more in mind. I found Al in the bar, he tossed me the car keys after I had established this supposed potential buyer was nowhere near close to finding the money.

"Where you headed?" was his only comment but I thought I sensed a bit of doubt in his voice.

"Someplace," I said. "Up the coast a little."

Betty stood at the door of the bar, Martini in hand, watching me pull up in the Land Rover, Loretta clambered into the front seat. Al was there, too, and for a moment, I thought he was going to suggest they should come along for the ride. I knew he was still suspicious of Loretta, perhaps even more so following the brawl.

"Where did she learn to throw a left like that?" he had said to me. "You think at nursing school? Hell, no, boy."

I watched them as they gradually diminished in the rear view mirror. Betty waved. Al stood in the road, not moving. I watched him until we were out of sight. As soon as he had given me the keys, there was something wrong with him, something more than his concern about Loretta, which I was determined to banish from my mind at least for the duration of the weekend away. He was worried about something else, I couldn't guess what.

I almost collided with a bus and remembered I was driving in a country where there were no rules of the road. We set off on route 35. The sun was low in the sky. The Western music radio was playing. Loretta had her feet up on the dashboard, headscarf drifting in the breeze from the open window. Hendrix came on. *Wind Cries Mary*. Cars and trucks went by. Loretta had the map, it was a straight run, we headed for Hua Hin, about three hours away to the south west, we had decided to go as far in the other direction as we could from Vietnam. The sun was setting as we turned onto route 4.

"On the weekend," Loretta said. "We would take the pick-up sometimes, a few of us, from school, drive down to the Keys, in Florida. Hang out on the beach. Light a fire, play the radio, dance, drink soda, a beer maybe. Eat marshmallows."

"It sounds idyllic," I said, negotiating another difficult manoeuvre concerning whether to overtake a loaded bicycle and run the risk of ploughing straight into a truck coming in the opposite direction. "Have you ever been to Blackpool?"

I realised straight away its inferiority in the glamour stakes compared to the Florida Keys.

"Blackpool, huh?"

"It's by the sea."

"In England, I guess?"

I suppose it was unlikely Loretta or any of her immediate contemporaries had set foot in a seaside resort in the North.

"Yes. It's a bit breezy but there's a pier and a very good funfair. And the tower, of course. Like the Eiffel Tower. Slightly less impressive, I have to say."

I braked sharply as a skinny pale cow wandered off its intended path and encroached onto the highway before slipping back towards the fields.

"No, I've never been to Blackpool."

"You can buy sticks of rock, a cowboy hat with Kiss Me Quick on the front, fish and chips."

"Like an American cowboy hat?"

"They're very popular."

I concentrated on the road, which was less busy with traffic but still full of hazards for the unwary.

"It's in England?" she said.

"Yes. If you want, I'll take you there."

Loretta tapped her sunglasses on her knee.

"Think we got enough gas?" she said.

I took my eyes off the ever-changing landscape, the winding road, the end of the day heat haze over the fields, mountains in the distance reaching towards the red purple sky, to look at Loretta leaning back in her seat, gazing through the window.

"First time I left America," she said. "Was on a plane to Vietnam. I looked for the funfair in Saigon. Couldn't find it."

I waited for a second or two for this sombre reflection to hang between us.

"Probably closed," I said. "Isn't there a war on?"

She laughed and slapped me on the arm.

"Shall we keep driving, Scooter?"

"For a while," I said.

"That's not what I meant."

"Have a look on the map. I think Hua Hin is just a few miles, we should see the sea soon. You know, when we used to go on holiday in the summer when I was a kid, we'd play a game, first one to spot the sea, you had to look out for it."

"Okay," she said. "What then?"

"Well, that's it. You just have to be the first to see the sea. Then you win. It means you're nearly there. I think my mum and dad let me win."

"Your mom and dad, huh? I got a mom and dad, too, are your mom and dad like my mom and dad?"

I had no way of answering that, never having had the pleasure of meeting them but I saw what she meant and I concluded they probably were.

"My mom and dad, they're good guys. Are yours?" she asked.

I had not considered them to be anything other than good guys. They were honest people, loving, their faces came into my mind sometimes, every day, and I suppose they wondered a lot what I was doing. I had sent them a postcard or two in the early days after we set out but postcards were harder to find the further East we went, so they would have been starved of news. Dear mum and dad, I'm driving down the coast in Thailand. It's sunny and hot. Keep the home fires burning.

"Different generation," I said. "Are yours?"

"Same, I guess. They got things they do, like they got to do, like most folks."

"Do you live in one of those houses, like in the films? Painted white? With the front garden and the mailbox is a little metal container on a pole?"

"Yard. It's called a yard."

"It's actually a garden."

"Yes, we do, our house is just like that. And it's a yard. We got one out back, too. It's a backyard."

We rounded a bend. Loretta sat up in mock excitement and pointed. The blue expanse spread out to the horizon, breathtaking, blue and clear.

"There it is! There it is! The sea. I win! Look, it's over there. I win! I win!"

I suppose you had to have grown up in a place a long way from the coast to really understand the significance of this activity. I suppose it was fun because your dad and your mum were in the front seats of the car and you were going to be with them for a week, maybe two, and you weren't at school.

"I don't think you took that game very seriously," I said.

"I win! I win!"

"Quiet now," I said. "I let you win."

We approached Hua Hin to the sound of Loretta's laughter filling the car and sailing out across the waves. There were golden sands, a few buildings, a couple of places to eat. We found a small hotel, the friendly proprietor greeted us with the usual wai, the little bow with the hands clasped together and we returned it politely and found our room on the first floor, its window looking out across the beach to the sea. A few fishing boats danced on the sparkling water, heading home. We dumped our bags. It was starting to get dark. We went for a walk outside. The night was clear, the stars were out.

"Guys on the moon. There's gonna be guys on the moon. How weird is that?" she said. "We can get guys to the moon, we can't get them out of Vietnam."

"Do you know the stars?" I asked, pointing up to the sky where they shone out against the blackness.

"Yep. They're right up there. Those shiny things, right?"

"You can see them so clearly here, they've all got names, all the shapes they make, the constellations."

"I know. You think I'm some dummy?"

"Name one."

"You name one."

"Okay," I said. "See that up there?"

I pointed to a collection of stars in a vague semblance of a shape.

"Uh-huh."

"That's the Big Wheelbarrow."

She laughed.

"You're kidding me, right?"

"And that's the Great Bucket," I said, picking out another shape. "And that one there, that's the Long Stick. And there, right there, see, that's the Phone Box."

"And there," she said. "What's that? Don't tell me, it's the Stupid Jerk."

She slapped me on the shoulder and we got up and went to our room. Loretta came up behind me as I stood for one last look at the window and put her arms around me and nestled her head between my shoulder blades.

"There's only one bed," she said.

"I'll be fine on the settee."

I could feel her shaking her head against my back.

"You don't learn, do you, Scooter?"

* * *

Maybe it would be wrong to say that weekend was the most perfect I had ever spent in my entire life up to that point. Maybe there had been others equally good. If there were, I couldn't remember them.

We stayed in bed late. The proprietor made us some pancakes for breakfast. He didn't speak any English at all. Nobody spoke English. A few little kids followed us for a while, squealing and skipping, when we ventured out into the heat to walk on the beach. Well, I say followed us around, they followed Loretta really, in her shorts and her blouse tied in a knot around her midriff. She hung onto my arm. We found some rocks to give us shade. The sea stretched ahead of us. It was quiet, apart from the occasional bird call and the sound of the kids playing a little way away.

"It's beautiful, isn't it?" Loretta said.

"You're beautiful," I said.

"You might want to rethink that one, Scooter. Cheap shot at a compliment."

"You reckon?"

"Uh-huh."

"Okay. You're not beautiful."

"Maybe not rethink it quite so much."

One of the children pitched a pebble towards a rock. It fell short. I could see which one he was aiming at. I leaned down and picked up a small pebble of my own and threw it. It hit the target and skimmed away. I could tell the little boy was impressed with my accuracy and I considered trying to improvise a game of beach cricket with the assembled youngsters. Perhaps not the right moment. The boy tried again, hit the target rock and looked at me and smiled. I gave him the thumbs up.

"Howzat?" I said. "Say it. Howzat!"

He looked at me mystified. He lobbed another pebble towards the rock. It just missed.

"Hard cheese," I said.

"He doesn't speak English," Loretta said. "Neither do you, buddy. Howzat? Hard cheese? What the hell?"

My turn. I sent one just wide.

"Is this day five?" I said to Loretta.

"Maybe."

"I don't want it to be day five."

The boy bounced one off the target rock and jumped up with his arms in the air.

"Howzat!" I said.

"We could just drive," she said. "That's what I was talking about on the way here. Drive away so day five won't ever catch us. Drive so far it won't ever find us."

I pitched one a little short. It sank into the soft sand. The boy gave a wide grin.

"A beautiful woman has just asked you to drive her away into the sunset, you do realise that, don't you, Scooter?"

"You're not beautiful."

"Stop that."

"Okay."

"You're thinking it over," she said. "You know he's guilty. I know he's guilty. Even Al knows he's guilty."

The road out of all this lay just beyond us.

"That's not it," I said.

"Really? You're not thinking you have to go back because of Al?"

I picked up a nice round pebble, smooth. It curved through the still air and caromed off the top of the rock.

"Howzat!" I said. The boy danced a little jig.

"If we go back, I can't be sure day five won't be waiting for us," she said.

I looked into her face, her eyes never far from laughing and never far from crying. I wanted to pick her up, lift her in my arms and put her in the Land Rover and do what she wanted, drive and drive and drive.

"What about the elephant?" I said.

She stood up, reached down and took my hands. We started to walk away. The boy watched us. He looked disappointed. He slammed another pebble into the rock. I heard it bounce off as we wandered back towards the hotel and I heard his voice.

"Howzat!" he said. In a Thai accent. I had done my bit for the next generation of cultural relations.

Loretta and I spent another night in the hotel, in each other's arms. The window had no curtains, it just looked out onto the stars and the sea. As we were drifting off to sleep, she pointed up to the stars.

"What's that one there, Scooter? Can you see it?" I looked. She wasn't pointing at anything, she was just pointing to the sky, to the scattering of planets and meteors and whatever else was up there. She closed her eyes. "No, you can't see it anymore. It's gone."

We got back into the Land Rover the next day and we hit the crossroads on the outskirts of the little town. A couple of cars were in front of us heading to the junction. One way was Bangkok. The other way was the other way. We looked at each other. Loretta pointed. Towards Bangkok.

"We can pick up the elephant," she said. "Then we can leave."

I nodded. We drove through the afternoon and when we got back to Bangkok, we discovered Al had been arrested.

27

"What happened, Captain?"

I was pacing in front of the desk in the small office McMichael had again ushered me into.

"Sit down, Benson."

"Never mind the sit down." I pointed in the general direction of the back office where I suspected Soames and Raniero would be working. I was ready to confront them for banging up my client but I wanted to get the story first. "Military police picked him up?"

All we had heard from Betty was that two MPs called at the bar on the Saturday. They had spoken to Al and he had gone with them, surprisingly, without any fuss and bother. I suppose he didn't have much choice. Betty had no way of getting in touch with me. When she told us about the military police, there was one thing I did notice but it didn't seem significant at the time. It was just that Loretta went very pale and had to sit down.

"Are you okay?" I asked.

"Maybe too long in the sun," she said. "I'm fine."

She was quiet all evening and I don't think she slept much.

"You know he disappeared for a couple of days?" McMichael said. "Do you know where he went?"

"He didn't tell me. You know Al. He's not the sharing kind."

"He went back to the motor pool."

"Jesus Christ."

"He hitched a ride."

"He knows a lot of guys."

"Yeah. The prosecution says he was interfering with witnesses, put out a warrant. They want him in jail until the trial."

"He's entitled to see his counsel," I said. "Where's he being held?"

"That's the thing. It's at the airbase. Outside of town. We have a small holding cell next to the court room but otherwise we don't have the facilities here for anything longer than one night."

I looked up as Raniero passed by, rather conveniently and, I suspected, quite deliberately, in the corridor. He was holding an armful of files as if he was on his way to do some work. He glanced in and smiled. McMichael sighed.

"Mr Benson," Raniero said. "Your client with you today?"

"You know where he is, Todd," McMichael said.

Raniero clicked his fingers as if he had just remembered.

"Oh, yeah, I did hear something about that. He took a little vacation back to Nam and now he's staying in one of our very own luxury establishments."

"You think I'm going to let you keep him in there? Do you have any proof?" I said.

Raniero pretended to look at his files.

"Let's see," he said. "He was spotted going into the motor pool. He was heard asking for Private Saunders, you remember Private Saunders? The main witness guy? The guy he's not supposed to talk to because he's the main witness? That guy?"

"Did Sergeant Moreau talk to him?"

"Private Saunders was absent on that day, it so happens. Moreau waited, asked around a little more, saw a few more people, social calls, I'm guessing, maybe just to make sure nobody else gave any testimony."

"Speculation," McMichael said.

"Well, just to be on the safe side, just to make sure the justice system runs smoothly, Moreau is out of harm's way. Maybe he'll reconsider his plea, who knows?"

"You have witnesses to back this up?" I asked.

"We've got all we need." Raniero oiled his way out of the office. "I might just add, thanks for the tip-off."

"What tip-off? I didn't give you a tip-off," McMichael said.

"I'm talking to Chummy here, when he said Moreau had been gone for a couple of days. We followed it up and what do you know? We caught us a whopper."

I knew I had said something wrong at the time. If it had been possible to kick myself under the table, I would have done it.

"Toodle-pip, old boy," Raniero said. "Maybe we won't see you in court after all."

*   *   *

The airbase was a half hour drive away. I didn't know the directions; if I took Mary Jane, I could end up in Chiang Mai by the time I realised how lost I was. McMichael knew the way but it would take two, three, four hours out of his day and he couldn't do it. He had more cases. I only had one.

"I could fix you a lift in one of the trucks?" he said. "Won't be very comfortable."

"Today?"

"What's the hurry? At least we know where Moreau is as long as he's in jail."

"I don't want Al in jail any longer than absolutely necessary. He can't handle it. I know he can't."

I thought back to the cinema, to the moment when the lights went down and Al was in the dark. It had something to do with the war, maybe he would tell me one day, maybe he wouldn't. All I knew was I had this feeling, tough guy that he was, he was afraid of being in the dark, in a confined space.

"While I'm gone, can you set up a bail hearing? For tomorrow?" I said.

"That's pretty short notice," he said.

"We have to get him out."

"I'll do my best. I can't guarantee it."

"Tell the judge I'll be there and I'll wait all day if I have to."

"Jackson? You don't know him like I do. He's a hard ass."

"Yeah? Well, so am I."

I spun the phone round on McMichael's desk, fished the card from my pocket and started to dial.

"That's for military personnel only," McMichael said.

"Two seconds. Local call. It's important."

"Make it quick. I'll see about the truck," he said and went out. I was left alone in the office. A desk, a phone, a typewriter, a filing cabinet. I could have been in my own office just like this, only without the mosquitoes, doing a little conveyancing, some trusts, perhaps a restrictive covenant or two. Then a bigger office, a secretary of my own. A familiar voice answered the phone, speaking in Thai.

"Preed?" I said. "It's Matt Benson. Matthew Benson. Can you get Betty? Betty?"

I had tried not to pronounce it too loudly and extra carefully but I realised I was still sounding like an Englishman in a foreign country, trying to get the locals to comply with a simple request. The fall-back position of every English speaker the world over.

"Mama-San Betty?" Preed asked.

"Yes. Betty."

"Coming right up."

I smiled. It was, I thought, one of the reasons for the war. The Vietnamese couldn't speak English so they must be backward. Even though their culture stretched back thousands of years further than the Americans. If the whole world spoke the same language, would there be any wars? I was sounding like an O Level history exam paper. Discuss in 500 words.

"Mister Matthew?"

"Betty? Hi, yes, it's me."

"Moreau?" she said.

"I'm going to see him. I'll let you know later. Can I speak to Loretta?"

McMichael reappeared at the door.

"Truck," he said, gesturing for me to put the phone down. I held up a hand and waved it in a circular motion I fondly hoped indicated extra time was required on his phone.

"Betty? Is Loretta there?"

There was a pause on the other end.

"The driver will stop by here. Five minutes," McMichael said, holding up five fingers.

"Betty?"

"She is not here, Mister Matthew. She went out."

I could hear music in the background. It must have been the band on their afternoon set.

"Where did she go?"

"She didn't say."

"Four minutes," McMichael said.

"If she comes back, tell her…when she comes back, tell her…"

Tell her what?

"I pulled strings to get this lift, Benson, move it out."

"Tell her the elephant is packing his trunk."

I put down the phone. McMichael gave me a puzzled look. Why wouldn't he? The message I had just given Betty couldn't mean a thing. I headed for the door.

"Thanks, Captain."

"Three minutes."

I hurried out through the front office. The bored Lieutenant looked up, threw me a paper ball, I caught it reflexively, slammed it into the waste bin from ten yards.

"Smokin'" he said and held up his hand for a high five. I slapped his palm. I laughed to myself because I realised what I had said: 'He's a hard ass.' 'So am I!' I couldn't believe I had said it. I went out the front door to wait for the truck. I didn't even notice the heat.

28

It was not a comfortable ride. The army truck with a star on the side door, canvas exterior, arrived some thirty minutes later and it was packed. I headed for the passenger door, hoping to get a ride up front but the man already occupying the seat thumbed me towards the back and the driver set off before I had gained entry. The back, which might once have had a tailgate, was open and I hurried along to try and grab a foothold. The truck stopped at a junction and I scrambled up, helped by the soldier on the end.

"All aboard, cowboy," he said, shuffling along to make room.

"Thank you so much. Very kind," I said, perching on the end of the bench and clinging on to a grab bar. I was perilously close to the open back. I took a look along the truck. Twenty or so young soldiers sat hunched on the benches, kitbags by their feet, mostly looking down, looking like the day after a big party, looking like boy scouts heading for a jamboree they didn't want to be at.

"You English?" the soldier next to me said. His leg was perpetually jerking up and down, his eyes were wide and staring. "This guy's English."

"Who cares?" someone mumbled.

"You a reporter? You're a reporter, right?"

"Actually..."

"Tell my story, man."

"Shut the hell up," came from the gloom along the truck.

"No, listen," the soldier persisted. "Private First Class Abraham Lincoln. I'm a goddam big war hero."

"Abraham Lincoln, Jesus Mary," a voice said. "General Westmoreland is driving the truck."

There was general laughter.

"LBJ, he's riding shotgun," the voice said. "Only job he could get."

It was a red-haired man with a round face, holding a cigarette. Snickering from the assembled company. The soldier next to me – Abe, though I doubted that was his real name – laughed and slapped his thighs in a solid four drum beat.

"Write this," he nudged me. I almost toppled from the back. The newly surfaced road blurred below me, palm trees and paddy fields sped by as we shook along. "Private First Class Abraham Lincoln single handedly took out a whole platoon of VC at Tan Can, armed with only a pop gun, like this…"

He aimed a finger out of the back and made shooting noises.

"You don't believe me? Here, I got me a little souvenir."

He reached down to his kitbag. The sullen soldier across from us nudged it with his foot and shook his head in a warning. Abe looked at him.

"He don't need to see that," the other soldier said. Abe leaned back. A figure loomed towards us, kicking his way past the kitbags. No-one complained if he trod on their boots.

"And after that," Abe was saying. "Private First Class Abraham Lincoln went on R and R. That's Rest and Recuperation."

"I and I," the red-haired joker said. "That's Intercourse and Intoxication."

Abe laughed then fell silent as the big man stood by us.

"Write about this," the big man said. He opened his shirt. There was a livid scar running from his left shoulder all the way to his right hip. I didn't know what to say. Without another word, he buttoned his shirt and returned to his place. The truck rumbled along. I hoped the airbase was not far.

"And on that R and R," Abe said. "Private First Class Abraham Lincoln screwed three little honeys and two Yankee nurses."

There was a splutter from along the truck.

"You didn't screw no nurses, asshole. Officers screw nurses."

Laughter. Nurses clearly had a reputation across the ranks. I wanted the subject to change. There was a grim nervousness pervading the truck. The red-haired man started to sing to himself.

"Ain't no use in going home. Jody's got your girl and gone."

The others listened. No-one joined in.

"Ain't no use in feeling blue. Jody's got your sister too."

The song tailed off, giving way to a general despondency as the airbase got closer. Even Abe was quiet. The guards manning the red and white hooped barrier pole must have left their hut to open it as they saw us approach then closed it behind us as we pulled into the centre of the airbase. I jumped out first. My travelling companions filed out slowly behind me, herded up by a man with a clipboard. I stood aside. They slunk past, kitbags trailing in the dust, not looking at me, the intruder, the man who shouldn't have been there. The red-haired joker smiled at me.

"Ain't no use in looking back. Jody's got your Cadillac," he sang quietly as he passed by. He gave me a friendly little salute with his index finger to his forehead and joined the others.

I watched them go, marching, heads up, a sergeant or someone yelling at them to get in step, out towards the landing strips separated from the few scattered buildings by a high chain link fence. The aircraft lurked like grey prehistoric beasts at a watering hole. The air was busy with these monsters taking off and landing, the acres of tarmac didn't seem big enough to contain them all. Eight motors roaring on each one. Aircrew bustled around, some in uniform, some in overalls. All the buildings were single-storey except for a control tower elevated on wooden stilts. Paths were marked out by white painted stones and one appeared to lead to the main building with a porch in front of it shielding the interior from the sun. I headed in that direction. It was late afternoon. It occurred to me I hadn't got a ride back into town.

29

"What you doing here, boy?" Al was sitting on a bench, his head resting against the concrete block wall. I could see him through the bars of his cell.

"I could ask you the same," I said in an attempt at levity as I approached from the front office. Getting in had been surprisingly easy, McMichael having called ahead, and the Lieutenant at the front desk pointed me through. I asked him about a ride; he said he would see what he could do. I thought that was jolly decent of him and I said so though as it turned out I would probably have been better off staying in a cell.

There was an alcove where the corridor ended, occupied by a desk and a guard who was leaning back in his chair, playing jazz on a portable transistor radio and reading an old copy of *Playboy*. There were maybe half a dozen small cells but Al was the only inmate. The guard snapped upright when he heard me approach.

"You the lawyer? Got some ID?"

"Come on, Clyde, who the hell else would want to see me in this shithole?" Al said.

The guard shrugged.

"Procedure, Al, it's not my rules."

"Chrissake." Al opened the cell door. Without a key. He stepped aside to let me pass into the small space with him and closed the door behind us. Clyde sat back down and resumed his perusal of the magazine.

"I went to the *Playboy* mansion one time," Al said.

"Like hell you did." Clyde shuffled in his seat. He was playing Miles Davis. *Sketches From Spain*. There was a small barred window and outside, the muted aircraft noise provided a ceaseless background. The sky was turning from blue to purple. I sat down next to Al on the bench.

"How are they treating you?" It seemed like a lawyerly thing to say.

"How you treating me, Clyde?"

"We treating him like the crooked asshole he is," Clyde said, turning a page.

Al chuckled and leaned closer to me.

"You got to get me out," he said quietly. "Seriously."

"I'm trying. What happened?"

"It was 1964. I was on leave in Chicago, a buddy of mine, he got us an invite." Al had raised his voice for Clyde's benefit. "You wouldn't know it from the outside, it just looks a big old regular place but inside, oh boy."

"You ain't never been to no *Playboy* house."

"I meant what happened when you got arrested?" I said. "Could we have some privacy, Corporal? This is an attorney client meeting."

"I ain't no Corporal."

"Clyde's a five-star General," Al said. "Fallen on hard times."

Clyde gave a throaty laugh.

"Hell you say."

"You want to hear about this?" Al asked him.

"No. Okay, go on."

"Inside the mansion, they got all these rooms, see, and a pool, two pools, jacuzzi baths full of girls, they bring you champagne, man, there's red velvet everywhere. This girl comes up to me, they're all over you as soon as you go in, she says, hey, soldier boy."

"You wearing your uniform?" Clyde peered over the top of his magazine.

"Hey, you know what it's like, Clyde, girls go wild for a uniform, ain't that right?"

"I'm trying to get a bail hearing as soon as I can," I said.

"Shush. Yeah, that's right," Clyde said.

"She had this yellow hair down to her waist and she's wearing this pink shiny bunny outfit, fluffy tail, ears, everything, she says she was Miss January. I said, sugar, you could warm me up any time of the year."

Clyde laughed.

"You said that? Goddam."

"She had thighs like Jane Fonda, and man, you know, up top, watermelons."

"Like Raquel Welch?"

"Bigger. And she took me into this room, there was a bed, a four-poster bed, all covered in these satin sheets."

Clyde put down his magazine. I had never heard Al talk so much. I was beginning to realise how he managed to get so many people to do whatever it was he wanted. Maybe I should put him on the witness stand.

"It would help if I had some details," I said.

"I was just thinking the same thing," Clyde said.

"And I tell you, man, she was a genuine blonde."

He pronounced it gen-u-wine. It sounds better that way.

"And she says to me after, she says, that was good, Al, but if you ever meet this guy called Clyde, he's a soldier too, give him my number. I hear he's the best lay this side of the Mississippi."

Clyde threw down his magazine and got up to leave.

"Hell with it," he said, and shambled away down the corridor.

"Two coffees," Al called after him.

Clyde turned briefly and raised his middle finger in Al's direction.

"Okay," Al said as soon as he had gone. "Listen up, I'm going to be honest with you, boy."

"I wish you would."

"One night, like last night, I can take, there were a couple of other guys here, it wasn't so bad. Now I'm on my own, just me and Clyde, he's a nice guy, but he ain't no Betty, hear what I'm saying? He won't hold me when it's dark."

"I think that would be above and beyond his guard duties."

Al looked thoughtfully at the concrete floor.

"I tell you this just one time. It was in some goddam Nang or Drang, I don't recall exactly, an ambush, always an ambush, that's what they do, the VC. I got hit, on the helmet. Out cold. When I woke up, I could hear them moving around. I was under some trees, in a hole. I pulled some branches over me. It was dark as hell. I waited for the morning. When I came out, all I could see were bodies. My men. The VC, they'd gone, slipped away, like they always did. Dark as hell, man."

He looked up, straight at me, as human as I had seen him.

"Mostly it's okay in the night. Sometimes, it ain't."

"I'm trying to get a bail hearing for tomorrow. It's too late today."

Al glanced around, panicked, possibly looking for a way out.

"Where did you go?" I said.

Al looked up towards the window. It was too small to climb through.

"I went back to Saigon. I had some business, guys to see."

"The prosecution says you went to the motor pool. They say you were interfering with witnesses. They want to keep you in here until the trial."

"Hell, no, I met a guy, I didn't go nowhere near there. I have interests to look after."

"You didn't go to see Private Saunders?"

"I don't need to do that."

"The prosecution knew where you'd gone."

"I told you, boy, I know a lot of guys. A lot of guys know me. They ain't all good guys."

He grabbed my arm as if a realisation had just struck him but I don't think it had, I think he had been preparing all along to voice it.

"Your gal. She knew."

"That's not right. For goodness sake, get over this idea she's working against you."

"Then how did they know?"

I shrugged his hand away. Raniero had told me but I was reluctant to let on to Al that it was me who had inadvertently given the game away. Also, I found myself thinking Raniero could actually have been bluffing to protect her cover but I quickly set that aside – it would be buying in to Al's ridiculous notion. Still, I couldn't help thinking it. The door at the other end of the corridor opened and Clyde came in, carrying two coffees. The sun was low in the sky outside the window.

"Lieutenant says if you want that lift back to town, you go now."

I stood up. Al clutched at the hem of my jacket.

"Get me out," he said. "And don't never tell no-one you seen me like this, understand?"

I nodded. That would be the worst thing that could happen to Al, worse than spending a night in the dark, in a cell.

"Have you really been to the *Playboy* mansion?" I asked.

"What do you think?"

I thanked the Lieutenant on the way out. He had found me a ride, this time a pick-up truck. Both the seats were occupied, by two taciturn individuals of indeterminate rank and age. I climbed into the open back, along with some shovels, a pickaxe, a small generator. Smells of oil and petrol mixed in the breeze, blowing up for some rain. I could feel it in the air. I appeared to be with a special animal unit and a cage was in the back with me, covered over with a tarpaulin. I could just see big hairy feet inside, pacing up and down, and I could hear slavering and growling and drooling. Rain started to fall. If it was anything like the usual downpours, I feared for my suit. But the only way to stay dry was to lift up the tarpaulin and share the cover with whatever was in the cage.

"Good doggie," I said. "Nice doggie."

I lifted the corner. There was a scrambling of claws, barking and clashing of teeth on the bars. I dropped the cover fast and huddled in a corner of the truck as big drops began to splatter around me. In the morning, I would go to court and get Al set free. I hoped Loretta would be waiting for me. She was not a secret service agent, no, sir. I couldn't believe she was anything other than gen-u-wine.

30

The driver dropped me off in the city without making any attempt to find out where I wanted to go and I made my way to Betty's, collar up in a rather futile attempt to stave off the rain bouncing from the pavements, trying to preserve my shoes, my jacket and trousers that were rapidly changing colour. Huge drops battered down, releasing a pungent vapour from the pavements, refreshing and cooling. And wet. I hoped my clothes would dry before the morning and it was with some relief that I pushed open the familiar door of Betty's and oozed in, shaking myself in the manner of my erstwhile travelling companion.

The bar was warm as usual, steam rising from those who had been caught in the shower, like a school cloakroom after a winter nature walk. It mingled with the fug of cigarette smoke. I looked for Loretta but I couldn't see her.

The girls were dancing to the band, a number I didn't recognise, a new one they must have been working on over the weekend. It sounded like it could have been *Honky Tonk Woman*. The Rolling Stones. Ambitious. I was heading towards the stairs, hoping Loretta would be in our rooms when I spotted a figure on his own at the bar.

"Captain McMichael," I said, sitting down next to him in the considerable space that had been left around him. He was still wearing his uniform with his rank insignia.

"Jesus," he said, assessing my dishevelled appearance. "Been for a swim?"

I had to wring some of the water from my cuffs onto the floor. Preed brought me a beer with a smile, without me asking. I thanked him. A cup of tea would have been nice.

"I didn't want to talk at our place," McMichael said, looking around. "But I sure as hell feel like one damn big party pooper in yours."

The enlisted men had given him a wide berth, casting the occasional sideways glance, reluctant, in the presence of an officer, to let it all hang out the way they usually did.

"Join in the fun," I said, loosening the laces on my shoes to try and air my socks.

"Got the hearing set for tomorrow."

"Fab."

"See Moreau?"

"I told him we'd get him out."

McMichael shook his head.

"There's more to this case than we thought," he said.

"How so?"

I took off my jacket, looking for somewhere to hang it up. I couldn't linger in the bar. I had to dry my clothes.

"Captain, it is an honour," Betty said, slinking through the tables, black cigarette in its holder lighting the way. McMichael couldn't resist turning around, jaw dropping, at the sound of her voice. Nobody could. "We see so few men like you in our humble establishment."

McMichael was lost for words. Betty leaned over him closely to tap some ash out in a glass on the bar.

"Moreau?"

"Sends his regards," I said.

"I have to talk to him. I have a proposal."

"He'll be back soon."

"That's good." Betty brushed against McMichael as she moved off to mingle some more. She dipped towards him to whisper in his ear and he tried hard to avert his eyes from the low-cut jet black sparkling evening gown she almost had on. "Don't go away. Mister Officer."

McMichael took a long gulp of his beer.

"What the hell?" he said. "Is that Moreau's squeeze?"

"A little blunt and colloquial but I suppose so, yes," I said. "There was something you wanted to talk about?"

I had forgotten to ask Betty if Loretta was around and I wanted to hurry upstairs to find out.

"You know I said there's something going on with this case?" McMichael said. "Raniero said they were acting on the tip-off you gave them in court?"

"Careless on my part."

"It was. Anyhow, they checked it out. How did they know he'd gone to Vietnam? Could have gone anywhere. Here's the thing. We don't have the resources to do that kind of investigation at the Justice Centre. Some other agency was involved, that's my thinking."

"Like who?"

"Could be anybody. I've never seen Soames and Raniero so worried. They don't want to go back to field courts doing summary cases in Nam. It's a damn sight easier to work on cases in Bangkok, let me tell you. Status of forces agreement, when they came up with that so we could hold courts here, great day in the morning."

He got up to leave and put his money on the bar. I picked it up and gave it back to him.

"On me," I said, knowing they would put it on my rent and I could settle when Al paid me some more of his fee, which was surely due.

"I'll keep listening," McMichael said, putting on his cap but not heading for the door. He wasn't finished. "If I'm right, this is not only about Moreau. This is what I'm thinking. The US is shipping out a load of equipment to Nam. And there's other stuff, there's currency fraud. You know the troops in Nam have got diplomatic immunity from the country's laws, right? There's no import duty. The black market is widespread. Everything from TVs to diamonds. It's hurting the economy."

"I can't believe Al is working on that scale. Is he?"

"That's my point. They want to keep a lid on it. If they can nail a guy like Moreau and make an example of him, it sends a message to the others."

"It's a theory."

"It's a damn good theory. All I'm saying is, be careful."

"I can't let myself be distracted by all that. I have to treat it as a theft case, pure and simple," I said, as if I had dealt with pure and simple theft cases every day for years, which I hadn't.

"Up to you," he said. "All I'm saying is, be careful."

Surely, McMichael was a conspiracy theorist. He wanted to liven up his daily routine. I did the mental equivalent of putting my hands over my ears and singing la, la, la.

"Thanks for the advice," I said.

"See you tomorrow," he said. "And one other thing."

I waited expectantly. As far as I knew, he wasn't aware of my involvement with Loretta but even so I thought he was probably going to say, watch out for the girl and that would be one more piece of advice I wasn't going to take. I was wet through and I didn't want any more help or platitudes.

"What?"

"I wish my office was like yours," he said.

*　　*　　*

My shoes left wet trails along the stairs as I went up to my rooms. This had been a long day and I had all these thoughts in my head and soaking trousers clinging to my legs. It was no secret the CIA were all over this place, it was in the papers, on the news, they were everywhere in South East Asia. They had been involved a long time, long before the military advisers had turned up in Vietnam, long before they had put boots on the ground. So maybe McMichael was right. I opened the door to my rooms. It was quiet. I kicked off my shoes and pulled the trousers damply down my legs. There was some movement from the bedroom.

"Loretta?"

The movement stopped. For a second, I expected some knife toting assassin to come storming out, it wouldn't have surprised me. I hesitated, holding my trousers as they dripped on the floor. Maybe that wasn't far from the truth. Betty's place was not exactly Fort Knox. Or it could be Stan Bronsky, or whatever the hell his name was, except he was on his way back to Montana. A figure appeared in the neon-lit doorway, surveying my state of undress.

"Wow, you're sure in a hurry, Scooter," Loretta said. I threw my trousers to one side, they landed inelegantly across the elephant, and I picked up the pace over a few steps and pulled her to me and grabbed her in a hug, sighing with relief.

"I thought you'd gone," I said.

"No, I haven't gone," she said, laughing, pushing me gently away. "Get off of me, you're soaked through."

"Rain."

"Take off your things, I'll hang them up. Get in the shower."

"Yes, Ma'am."

I didn't care who or what she was, she could be the secretest secret service agent in the world, she could be the President in disguise, no, maybe draw the line at that, Nixon could never be that attractive. I only cared that she was there. I stepped out of my clothes.

"I thought when I went to see Al, I didn't know if you'd still be here," I said. She fished my trousers from the elephant.

"I don't know when these pants will be dry," she said, arranging things on the back of the settee and over the coffee table. The band downstairs moved into *Shakin' All Over*. "How was Al?"

"Listen," I said. "They're playing our song. He was worried."

"Is this our song? Isn't it the only one they know? This your new jacket? Just look at it. What are these long hairs doing all over it?"

She stopped and put her hands on her hips and glared at me.

"Scooter, how could you? What's her name?"

"I think it was probably Rover. Or Fido."

I recounted the story of my uncomfortable ride back as I stripped off the remainder of my clothes and went into the bathroom. I could hear her laughing. She could have been with anyone. Officers screw nurses. It's a rule. But she was with me. I didn't know why.

"You wanted to go away," I said. "You weren't here."

"I always want to do a lot of things I want to do," she said, bustling around, smoothing out my shirt. "Maybe I couldn't not stay. Have you thought about that?"

"Why not? Or why, possibly?"

She didn't reply. Even though it was raining, the night was still warm. I wanted to ask her to describe everything she had done while I wasn't there, the dead-letter drop she had been to, the handler she had been meeting. The constant questions, McMichael, Al, Raniero, were nagging me. I watched her from the doorway as she spread out my clothes, then she turned around and I felt embarrassed at being in the nude so I covered up with my hands like I was defending a free kick on a football pitch in some strange dream and dodged quickly into the shower.

"You want me to scrub your back?" she called after me as I turned on the tap and revelled in the lukewarm water that sprayed down.

"No, I'll be fine, I think there's a loofah," I shouted.

She came into the shower room, shaking her head, unbuttoning her blouse.

"You really don't learn, do you, Scooter?"

31

Luckily, the warm air had dried out my clothes to the extent that they were merely a little bit damp. It was uncomfortable, certainly, and the humidity in the courtroom didn't make it any less claggy around my armpits. Also, there were one or two little watermark stains that kept catching my attention. Nevertheless, I had made it on time and I had a chance for a brief chat with McMichael before the prosecution arrived.

"I think these guys have overstepped the line," he said. "That Betty is some woman. That was Betty, right?"

"Yes. How so?"

"The Military Justice Act, quote that. There's been a general shift in attitudes towards civilianisation of the military trial procedure over the last few years."

I memorised his line though I wasn't quite sure what it meant or how it was going to help us. McMichael knew his stuff, no doubt about that. The double doors opened and Raniero and Soames came in, chatting to one another.

"Okay, here come Laurel and Hardy," McMichael said. "They'll be feeling pretty good but I know this judge. He's tough but he won't want to break any rules. He won't want to set any precedents. Got it?"

I jotted down his suggestions in my notepad, carefully placed it on top of the sizeable folder I had brought with me. Earlier that morning, I had worked on it at the table in our rooms. I called them ours now. Loretta had come up behind me and draped herself around my neck.

"Whatcha doin', Scooter?" she asked in an exaggerated drawl.

I confess I had closed the files when she appeared. I couldn't help myself.

"A few things. Getting ready for court."

She pouted.

"Arentcha gonna let me see?"

I turned and kissed her. I had made all the notes I wanted to, I had been through the Code, I had picked out the facts I needed and with McMichael's help, I thought I could formulate an argument.

"What am I gonna do while you're at work, honey?" Loretta said, swaying coquettishly, hands behind her back. "Some housework. Get my hair done?"

"As long as you have my tea on the table as soon as I come home, you can do whatever you like, sugar," I said. "Go buy yourself something pretty."

She laughed. We had moved on to Day Seven at least, maybe Day Eight or Nine but we were still waiting for Day Five to catch up with us, when she would have to go. She didn't seem concerned. I had tried to stop counting but I couldn't.

"I guess I'll just sit here waiting for my man," were her last words before I went off to work.

This courtroom was becoming a familiar setting to me. The clerk and the stenographer wandered in.

"Betty and Moreau. How close are they?" McMichael asked, twisting the wedding band on his third finger reflectively.

"Howdy," Soames said. Raniero gave his twisted, arrogant smile, the one that made you want to kick his shins. McMichael said nothing. I returned the greeting to Soames.

"As soon as the hearing is over, I expect Sergeant Moreau to be given a ride back to town from the wholly inadequate custodial setting he has erroneously been placed in," I said.

"He's behind bars, if that's what you mean," Raniero said. "And that's where he's staying."

"We'll be arguing for Moreau to remain in custody until the trial," Soames said.

"On what grounds? Considering you had him picked up without a warrant when he had not committed any crime."

"Interfering with witnesses."

"You got anybody who saw him at the motor pool? Anybody see him talking to Saunders?"

They were silent.

"Thought not," I said.

"Also, he's a flight risk," Soames said. "He might not appear for the trial. If there's going to be a trial."

"Come on," I said. "He has ties to the local area."

I was stretching my point but I saw McMichael nodding in agreement.

"Have you seen Moreau's ties to the local area?" he said vaguely in the direction of Soames, half-dreaming. "Believe me, he is not going anywhere."

Raniero and Soames gave each other a puzzled look.

"Have you lost your mind, Travis?" Raniero said.

"There is going to be a trial," I said. "Sergeant Moreau is not guilty, as he has said all along."

"Get back in the playground, sonny," Raniero said.

McMichael was right. They were taking this so seriously. It should have been no more than another job to them, they were lawyers, but I could tell the pressure was on, they were being watched. They needed a result. I was in their way.

"I am not even going to suggest any recognisance," I said. "Sergeant

Moreau is on Army pay, he has no funds to put up. He will be released on his own word."

Soames snorted.

"Good luck with that," he said, standing up. I stood up as well. So did Raniero. And McMichael. We glared at one another across the aisle. The clerk and the stenographer watched us. The two MPs tensed, thinking their shift had become a lot brighter and they might have to break up a brawl. The side door opened and Major Bill Jackson strode in. Whenever he entered, it seemed like there should have been a fanfare from a full marching band. He paused at the dais and saw we were already standing up well in advance.

"Gentlemen," he said, indicating with a grand gesture that we should be seated. "We meet again. And yet, it is not for the trial. Therefore, what do we have on this lovely day?"

Soames outlined the position. He steered clear of suggesting that Al had been spotted at the motor pool, merely hinting that was clearly his destination. Another careless mistake on my part. I had tipped him off about my best point. I could still make it; it wouldn't have the same impact because they no longer relied so heavily on it. However, their position had been weakened. They didn't have a witness and the judge would know it. Soames made his arguments carefully and thoroughly.

"And so, Mr Benson, I imagine you don't want your client in a cell, is that right?" the judge said. "It is your application. You should have gone first, before Captain Soames stepped up and stole your ball."

It was such an elementary blunder. The judge had let him go on, probably waiting for me to object. I hadn't. And neither had McMichael, who was supposed to be watching my back, instead of day dreaming about Betty. Soames smiled to himself.

"I apologise, Your Honour. I was merely waiting to hear what Captain Soames would say next. He speaks so well."

"He does, doesn't he?" the judge said. "He should know though that I don't appreciate anyone taking advantage of my well-known good nature. The procedures are there to be followed."

The smile fell from Soames' face. He stood up.

"I was trying to assist the court, Your Honour. Mr Benson is not familiar with the proceedings."

"We are all grateful," the judge said. "Please don't do it again."

I had clear ground. I stifled a smile, put on my professional face, the one I had been practising in the bathroom mirror that very morning, I fancied it was a mixture of Gregory Peck and Gary Cooper with perhaps a soupcon of James Mason. I outlined my arguments. Al had not been to the motor pool, he had not spoken to the main witness and the prosecution could not bring forward anyone who could prove otherwise.

"As to the flight risk, Captain McMichael and myself are familiar with the address Sergeant Moreau has in Bangkok. He is well established there and we have personally checked it out."

"Objection," Soames said, rising to his feet. "It's a Go Go Bar and Mr Benson also lives there."

The judge raised an eyebrow. They knew where I lived. I doubt McMichael had furnished them with the information. All contact had been through him, it was easier that way, he shared the same building as them.

"Is that right?" the judge asked.

"All the more reason, I would suggest, for this to be a secure address," I said. "Your Honour, I can personally guarantee Sergeant Moreau's appearance in court for the trial."

"It's a bar of ill-repute frequented by enlisted men. Not officers. Except for Captain McMichael. There are young girls there for sale."

"What the hell do you mean by that?" McMichael half rose in his seat.

"Young girls luring young American men, good Christian boys, into the ways of the devil. The depravities that go on in these dens of vice are insulting to any God-fearing men – and women, yes – an insult to the Lord. There is drinking. There are girls there without a stitch of clothing on and they dance, yes, there is dancing. There is fornication..." Soames faltered, looking maniacally around, realising he was not in a pulpit and we were all staring at him, even Raniero. "I am saying. It is not a suitable place. Your Honour."

He sat down, staring at the hands he had folded prayer-like on the desk. The judge considered for a moment. He cleared his throat.

"I saw when I came in there had been some discussion between counsel before the hearing and it will probably continue after. Don't bring your values into my court room, any of you, and if you have arguments, they will be aired before me. And not before the Lord, though he might interject if he sees fit. Anything else, Mr Benson?"

The judge was losing patience. Soames wisely kept his seat. I quickly gave a rundown through my notes on the Military Justice Act, procedures, how it was undesirable for defendants to be incarcerated before a trial and sat down before Soames could object. We waited while the judge pursed his lips and steepled his fingers and considered.

"Bail granted," he said. "Sergeant Moreau will be freed today. I see no reason he should be locked up, it has yet to be proved he has done anything wrong."

He turned and pointed his gavel at me, a small hammer with a powerful blow.

"Mr Benson, I am releasing him to you. I require no surety. But you will make sure he appears in court for the trial. I am increasingly concerned about the way this case is being pursued."

He glanced towards the prosecution when he said that, I was relieved to see.

"These are issues of law. Nothing else. They will be tried here. Properly, in a court. I don't know what else is going on. I don't want to know. Monday next week. Sergeant Moreau will be here." He looked pointedly at me. "The trial will begin on that date. If you are not here, there will be hell to pay. The punishment of the Almighty in Captain Soames' eyes will be nothing compared to the punishment I will hand out. Got me?"

He banged the gavel, rose and departed in one swift movement. The marching band, had they been there, would have followed him out. I waited for his door to close. Soames and Raniero sullenly gathered up their papers. McMichael clapped me on the damp shoulder.

"Hallelujah," I said.

32

Outside in the blasting midday sun, I felt like I wanted to walk back to Betty's, no, dammit, I wanted to skip back to Betty's, all the way, like a little kid. But when I tried it, I looked like a crazy man and I started sweating straight away so I walked again. It was tough going, like I had lead in my soggy shoes.

McMichael had gone back to his office, he had other cases to work on, we had arranged to meet again the next day because I wanted to run my defence strategy past him, I wanted him to consider the flaws I had found in the prosecution case. He wanted the meeting to be at Betty's. I deflected this suggestion, conscious of a possible ulterior motive re Betty. Al would be back and the last thing I wanted was for McMichael to turn up in the bar with a box of chocolates. I needed McMichael, preferably without a chair wrapped around his head.

A bicycle rickshaw driver cruised slowly alongside for a while. I waved him away. The rain had all gone. It was a beautiful day. There was a heat haze along the pavement and I thought I could see an image of my dad walking alongside me, his grey suited figure shimmering.

"Well done, son. Good work. Your client will be pleased."

"Thanks, dad. See, I said I could do this job and I can, I can, I can."

I wanted to phone him. Talk to my mum. See Pete and Alfie and Mike but they were too quick, they had disappeared around a corner before I could grab them, hey, guys, wait for me. There was a parade along the street, Buddhist monks in their bright robes, a small procession, others following them in smart clothes. They were chanting, chanting, chanting. It seeped into my head. My thoughts were scrambled. Thai people were fond of parades, celebrations, it might have had something to do with the Royal Family, pictures of the King were everywhere, this was a monarchist country. I could see why they were on the side of the Americans, not just because of the millions of dollars being poured into the infrastructure, the roads, the buildings, the economy was booming. It was an ideological thing. They had their own ideas of freedom. Like my dad said, there's two sides to every argument, always look at the other side, then you know, it's like a mirror. Until you can see behind it, you can't see yourself. That might not have been quite what he meant. It sounded more like something Loretta would say.

"Will you be home for supper, son?"

But I don't know where home is any more, dad. After the trial, what then? Al knew a lot of guys, there must be some legal stuff they needed doing, something legitimate hopefully, though that wouldn't be of any use if I lost and he was shipped back to Texas facing four years inside. And anyway, if I knew what was good for me, I would get right out of Tombstone before I was under one. I slowed down, considered getting a cab to the British Embassy. Ask for help. A ticket to another dance. Loretta was waiting for me back at the apartment. Maybe that was home. Because she was in it, hanging up my clothes, wearing a pinafore, dusting. A home that could burn down any day. Or back in my parents' house, with the green lawn and the flowerbeds. I was walking alone. My dad waved goodbye.

Something had happened to my mood and I was thirsty, so thirsty. I had kicked the proverbial ass in that court room. Soames and Raniero had gone slinking away without a word, back to report to the higher-ups. They would be back, particularly now we all knew Soames genuinely believed he had the power of the

Lord on his side and he was fighting the good fight, but for the moment, I was ahead of the Great Redeemer's servant on points.

I passed what seemed to be an ironmongers shop. The craftsman was working on a small bench at the open front of the store, making something out of metal, a jug, perhaps, an intricate candle holder, sitting on a small stool. He had a hammer and nails. I could get a hammer and nails. I could use them to fix the elephant. The trader stopped and smiled up at me from his little stool. I mimicked the action of a hammer and nail, tried to describe the shape of an elephant with my hands, an arm waving like a trunk.

"Sell me hammer? Nails?" I said.

The smile slipped from his face. He didn't know what I meant. I was standing there miming the action of hammering nails into an elephant. The sun beat down. I didn't have a hat. Steam was rising from my still damp clothes. I walked away, clutching my document folder tightly, fearing it could slip from my loosening grip. I accidentally bumped into a woman carrying fruit in baskets suspended from a bamboo pole across her shoulders. I stepped into the road, horns blared. How far was I from Betty's? It couldn't be far, I had walked a long way. Across the road, through the haze, I saw my dad again. He was talking to a man with one arm. Bronsky. I pointed at them.

"You're on your way to Montana," I shouted.

"Well done, son. Good work," my dad said.

People avoided me as I weaved along the street. Bronsky followed me, laughing. Ahead, I could see Soames, hovering just above the pavement, pointing a finger, a golden halo glow all around him. A lightning bolt flashed from his finger. I dodged it. Next to him, Raniero was swinging a baseball bat.

I carried on putting one foot more or less in front of the other. Sweat was pouring from me. The Petchaburi Road had never seemed so long. I was staggering like a drunk, my legs were jelly.

I leaned up against a wall, my eyes started to close. Passersby gathered around. I tried to smile and reassure them I was okay. I pushed myself off the wall. It wasn't far to Betty's. In the middle of the road, soldiers spread out, American soldiers, with guns, with M16 rifles. I could hear artillery fire, I stepped over bloodied bodies on the pavement with an exaggerated step, the air filled with black smoke, the rattle of machine gun fire.

"We never have sun like this in England," I said by way of explanation, unnecessary as no-one could understand me. I went on as quickly as I could, trying to escape the fighting, the black-clad Vietnamese, young boys, young girls, falling to the ground, screaming, the red-haired guy from the truck striding along, singing, *Jody's got your Cadillac*, rifle slung over his shoulder. A hand grenade came spinning through the smoke towards me, I reached out and plucked it from the air. It didn't explode. When I uncurled my fingers, it was a cricket ball.

Above, not too far but a million miles away, I could see the neon sign hanging over the pavement. Betty's. I lurched up to the group by the door. The two guys were there as ever, sitting on their little chairs, eating. Three or four of the girls were with them, getting some fresh air, trying to entice some customers into this den of vice, filing their nails, chewing gum. They looked up.

"Mister Matthew," they said in a concerned chorus. They got up to hold me. I fell against them. I realised one was Number Seven.

"Kannika," I said. "Hello, dear."

She took my arm and led me through the doors into the cool. It hit me like a shovel full of ice. Kannika called out for help. There weren't many people in the bar. I couldn't count them anyway, they were a blur. *Mr Tambourine Man* sounded very loud and off key but then it probably was.

"Mister Matthew?" I heard Betty's voice nearby.

"Betty?" I said, sinking closer to the floor. "Al's coming home."

33

"Lucky you have your own live-in nurse, Scooter."

I could hear her sweet voice as I opened my eyes. I blinked, painfully. She was sitting on the side of the bed near me. She wiped a damp cloth on my forehead. I had a vague recollection of things that had happened. I didn't know where I was. In my room. Our room. I reached for her hand.

"Am I alive?" I said. "Or is this heaven?"

Loretta slapped me with the cloth.

"Because you've been ill, you get one cheap shot."

"Are you an angel?"

"One, I said."

She got up from the bed, fussed around a little, tucking in the sheet, not that it was needed, the sun was still high and the room was hot, or maybe that was just me. I pushed myself up against the pillow. Memories of what happened came slowly back to me. Loretta had been sitting by my bed, talking to me. She had been telling me stories, I could remember some of them, about practising intubations on anaesthetised goats, the sound of the dust-off Medevac helicopters bringing in the wounded and the dying to lie in their beds and think the nurses were their wives or girlfriends or mothers. I remembered the moment when I staggered up the stairs, hanging on to Preed. She had been standing in the corridor.

"Nursey, dear," I said.

"Don't get familiar or I'll call Matron."

"You like being back in action?"

She paused in the middle of smoothing down the sheets. What an inept thing to say, even for me.

"If you're asking me am I desperate to get back to look after crying kids with their legs blown off, no, Scooter, I'm not."

She stomped out of the room. I closed my eyes again and rested. My head was throbbing. I knew what it was because it had happened to me before on the journey. We had got a little too close to the Sahara before we realised our mistake and turned back. Mary Jane had offered us little protection. We had all suffered. Alfie had looked after us then, she was a brick. Mild heatstroke. I had this stupid way of failing to put on a hat in the middle of the day because I didn't like the sweat messing up my hair. That, coupled with the soaking I had got in the rainstorm, had laid me out temporarily. I would be fine after a short rest.

"What time is Al getting here?" I asked. "We had the bail application granted this morning, did I tell you?"

She came back into the room, arms folded crossly.

"I heard," she said.

"Who from?"

"From Al."

"That was quick."

"You don't know how long I've been sitting there watching you?"

"Couple of hours? Isn't he due back later today?"

Loretta softened and came over to me and sat down again. I could remember more details about my arrival, it was coming back to me but I didn't want to mention it.

"Baby, this is not the same day," she said. "This is not the day after. You've been out for two days."

Two days? Jesus. I sat upright.

"Whoa, tiger, take it easy," Loretta said, pushing me back onto the bed. The effort of sitting up had taken it out of me. Two days? Forty-eight whole hours? That meant I had missed Al returning from jail. It also explained why I was ravenously hungry. Not only that, we were two days closer to the trial. It was Saturday. I hadn't done the work. And that meant it was Day Ten. Or Eleven. Not Day Five.

"Why didn't anybody wake me up?"

"You mean, thanks, Loretta, honey, for looking after me all that time, for watching me dribble all over the pillow and shake and sweat and burble about cricket? Is that what you mean?"

"Gosh, yes, of course, I'm terribly sorry, yes, you didn't have to do that."

"No. I didn't. But I couldn't not have done it."

I remembered then, when they brought me up the stairs. She had been standing in the corridor. In one hand, she was holding her suitcase. In the other, her kitbag. She was wearing her headscarf and sunglasses and her jacket. When she saw me, she dropped them and grabbed me and hauled me into the room and put me to bed and she had stayed with me for two days. I had to pretend I didn't remember. At least, until I could stand it no longer and I would have to ask her if she had been on her way out. If she would have left and only me being dragged back home had stopped her.

"Tea? Ginger? Cinnamon? Mint?"

"Mint would be lovely, thank you."

She set off to get it from the bar. I stopped her, holding tightly to her hand and giving her what I hoped was a searing soulful gaze but probably just looked like I had gone doolally again. "Loretta…"

I had something meaningful to say. I knew I did. Something ground-breaking, something momentous. Instead, I was seized by a fit of coughing, a dry hacking convulsion that caused me to loosen my grip and she eased away from the bedside with an apparent sense of relief.

"Save it, Scooter," she said. "Dying men always love nursey."

34

"Hurry back, Scooter. You know I don't feel good when my man's not by my side."

She laughed. Sometimes, I felt as if she didn't really mean it, like she was just reciting the words from a Country and Western song. That could just have been because of her accent. She had decided not to venture out on this occasion. She said she was finishing off the *Reader's Digest* version of *Moby Dick*. The band was playing *Mr Tambourine Man*. The singer danced to the side of the stage as I passed.

"Mister Matthew, I have not seen the lady today," he said, ignoring the fact that he was missing half a verse.

"Loretta? She's upstairs, Roger."

He called himself Roger. I don't think it was his real name. I had noticed him casting glances at Loretta once or twice when we had been in the bar and in the most amorous passages of his limited repertoire, he gazed earnestly in her direction. He looked disappointed that she wasn't with me.

"I have written a song for her."

I didn't know what to say. Nor could I come up with an idea of what it would sound like.

"Save it for her," I said. "She would love to hear it."

He gave me a thumbs-up and went back to pick up the song nowhere near where he had left off. I couldn't wait to tell Loretta. She would be thrilled.

The girls were swaying in front of the stage. Several of them approached me solicitously to inquire after my health, which I thought was very good of them. There was a decent crowd. I took my regular stool, next to Al's at the corner of the bar. Betty perched next to me, not quite sitting, languishing. If it is possible to languish on a bar stool, Betty could do it.

I was hoping to see Al but he wasn't there and had been absent for a while, Betty informed me. No great surprise. At least that explained why he hadn't been up to visit me while I lay deliriously on my sickbed, thanks for nothing, pal. The trial was on Monday. McMichael wouldn't be there over the weekend. I had my notes, I had my diagram tree worked out, the questioning trail I wanted to follow but the whole strategy would have benefited from a discussion with Al, especially since he had decided I couldn't drag anyone else into this mess. I had made my own decision about that. I wasn't going to tell him. He wouldn't like it. I ordered a beer. Not only that but if he had skipped off, Major Jackson would come down on me like a firestorm and I didn't want that.

"Mister Matthew, the lawyer," Betty said, probably the only person in the world who could make that job title smoulder. "Now you are fit and well, I have something to offer you."

"If it's anything to do with two-and-a-half ton trucks, I don't want to hear it."

Betty's laugh was like sugar in a cement mixer, a sweet rumbling.

"I have work for you?"

I paid more attention. Work. Cash. Al, it turned out, had paid my rent and my bar tab, or at least it had been written off due to his bidding. Unfortunately, he had yet to stump up any further hard currency and until Mary Jane finally left my possession, I had but a few baht.

"I'm listening."

"This place," Betty said, gesturing around the bar with her cigarette in its long holder, ash toppling onto the floor. I followed the sweep of her arm, taking in the new card tables and chairs, again in softwood, incongruously showroom perfect on the dirty parquet floor. Betty had replaced furniture with brand new very quickly. Business must be good in her seedy trap for the unwary, to use the words of Soames. This comfort station for the troops. And in the satellite industries; the chair and table manufacturers, for instance. Money was pouring into this country and everyone was doing what they could to grab a little. The inhabitants of Betty's were here by choice. It might have been a choice forced on them because they had nothing else and some choices were much, much harder than others. But they were people. They lived. They did what they could. Amoral times.

"Yes?" I said.

"The plans I told you, such plans, Mister Matthew."

"Right. Yes."

"It is a great opportunity. I need investment, I need help to run it."

"I don't think it's really my line of work," I said. "I'm afraid I wouldn't know how to run a bar, I couldn't charm the customers the way you do. Or clear out a riot the way Al can, hold on, you don't mean me, do you?"

"Of course not," she said, rather too quickly for my liking. "I want you to draw up a contract. I want Al to join me."

Al the legitimate businessman. Well, more legitimate than he had been before.

"When we marry, we can get tax break, is that not so?"

Al the married man. Al the bar owner. Al's future sketched out for him in a way he could never have imagined. Oh, if only. If only he had been a man with imagination. If only he could have seen another way.

"Have you asked him?" I said.

She shook her head, her hair falling around her face like stage curtains halfway through a major operatic performance.

"Asked him what?"

Somehow, Al had regained his regular place on his stool without either of us noticing his entrance into the bar.

"Moreau," Betty said.

She put a finger to her lips and I inferred that Al was still not to be told anything about the proposed venture. She swung away across the bar, not short of willing customers eager to be enchanted.

"I been selling your piece of crap," Al said.

"You mean my beloved?"

"Got you some bucks." He slid a packet of notes across the bar. I picked it up, started to open it. He snapped out a hand and put it on top of the cash.

"Not in here, boy."

I don't know if he was being cautious about possible theft or because he didn't want me to see how little it had sold for but I didn't quibble and put the proceeds in my pocket. That was it. Mary Jane gone. I would put three quarters aside for the others. Or should Pete and Alfie just get one as they were now together? It was a thought. I would have to discuss it with Mike. If I ever saw him again. We got drinks. I drank to the sale. I drank to the memories. No chance now of driving off into the sunset with Loretta.

"Been taking care of some business," Al said, a phrase that did not always augur well from him. "Putting my affairs in order."

"How so?"

"This and that," he said. "You wanna hear a story?"

"Is it to do with marching fifty miles through jungle carrying a 60lb pack? Heating up your coffee with plastic explosive while the rain beats down on your poncho? Because if it is, I don't want to hear it right now. I would prefer to develop a trial strategy."

"I do got one you ain't heard," he went on. "You know the way the bad guys bring down all their supplies, down the Ho Chi Minh Trail?"

"You mean the North Vietnamese?"

It was a measure of the way we now were that I could say this to him. I no longer felt he was going to take violent offence.

"Right. Every corps brings with them an artist, like an actor, somebody to tell stories, they love all that."

"Yes, you do know, don't you, it's because their culture and history is so strong? They aren't just the piss-ant country the US thinks they are and I'm using the words of Lyndon B. Johnson here. He couldn't understand how a piss-ant country was winning the fight."

"They ain't winning," Al said. "Nobody beats the USA, boy, lemme tell you that, you want to hear my story or not, asshole?"

I shrugged. I supposed I had nothing else to do than listen to some jingoistic blowhard and besides, I liked his company, goddammit.

"Thanks for asking me how I am," I said.

"Yeah. So I was out on patrol. There was a little cadre of them. I knew where they were, and for like three or four nights, night after night, they would come outside and they would sit in a circle and listen to this guy telling the stories, acting them out. They never knew I was watching them, sitting with my rifle behind a coconut tree. Yeah, they would listen to stories, man. It was cool."

"That's somehow life-affirming," I said.

"Yeah, then one night, he didn't turn up. There was no story, there was no performance from the storyteller."

"That's a pity," I said. "Why was that?"

"Because I shot him."

The band struck up *Rock Around the Clock*. Sometimes, I didn't know if Al was pulling my leg. I rather hoped on this occasion, he was but I didn't get chance to ask him.

"Evening, gentlemen. Not seen you in a while," McMichael said. At least he wasn't carrying a bunch of flowers though he did look earnestly around the room, clearly hoping to catch a glimpse of Betty.

"I was passing. Thought I'd drop off these papers." He put some documents on the bar. "Couple of things to talk about, couple of things the Sergeant said you wanted checked out."

"Did he now?" I said.

Al made a move to take the file but I got there first. As far as I could recall, I hadn't asked him to talk to McMichael without my presence or consent. Al clearly didn't think much of McMichael, though I suspected this animosity extended to all of a senior rank. I was surprised he had sought him out for a tête-à-tête. Al seemed uncomfortable.

"Another time, Captain," he said.

"Now's a good a time as any," McMichael said. His eyes lit up when he saw Betty. I thought I would have to scoop up his tongue as it dropped to the floor. She gave him one of her special little waves. There was nothing in the file that couldn't have waited until the trial started, nothing to get McMichael to go out of his way on a Saturday. Apart from ogling Betty.

"First off," McMichael said, lowering his voice. "They brought Saunders in. Put him in a cell."

"He's a witness," I said.

"Exactly. Highly unusual. I'll try to find out why, might give us something."

"How is the kid?" Al asked.

"I don't know. I haven't seen him yet."

"Poor kid."

"So there's still just him and the other witness testifying to the documentary evidence?"

"Sergeant Madison. He's the front guy. I am damn certain the secret service has done the leg work on this, all the investigating, but Madison will answer the questions in court. Soames and Raniero think it's a slam-dunk anyhow."

"They think my case is a slam-dunk?" Al asked.

"Yes," McMichael said.

"It's not," I said.

"Assholes."

"One other thing." McMichael turned to Al. "You know that girl you wanted checked out?"

Al shuffled on his stool as if he was ready to pounce and eject McMichael from the bar.

"What girl?" I said.

"She's not secret service. She's not working for the prosecution."

I had an idea who they were talking about. I just didn't want to believe Al had done this.

"Loretta?" I said.

"Yeah, that's her," McMichael said.

"You had Loretta checked out?"

Al had the good grace to stare balefully into his glass. He wouldn't meet my eyes. Betty swayed across the room to us. McMichael broke out in a cold sweat as she approached.

"Mister Officer," she sang. "Drink?"

"He's in a hurry," Al said.

"Don't mind if I do," McMichael said, sitting down next to me. Betty waved to Preed. And then the world came crashing down.

"I did find this out. About Loretta Maine."

"Loretta?" Betty said. "She is our friend. Isn't she, Mister Matthew?"

"That so? Maybe not for much longer. MPs are on her tail. She's AWOL. Been absent without leave for three, four weeks."

Al had known something was wrong all the time, he just didn't know what. McMichael took a sip of his beer.

"Yeah," he said. "She's a deserter."

35

"Whatcha doin', Scooter?"

I had all my papers spread out on the coffee table, sifting through them for the possibility of another defence. Loretta tossed *Moby Dick* onto the settee and stretched out her legs, yawning.

"Working on something for Betty."

"Like what?"

I put down my pen and looked across at her as she sprawled on the settee. I had been looking at her a lot. I don't know if she had noticed. She picked up the elephant's trunk and started absently tapping it against her knee. I hadn't known what to say. I had stumbled up the stairs, leaving the others at the bar. I was furious at Al but I could see why he had done it, he just hadn't found out what he thought he would.

"You want to go out, maybe? Get something to eat? See some things?" I said. "There's a lot of temples we haven't seen yet."

She hadn't been out of the apartment for days. I had worked it out, I knew why. She had gone downstairs into the bar. She hadn't gone outside in case she was seen. She was using my place to hide. Using me.

"Not today," she said. "It's hot."

I couldn't sit there and pretend. I wanted to persuade her to tell me it wasn't true but I think I knew it was. She had been with me for too long. I hadn't wanted to ask her, tried to convince myself she was on some special extended leave or something, some mission, some Army nurse thing she hadn't wanted to disclose. I hadn't wanted to ask her because I didn't want to find out, because of the old lawyer thing, the courtroom mantra. Never ask a question if you don't already know the answer.

"I'll go out, get us some food," I said.

"Maybe buy a hat?"

For a second, I tried to avoid her eyes but I couldn't. I think at that moment, she realised the play-acting was all done. I had kept it going for a night, part of a day. No more.

"Maybe I will come with you," she said. "I don't think you can choose it without me."

She put on her headscarf as usual and sunglasses, of course, scanning the crowds so carefully. She was looking out for the military police. She took my arm and walked right close beside me as we made our way through the Sunday streets. Back home they would be quiet. All the shops closed, probably grey skies, cold. Sunday was the greyest day of the week, a day lacking in any joy. People went on Sunday walks, families dressed in their best clothes, visiting relatives. Instead, I was here, in the sun. Let's not go and visit Grandma today, dad, let's just hang out.

"I got this idea," Loretta said. "Buy some glue? Let's buy some glue."

"Glue?"

"Some glue. Fix the elephant. Don't you want to fix the elephant?"

"Sure," I said. "Fix the elephant. And when the elephant is fixed, you can go."

I had said it. The words just came out and I couldn't stop them. She eased her grip on my arm, she looked away. A guy tried to sell us cigarettes from a tray he was carrying. We were heading through the city. Neither of us knew where.

"I didn't ever want to go back," she said. "I would do anything."

"Even sleep with me? You were that desperate?"

"That's not what I meant."

The road led out into a square. It was bustling. Cars and rickshaws and cycles and trams circled it. There were American soldiers with their girls, pointing out the sights. Another day in Bangkok and I was teetering on the edge.

"There's a store, let's see if they got glue," Loretta said, pointing across the street, trying for a normal tone in her voice. I nodded, in a daze. She let go of my arm. There was a brief break in the traffic. Loretta ran across. I saw a tram coming. I had to wait. She got to the other side of the road and turned and looked back. She was standing there in her headscarf and sunglasses and her blouse and shorts and sandals and she was the only person I could see in the crowds and she was waiting to see what was going to happen, knowing I wasn't at her side, knowing why. I could turn around, go back to Betty's, throw her bags out of the apartment, lock the door, except it didn't lock very well. She waited, her head on one side. She put her index finger to the dimple in her chin and posed with one knee bent. I started to turn away, I did, honestly. From the corner of my eye, I could see a gap in the traffic, a tuk-tuk the only obstacle and I ran across and dodged it and ignored the driver yelling at me and grabbed her and lifted her so her toes were just touching the ground and I kissed her. Because I couldn't think of anything else I really wanted to do.

*   *   *

We wandered the streets for a while. All the time, she was looking out for faces in the crowd, looking out for uniforms, looking out for those white helmets with the black letters on the front. MP. A couple of Western guys wolf-whistled at her, she just hung tighter onto my arm. We headed back to Betty's a roundabout way.

"What's going to happen?" she asked.

"McMichael doesn't know you're living at Betty's," I said. "Anyway, I don't think he cares enough to snitch."

"That's not what I meant."

"But if he knows about you, others will."

I had to get my thoughts back on the trial. I had the witness statement to go through, both witness statements in fact but the main target was Private Saunders. If I could take him out of the picture, the case was ours, I could throw enough of a cloud over the rest of it. For Al. The man who had gone behind my back. He was still my client. Everything could change in the next 24 hours, that's all it takes, that's much longer than it takes, it only takes a second.

The people in south East Asia have a different idea of time. It's circular, it doesn't end, it keeps going. That's part of the problem the Americans had in Vietnam. They took their Western idea of time – do it now, by a certain hour, by a certain day – and tried to impose it on the conduct of war. Against people who didn't share the same view; time to them is endless. They could spend days walking along a trail to deliver arms to their warriors. They could live in tunnels underground for as long as it took, waiting. That's what the Americans didn't realise. I probably said some of this to Loretta as we walked. She listened politely, most likely on the point of telling me I didn't know what the hell I was talking about but I wanted to avoid the real conversation. We bought glue from a little shop.

"Things don't fix as easy as they ought to fix, Scooter. I wanted so bad to fix those boys."

Loretta's war was not the same as Al's. This was not gung-ho, Sergeant Fury, leaping into battle, this was mopping-up, the dust-off, that's what they called the Hueys, the helicopters who carried the wounded from the field to hospital within fifteen minutes, very efficient. The dust-off. Like clearing up a spillage in your kitchen, swiping your hands together and looking back on the job done with some satisfaction. Loretta was hurt. I had become her dust-off.

"Switching hotels, waiting for the MPs to knock on my door, using false names. I'd never been on the run before. I didn't know what to do but I just knew what I didn't want to do. You know? And that was to go back," she said.

A few men and women were loitering around in the streets, sitting outside houses, chatting, laughing. Electricity wires were bundled together, hanging from lampposts, coiled and strung across the street into houses and shops. Music came from the bars as we passed, a waiter tried to entice us into his restaurant but we weren't hungry.

"I get it," I said. "I get why you were running."

"Maybe you do, maybe you don't. I can't tell you any more than the things I've already told you about what it's like to be there."

"I guess." We were both trying to retain something normal, something we could cling onto, something that would make us both believe we weren't frauds.

"That day was the first day I had been out for a while," she said. "I saw those guys running towards me. The police. I ducked into that alley and the next thing I know I get hit in the leg with a flying elephant and I'm thinking, Loretta, honey, you were right, these streets are sure not safe."

"So you're looking for somewhere new to hide? Then Mr Muggins comes along, right? Some sappy English guy wearing old clothes who just happens to be not too repulsive?"

"Nearly right. I mean, you're repulsive."

She stopped and looked at me, to see if I was smiling. I was, a little, I couldn't help it. She reached up and pulled the corners of my lips up at either end.

"I made you smile, didn't I?"

She leaned her head on my chest and I put my arms round her and we stood for a few moments like that in the middle of the pavement.

"I thought to myself, English, but you can't have everything. Talks kinda funny. You gotta believe me, Scooter," she said. "You were more than a hiding place."

"Were?" I said. "Past tense?"

No answer. We walked on. It was getting towards dusk when we headed back to Betty's where Al was sitting at one of the tables talking to some men we didn't know. Betty was watching them from a distance with some trepidation.

"Mister Matthew," she said. "I am so glad you're back. These men. They found Al."

36

I eyeballed them through the steel mirror as Al and the two men chatted at a table by the window. One of them looked like a second division footballer from some Soviet state, the other was Oriental, dressed like a stockbroker. They seemed like colleagues at a business meeting. The band played a song that might have been *Daydream Believer*. The Monkees. Good song, originally.

Betty hovered around near me behind the bar though I have no idea what she thought I was going to do if things went pear-shaped with Al's companions. They both looked like they could handle themselves and probably in their line of work, that was a minimum prerequisite. Loretta stayed with me for a while, drank a soda. She smiled at Roger, as he directed his vocals straight to her, his voice wavering from rock and roll to crooner.

"Something else happen, Mister Matthew," Betty said. "Al punch the officer. On the chin."

I closed my eyes and said a silent prayer.

"Jeez, Scooter, we missed all the excitement," Loretta said. "What happened?"

She was acting as if nothing was wrong between us. But there was, there had to be. Betty shrugged.

"You had better ask Al," she said. "He would not tell me. The officer left. I don't think he was hurt. Too much."

At least it sounded like Al had only given him a tap. I had no doubt he could have put him in hospital if he wanted to, so I was grateful for this restraint in punching my second chair almost on the eve of the trial. Loretta slid off the stool.

"Guess I'm going to be going upstairs," she said.

"What about Al?" I asked.

"He's a big boy. He can take care of himself."

"Maybe," I said.

"You'd rather stay here than come upstairs with me?"

"Not the way you mean."

"What other way is there to mean? It is or it isn't."

The sensible thing to do would have been simply to go upstairs with Loretta but sensible was somehow out of my reach. I let her out of my sight because I wanted to sit there acting as Al's bodyguard.

"Fine," she said and waved to Betty and Roger and a couple of the girls and I watched her walk away. It occurred to me I should follow her, let her drag me up the stairs behind her. But I couldn't tell if that's what she wanted so I stayed put, waiting to see if one of these men was going to produce a gun or a knife or something and I would have to step in. Dangerous men. Seemed an accurate description. I didn't like the look of them at all. Preed brought me a beer, smiling and bowing.

"Whisky?" he said. I shook my head. I wondered if I should suggest that he brought in the world's two worst bouncers from the front, the guys who had been so useless on the night of the fight. It had turned out they were relatives of Betty's, employed merely for the sake of nepotism rather than any door security prowess so I decided this could achieve no more than escalate the situation. No, I was on my own being the hard man.

Al turned and looked at me as if to demonstrate to his companions that he had only just noticed I was there. I knew he had seen me the second I walked in, the way he saw everything.

He jerked a thumb, indicating to the other two that I was there. They looked across to me like I was dangling on the end of a line, waiting to be fished out and thrown into a frying pan. Al said something to them and their faces changed, registered a different expression. I thought I noticed a kind of grudging respect.

"Is all okay?" Betty asked. She put her elbows on the bar and her chin on her cupped hands and let the cigarette holder dangle from her lips, the smoke drifting up around us. I think at that point I allowed my lip to curl slightly. I was aiming for a James Coburn face. I chewed imaginary gum. If I had had the benefit of a knife, I would have trimmed my nails with it. Possibly even given myself a shave.

"Sure thing," I said. "Why not?"

"Because you look sick."

"I'm looking tough."

"Of course. I will look tough, too."

We both tried to put on the appearance of being heavily armed and knowing how to use the heat we were packing. Al continued his discussions. I wasn't sure how long we could keep up this waxwork display so it was a relief when after a few minutes, the three rose from the table. I put my hand inside my jacket, searching for a shoulder holster. Betty stood and reached under the bar, as if she had a shotgun handy. The two men could have come towards us, pushed past Al, slalomed through the tables and confronted me. Called my bluff. It was with an enormous sense of relief that I saw them shake hands with Al and leave, without looking in our direction. Al came over, spreading his arms wide in a gesture of disbelief.

"What the hell were you two clowns doing?" he asked.

Clearly, our act had not been the deciding factor in whatever negotiation was going on. Betty burst out laughing, a sparkling mountain stream across diamond rocks.

"We were back-up," I said.

"Back-up? In what? Some Little League cheerleading tournament?"

"We were worried about you, Moreau."

She burred the 'r' in Moreau, rolled it and sizzled it. She leaned over the bar and ran her hand through Al's hair and onto his cheek then went away to work the room.

"Didn't believe those guys knew where I hung out," Al said. "Couldn't tell Betty. I don't want Betty to know, I think they went away okay. Ain't none too sure about that, though."

"I'm assuming they're part of the background to the trial?"

"Could be."

That was about as useful as any of Al's contributions. He was going to give me nothing. At that moment, I realised I still had another decision to make; whether to put him on the stand or not, whether to let him face Soames and Raniero. It could go either way. He could be the charming Al, the silver-tongued Al and he would win the day. Or it could be mayhem. He could start a fight with everyone, including the judge and the stenographer. I hadn't briefed him so it would be even more of a risk if I decided to play that card. If I didn't take the risk, I would have to win the case without him.

"You remember Stan Bronsky?" he asked.

I did remember Stan Bronsky. In fact, I saw him behind every lamppost, around every corner, and I even checked for him in my shower at night.

"I think he was working for them. They were a couple of the guys moved some machinery."

"La la la. Don't tell me any more about moving machinery. Wait. Hold it. You said you didn't know anybody called Stan Bronsky."

"That wasn't his name."

"Then how on earth do you know it's the same man?"

"I know."

Stubbornly enigmatic as ever. I decided to let it go because he was giving me his "you shittin' me, boy" look again.

"You had Loretta checked out."

"Don't matter none."

"It matters to me."

"She ain't CIA. That's all."

"That's all?"

"I know she ain't what you thought. Too bad. Okay?"

As far as he was concerned, there was no more to be said on the subject.

"So," Al said. "Those guys. I told them if for any reason I didn't make it out of the trial, you were the guy they should come looking for."

"You told them what?"

"Said you was my business partner."

"Good grief."

"Said you was a legal eagle. Wouldn't take no messin' around. That you was a tough guy. Now ain't this amazing?"

"What?"

"I think they believed me."

Once again, he had put me in the firing line. Although they had gone away without a murmur, should they return following the trial – and I didn't know which outcome they would consider favourable – I doubted even my James Coburn face would save me.

"No more," I said. "No more today."

I had reached the nadir. I had got to the stage where nothing else was going to trouble me, nothing could surprise me. Dad, you know that plane ticket? Send it now. I don't want to be a lawyer any more. I want to work on an oil rig. Something relatively safe. I started to leave, to go upstairs. Al grabbed my arm as I passed.

"Hey," he said.

"What now? You're about to tell me an assassination squad armed with nuclear weapons is heading this way and you'll be sending them straight up to my room?"

"I don't know what the hell you're talking about sometimes," Al said.

"Go on." I sighed. "What do you want to say?"

"Just this. Appreciate you sittin' there looking like some dumb cluck."

Once again, he had disarmed me. I think he meant it.

"Thanks."

"Don't mention it. We all set?"

"Yes," I said. He scanned my face to see if I was telling the truth. Whatever he found there, whatever veneer of confidence I had managed, it seemed to satisfy him.

"That's good, buddy."

He called me buddy. Not boy.

"Nearly forgot," I said. "Just a small thing. Is there a good reason for you punching my co-counsel in the face?"

"Sure," he said.

"Are you going to enlighten me?"

"He asked me if Betty was for rent."

Fair enough. I turned away. The only surprise there was that Al wasn't now facing a murder charge.

* * *

The lights were off when I went upstairs. The only illumination came from the signs flashing outside, on off, on off, purple, gold, green, lighting up the few sticks of furniture. And the elephant. He was on the coffee table. He was fixed. His trunk was back in place, where it had never been because all the time he had been my constant companion, it had been resting by his great big solid feet. Loretta had fixed the elephant.

The tube of glue lay partially squeezed on the table, its cap back on, a slight sticky residue around the nozzle, like there always was, like you tried to scrape off when you remembered you hadn't finished making that Airfix model of a battleship or a tank and you wanted to have another go because it had been a birthday present.

Her suitcase was by the door to the shower, her kitbag on top of it. I went to the bedroom. I could hear soft breathing. I should wake her up. I should have woken her up, of course I should, I knew that. But then, I thought, if I did, I wouldn't know what to say. Somehow, sometimes we all use each other, that's the way the world goes around. I could have said, hey, baby, it's cool, this is the Sixties, we had a good time, we had sex. We let it all hang out. Groovy. So long. Been nice knowing you. Peace and love.

I picked up the papers for the trial. I had work to do. I had been through them endlessly, my notes, the testimony from both witnesses, Saunders and Madison the MP, they were all I needed. All the disclosure had been made. I had seen the evidence. I heard the faint rustle of the bed sheets as Loretta turned over. I had half-expected her to be gone when I got to the room. All the things we had done, the way she looked at me. All a fake. All of it a subterfuge. And she hadn't even had the decency to walk out, to take the decision away from me. God, I wished she had gone, then I wouldn't have had to know she was still there and we wouldn't have had to wonder any more, it would just have been over. I closed my eyes, the folders and the documents clutched in my hand and lay back on the settee where I seemed to have spent quite a lot of time. I heard the band below play *We Gotta Get Out Of This Place*.

The papers fell from my fingers. It became the middle of the night. I couldn't go to my bed. Loretta was there. It wouldn't have been right. I stumbled around and picked up my papers but as I backed away as quietly as I could, I knocked into the elephant. The trunk fell off. It dropped onto the coffee table, it must have been still drying. It hit the top of the coffee table with a rattle. I stilled it, worried that the noise would wake Loretta up. No movement from the bedroom. In the morning, when she woke up, she might think I had done it deliberately. A couple of days ago, we would have laughed about it. Now, I didn't even plan to be there. Hell, I could kick the elephant all over the room. As the door closed, I thought I heard a voice calling behind me. If it had been, I would have stopped, I'm sure I would.

"Whatcha doin', Scooter?"

It was just a breeze outside in the night air, fizzing through the bar signs. Maybe the diluted noise from a motorcycle. I went downstairs, to the bar. It looked empty. The moon shone through the big window. A red light was still lit on one of the Marshall amplifiers on the stage. It was making a low buzzing noise. The floor was sticky with spilt beer. I stepped up onto the stage past the guitars propped up on stands, past the drum kit, nudging the hi-hat cymbals so they made a small tinny noise before I stopped them with my hand. Something stirred out in the bar. I switched off the amp. Silence except for a gentle breathing from the direction of one of the tables. Someone was still there, sleeping, head on their arms across the table, like it was afternoon in primary school. Betty didn't mind if that happened. The moonlight showed me who it was. Number Seven. Kannika.

"Ten per cent discount?" the breeze whispered.

I crept silently off the stage and went across to where she was lying. She didn't move. I was happy to have another person there with me. I didn't want to be alone. I sat across from her at the same table. I reached over, my hand raised in mid-air. I watched it trembling there in the moonlight. Those girls downstairs, Loretta had said, sorry for them. I almost stroked her hair as it lay spread out on the grimy beer-stained top of the card table. She was wearing little shorts and a shiny blouse. Her arms were thin. She looked as if she had lost her teddy bear. I took my hand away, leaned back in the chair, closed my eyes, listened to her sleep until morning.

37

The Justice Centre was busy. Monday morning busy. I had left Betty's early, I wanted to get to the courtroom, the tram was packed and I had to stand. Number Seven had woken up before me, rubbed her eyes, smiled. Waking up next to a man she didn't know too well was nothing new to her. I got her a glass of tea from the bar. I went into the downstairs bathroom, which was still as much of a health hazard as it always had been, I didn't know why Betty didn't clean it up, splashed water on my face and went out of the side door. No point in waiting for Al, he could have been anywhere. I got breakfast on the way. Some rice. I was in a bit of a daze. The MP was standing outside, reading the *Bangkok Post*.

I was the first to arrive. The courtroom seemed much bigger with no-one in it. I walked down the centre aisle like I was taking my first steps from the pavilion, swinging my bat to loosen up, in need of a decent innings with the score delicately poised. If it hadn't been for the Stars and Stripes on the wall, I was padded up, I was walking out at Lord's. The sun shining down on a glorious July afternoon, the soft green grass giving way beneath my spiked boots. I glance around, the fielders watch me, the bowler sizes me up. The crowd applauds. I want to keep walking, right across the square, past the wickets, back to our rooms, to explain about the elephant, explain about me, explain about us, explain about everything.

I had decided I didn't care how or why Loretta was with me. I only cared that she was. I would have to count the minutes until the end of the day, hoping she would still be there and I could make it right. Soon I would find out I should have left straight away, abandoned Al, swept her up and run off. Instead, I chose to stay because I had a job and I heard footsteps behind me on the tiled floor and a jumble of voices. It was time to take guard.

"Moreau here yet?" McMichael said as he took his place next to me, throwing his papers onto the desk. He fingered a small bruise on his chin that looked like he had tried to cover it up with some cosmetics, perhaps spot remover cream.

"Shaving?" I said.

"Walked into a door."

"Yeah. I heard."

"My own fault. I wasn't looking. Couple of beers too many, I guess."

I hoped this was not going to make things even more awkward than they already were but I didn't have chance to broach the subject because the side door opened and the clerk and stenographer wandered in silently, without acknowledging us, and took their places in front of the dais.

"Okay, here's how it works," McMichael said. I knew how it worked but I wanted him to tell me. I needed him on board. "The prosecution will open the case, run through the charges. We just sit and listen unless they slip in something we haven't heard about, so we keep an eye on our documents, got it? I think they probably won't put up the first witness until after the lunch recess."

Voices were raised in the corridor outside. Soames and Raniero. I couldn't make out all that was being said but it appeared things were not too rosy in the prosecution camp. Good for us.

"They only have two witnesses. They don't think they need any more so I guess this could last two days, maybe three, depending on if you want to put Moreau on the stand. Want my advice?"

I looked around. Soames and Raniero were face to face in the doorway of the court, clearly arguing. I nodded to McMichael, though I already knew my answer.

"Put him on the stand," McMichael said.

"Do what? That's your advice?"

The prosecution would take him apart. Unless he lied. Which he was quite capable of. And that could go even worse for him. Maybe McMichael knew that. Payback for Betty's could have been on his mind.

"Sure," he said. "Moreau's a good soldier. His record speaks for itself, he's sharp, he can answer the questions. Unless you think he's guilty?"

"I'm his lawyer," I said. "It doesn't matter if I think he's guilty or not."

"Then put him on the stand."

"I'll take that under advisement," I said, shelving my real response, which would have been – 'Listen, I don't care what happened in the bar, in here we're professionals and we're on his side, got it?'

"As you wish," he said. "If you don't trust him."

I put aside any further discussion on this point, straining to hear what was being said at the entrance to the courtroom and looking at the clock on the wall, which read two minutes before the start of the trial. No sign of Al.

"You know the judge is going to tear us a couple of new ones, right, Todd?" It was Soames.

"What's this I hear?" McMichael said. "Trouble in the ranks?"

He rubbed his hands together, a grin crossing his face.

"Fifty bucks, Captain," I said. If anything was going to cheer him up, it was the thought of beating Raniero. He nodded.

"Let's do it."

"What else could I do?" Raniero was saying. "And keep your voice down, Blaine, for Chrissake."

He glanced over to us. We had both turned pointedly in our seats and were watching them, not trying to disguise the look of amusement on our faces. I waved. McMichael gave a salute. They clammed up and barged into one another as they tried to get into the courtroom.

"Morning, gentlemen," I said. "Nice day for it."

Raniero glared at me.

"You won't think so soon, Benson."

Soames forced one of his big cheesy Evangelist smiles onto his face.

"Your cowboy client coming on horseback?" he said, looking past me to the empty space where Al should have been. "Stuck in the saloon?"

"He'll be here," I said.

Soames looked at his watch. He put his cap down on the table, the solid shiny peak hitting the wood sharply. The MP by the double doors had come inside and closed them. McMichael looked nervous.

"If he's not here, the judge will probably take that as an admission, would you agree, Todd?"

"He'll probably think we should put out a warrant for Moreau and have him kicked out of the United States Army, hell, probably out of the United States, what do you think, Blaine?"

McMichael half rose in his seat.

"Hey, Abbott and Costello," he said. "You hope he's not coming because that's the only way you can win your lousy case."

"Someone got out of bed the wrong side, Todd," Soames said.

"Yeah," Raniero said. "Maybe it wasn't the bed he wanted to be in."

They both laughed. They couldn't possibly have known what had gone on. Could they? It had to be a coincidence. Though if they had the entire place bugged and a camera hidden in Roger's bouffant hair I would no longer have been surprised. The door opened to allow the entrance of Major Bill Jackson, robes flowing, marching, the band he should have had with him playing the national anthem. We all stood up. Soames, Raniero, McMichael. The clerk. The stenographer. Major Bill Jackson surveyed his domain like a Roman Emperor and then, seemingly satisfied, he indicated we should all regain our seats but he couldn't have been satisfied because we were lacking a key component, namely the defendant. As I stood up, his chair had been empty. When I sat down, he was right next to me.

"Your Honour, I think we might have a problem…" Soames said. Raniero nudged him and nodded to where Al was sitting, looking calm, looking soldierly in his dress uniform with his ribbons of medals. Weird thing to say, I was kind of proud of him at that moment. I was proud to be sitting next to him. I was proud he had called me buddy.

"And what would that be, Captain?" the judge said.

"We don't have a problem, Sir," Soames said. He sat down, fiddling with the peak of his cap. There was clearly a lot riding on this case for Soames. He was feeling the pressure.

"Thank you for those opening remarks," the judge said. "Good to know. Now, are we ready to proceed? Properly and correctly? In military order. Except for you, Mr Benson, that doesn't apply. The court will make allowances."

"Grateful, Your Honour," I said. "I hope the court will not have to worry about the defence acting correctly."

I looked across to the prosecution bench and sat down. Nice. I was pleased with that one. First ball, nudged it away to the boundary for a quick single. The judge was contemplating. We awaited his instructions. The fan was even less efficient on this occasion and it was also emitting a high-pitched whirring noise. I wondered for a second if he was going to tell me not to be a smartarse but he decided to let it go and he nodded to Soames.

"Your turn, Captain. Let's hear it."

Soames stood, cleared his throat, picked up his papers and stood as if he was in a pulpit somewhere in the Deep South, the congregation yearning for his Sunday words of wisdom. We sat back. I looked at Al. His arms were by his side, he was straight backed, he was looking ahead. Just for a second, his eyes gave a little twitch. He was in the jungle. He was expecting a firefight. For the first time, I could see what he meant when he said he was scared most of the time. It was the way he stayed alive.

38

The charges flowed. McMichael checked them on his documents. It took the best part of an hour. Soames ran through the evidence as briefly as he could. We all had it before us, we had all been through it. I found my attention wandering a little, I couldn't help thinking of Loretta, back in our rooms, waiting for me. At least, that's what I was hoping. I had no way of knowing if I was right. McMichael was good. He spotted a flaw, nudged me, pointed to them on the files and I stood up and objected.

"Your Honour, with reference to US16001.4."

The judge found it among his documents and indicated I should go on. These were the holes I was looking for. This was the defence I was running without Al's consent. I was going to go for it anyway.

"You will see that on this occasion, August 22, 1968, Sergeant Moreau's name does not appear on this docket. He was not the person responsible for this consignment."

It was the two-and-a-half ton truck. I had no idea what had happened to it. I guessed Al knew, doubtless it had been shipped on to the Philippines or somewhere by one of the men he had been talking to in the bar. But he hadn't signed it out, there were three other names on the ticket, he didn't want me to put them up in court, he didn't want to land any of his men in trouble. I could feel his body tense next to me. I was expecting a sharp elbow in the ribs but what the hell, I was going to run this.

"Your Honour, the prosecution is aware that Sergeant Moreau's name does not appear on every one of these dockets," Soames said.

"There are quite a number," I said. "To avoid any delay, I can provide the court with a list of the charges to which we have an objection."

"That won't be necessary," Soames said. He had seen this coming. Raniero leaned across the desk, looked out around him, grinning at me. "None of the other men are on trial. None have been charged."

"Exactly," I said. The fielder had picked up the ball but I hadn't seen him. I was carelessly running for the wickets while it was already whistling towards the wicket-keeper's gloves. "They haven't been charged and yet their names are on these dockets. The defence suggests that Sergeant Moreau was not the only member of his company capable of signing out these vehicles, all of which could have gone on to legitimate use in the furtherance of the activity in Vietnam."

"They didn't," Soames said.

"There is no proof of that, Your Honour. The prosecution has no evidence as to where the vehicles could later be found."

"That is correct," Soames said. He was giving this up to me way too easily. "But if the vehicles went on for use in military measures, their arrival would have been signed for. The dockets would all have been filed. They have not. There is no record of them anywhere once they have left Sergeant Moreau's charge and that is the point here, if I may make it at this juncture, Your Honour?"

He was in full flow. The congregation was raising its arms. Soames was giving them the full fire and brimstone and it was all about to come raining down on my head. The judge raised an eyebrow, indicating Soames could carry on. He even stepped out into the aisle to give full vent to his righteous fury, waving a handful of dockets.

"Sergeant Moreau was in full and complete charge of this facility. Everything that happened there was under his control, he was, if you like, the chief executive of this company and according to that rule, no matter that he did not see each and every one of the transactions that took place, it was still his to control. He was the master of it."

"Objection," I said, trying not to sound too alarmed. My intention was to stop him in the middle of his oratory. "The prosecution can't possibly have been through every single vehicle movement in this war, there would be millions."

"There would be no reason for us to do this. As I say, Sergeant Moreau is responsible for every one of these transactions because it was his motor pool. The prosecution does not have to prove that his hand was personally involved in each of these occasions. We merely have to show that he was aware of what was going on and was personally involved in one, just one, that's all."

"It's still conjecture." I stood up. "Your Honour."

"And we have a witness to prove this," Soames said. "And the testimony of the investigating officer."

The judge considered in silence and then stood, sweeping to his feet like the golden eagle on the seal in front of him, gathering up his robes.

"We'll take a break," he said, banging his gavel on the desk. The Star Spangled Banner should have played as he marched from the room. Soames patted McMichael on the shoulder as he passed by. He didn't look at me. Why would he? He knew he had just kicked my ass. I had been so sure. He had made me look like an amateur. I braced myself for Raniero's comments but he didn't stop, he hurried out, ran past Soames, straight out of the courtroom without even gloating. McMichael gathered up his papers.

"Good try," he said. Al got to his feet. He didn't look at me. I was sure he had followed everything that had happened. He could see the hole opening up below him and it looked like I was about to push him in.

39

The recess was short. I tried to telephone Betty's from the small office in the Justice Centre. It took too long to get a connection and when it finally rang, no-one picked up. I sat on the edge of the desk in the office. McMichael was in the chair, fiddling with elastic bands he was wrapping around his fingers.

"Baseball season back home," was all he said. Al had gone somewhere, perhaps to carry out his last bits of business. I could feel a sense of disappointment. He had believed in me. The phone rang and rang. I wanted to tell Betty to pass on a message to Loretta to stay put until I got home, at least give me a chance to explain.

"I played a little, did you know that?"

"No. I didn't know that."

"Minor leagues, only for a season or two. Pitcher."

I had been rehearsing all the things I wanted to say to Loretta, stopping only a little short of begging forgiveness and pleading and I was happy to add them to my list.

"Tommy is still in a cell," Al said, appearing in the doorway. I put down the phone. McMichael moved away from him to a safe distance out of arm's reach but Al didn't bother with him.

"He's a witness. I can see they might have put him there initially while they found somewhere else but not right up until the trial," I said.

206

McMichael sat upright, clapped his hands.

"Wait," he said. "They have him locked up because they don't trust him. Probably brought him from Nam in handcuffs, too."

"If you're right, okay, what about the other guy? Madison?"

I was sharing his excitement, grasping at straws, maybe, but it was all we had.

"My guess is they're keeping him out of the way for a while. I haven't seen him but I wouldn't know what he looks like. There's plenty of MPs around here," McMichael said. "They only need him for corroboration. Saunders is the smokin' gun here."

"Can they do that?" I said. "Keep him in a cell?"

"Hell, no. You know how this judge feels about jail time without proof and this guy is not even a suspect, he's a witness," McMichael said. "Maybe they've given us a shot. Yes, Sir, the bases are loaded right now, let's hit this mother out of the park."

"Wait a minute," I said. "What if they got the judge's permission? What if they say Al would have got to him otherwise? Intimidating the witness? Like the trip to Vietnam? I mean, I know they didn't prove that but there was a suspicion."

"It's possible," McMichael said.

"Need to tread carefully." After the not exactly calamitous but none too successful opening, I was trying not to get too carried away. I wondered if I had time to try again on the phone but I didn't. The clerk of the court came out to find us.

"Back in five," he said.

"Okay, thanks, Marty," McMichael said. "This is it then, boys, second innings."

"That's cricket," I said.

"The hell it is. It's called an inning in baseball as well. In fact, you get a load more. You get nine. That's value for money."

I surmised he had not spotted the essential difference between the two sporting events but this was not the time to debate it. He gathered his papers and headed for the door, giving Al as wide a berth as possible and avoiding eye contact. I went to follow him. Al held my arm, the way he had done when we first met.

"Tommy is a good kid," he said. "Never done me no harm. You want to know why they locked him up?"

"Why?"

"Two things. I told you about the poppies, right? He's addicted to heroin."

So that's what he had meant. I hadn't given it much thought at the time.

"Guess they didn't want him out on the streets in Bangkok," Al said. "Second, he has a Vietnamese girlfriend."

"What's that got to do with this?"

"You're the lawyer. You figure it out," he said.

40

The rest of the morning passed with Soames detailing the outlines of the vehicle movements and weighing in with the charges they had added on, the ones concerning currency manipulation and black market trading.

I objected to every one of these on the grounds that it was fishing. They had no evidence. They had just tagged these on like throwing a load of bait into the water and seeing if anything came up.

"The prosecution has so far provided nothing to back up these charges," I said. "I would remind the court that US soldiers in Vietnam are given diplomatic immunity. They are protected from the laws of the country."

McMichael had given me that one. It wasn't directly relevant because using the military pay certificates to exchange for currency was technically a breach of US rules. The US government didn't like it. There had been so much black market trading in dollars, the Army had been issuing pay in the form of certificates for the last few years. The taint of corruption was not far from all of this. I could open up a can of worms. The prosecution knew it. The judge knew it. But my job was to get Al off the charges and I only wanted to raise the question, so they knew I had it in my armoury and it would go on the court records. There was so much money floating around, so many people looking to skim some right off the top; the turnovers in some of the American stores ran into millions of dollars, it was like Woolworth's Christmas Sale, only in the jungle.

"These are breaches of military conduct," Soames said. He was phrasing carefully.

"Keep going," the judge said. "I can't see what the objection is so you can talk some more, Captain."

I sat down. I had put in a bit of doubt, that was all I wanted to do. Soames moved on to the charges of dealing in electrical goods. Another area where it crossed over into Vietnamese law and should not concern the military. That was my argument. I put it. I didn't have much confidence in it. The judge ruled the charges could stand. I would have been surprised if he had said anything else but I was hoping he would now have to consider them lumped in with all the others. My argument in closing would be that all the charges stemmed from the motor pool and the motor pool was not entirely under the control of Al. That was all I had. The prosecution concluded its opening of the case.

"Lunch, gentlemen," the judge said.

"Before we go into lunch, Your Honour." I stood up. "Might I inquire as to how the witnesses are to be presented to us this afternoon?"

"How do you mean, Mr Benson?"

Soames and Raniero looked down, I was pleased to see, trying to avoid the Judge's eye. They hadn't seen this one coming, they weren't aware we had found out about Saunders. I had decided to get my shot in early, before lunch, give the judge time to mull it over.

"I understand, Your Honour, that the main witness is in custody. Is he to be brought into court in handcuffs and under guard?"

The judge spun round to stare daggers at the prosecution. Marty the clerk and the stenographer waited to see what would happen. It seemed for a moment as if they would have to dodge out of the way as Major Bill Jackson launched himself from his judge's seat to front up Soames and Raniero.

"Explain," he said.

Soames rose slowly to his feet.

"Your Honour, there has been some difficulty with this witness."

"Is he a felon?"

"Not exactly, Your Honour."

"Has he committed a crime for which he has been convicted in a court of law?"

"I wouldn't say so specifically, Your Honour…"

"Then what in God's name is he doing behind bars? Where is he? Is he in my court building? You had better come up with a good reason for that, Captain. I am not going to give you any more leeway, understand? Any more rope and you will hang yourselves. Lunch."

He got to his feet like a geyser shooting up in a national park and spun round and made a grand exit. The band played. It felt like a triumphal march. Soames and Raniero were talking urgently, plenty of arm waving, Soames was red in the face. We could have left at that point, in fact, I wanted to. I wanted to dash back to the office, get on the phone to Betty. But this was too good to miss. They realised the three of us were sitting angled towards them and stopped abruptly, mid-gesticulation.

"Makes no difference, Benson," Raniero said. "You're still losing."

"Luncheon, gentlemen?" I said to my companions, who got up with me to file out.

"You think the judge is going to care?" Raniero went on, pushing past Soames to meet us in the centre aisle. It was clearly his involvement that had led to Private Saunders being held in a cell, for at least one night, maybe more. McMichael stopped further along the aisle. Al was behind me, Raniero was right up in my face. "You won't win."

"You're in the way," I said, deliberately not giving him his rank or title. He glanced behind me. He might have been a Captain but he was only a lawyer. Al was a veteran fighter and I was on his team. He stood, as he always did, ready. Raniero stepped away, jabbing a finger at me, spluttering. The two MPs were watching us, amused, hoping for some action to liven up their day. Soames ushered him away.

"See you later," Soames said, winking at me. He was clever at giving the impression he always knew something nobody else did. Unsettling. He stopped at the door and turned. "Nearly forgot, Benson. You know that filthy Gomorrah you call home?"

"Don't tell me – the good Lord has seen fit to pour down his wrath upon it?" I said.

Soames' face darkened.

"Do not take His name in vain, Benson. Just doing you a favour. You might want to call. See who's there."

Al stepped forward. I edged into his way. Entertaining as it might have been, I didn't want the chief prosecutor with a broken jaw.

"See who isn't," Soames said and went out.

41

I got to the phone first, dialled Betty's. It rang out. Al was beside me. McMichael had left us to it, no longer preserving the sanctity of the phone in the little office for military use only.

"What did that trumped-up Holy roller mean?" Al said, clenching and unclenching his fists in that way he had. "He mean Betty?"

"Probably nothing," I said. "He's just trying to get under our skin."

The phone rang out. No-one was picking up. It was the middle of the day. It was hot. Maybe they had just decided to put the shutters up, settle down, have a siesta. Unlikely. There would be thirsty customers waiting to get a drink and sit in the cool. I sat on the edge of the desk with the phone to my ear.

"Let me try," Al said.

"What for? It's a telephone. It doesn't matter who dials the number."

"You shittin' me?"

"No. But there's no magic in dialling. The phone system doesn't distinguish between nationalities. Or indeed types of finger or matters of urgency."

"Lemme try."

The phone was still ringing. I put it back on the cradle and moved aside.

"Be my guest."

Al picked up the phone and spun his finger round in the dial, tapping his foot. I could hear it faintly at the other end, sending its plaintive message into an empty room. After the first ring, it was answered. I slumped into a chair. A bit annoying but at least we had got through.

"Betty?"

A pause as whoever was on the other end seemingly disappeared again.

"Betty didn't answer?"

Al shook his head.

"Preed. I guess he's gone to get her."

We waited.

"If she's there," I said. "Maybe that's what Soames meant?"

We waited some more. Sweat pooled on the side of Al's face where he was holding the receiver pressed tightly against it. I heard a voice.

"Betty?" Al said, springing off the table. There was a burst of speech from the other end.

"She's there?" I said. Al motioned for me to keep quiet, listening, clearly relieved no harm had befallen Betty, no bolt of lightning had crashed through the ceiling and pinned her bass player to the floor of the stage, for instance, though perhaps that would have been a blessed intervention, musically speaking. Al was nodding.

"What's she saying?" I said.

"Talk to him," Al said, and held out the receiver to me. I took it warily. If someone hands you a phone for a direct conversation instead of relaying a message, it bodes ill. Al's face, as usual, gave nothing away.

"Betty?" I said.

"Mister Matthew," Betty said. Even on a crackly line, her voice sounded as if we had somehow mis-dialled and got through to the place where they taught the sirens to sing. "They came."

"Who did?"

It could have been anybody. CIA. Secret Service. Gangsters. I don't know. The cast of *The Magic Roundabout*.

"Policemen," Betty said.

My stomach slid. Could only be one thing.

"Loretta?"

I could hear Betty taking a drag on her cigarette, possibly a sip of a Martini, and trying not to cause me to panic.

"Two men in uniform. Helmets with MP in big letters. They find Loretta. Take her with them."

I gripped the phone receiver. Raniero and Soames had tipped them off. If McMichael knew about her, then they surely would. Sinking pretty low, bastards. I had been treating them as professionals doing their job. Now they had made it personal.

"Where to?"

"To an airbase, I think."

The one outside of town. They were going to take her back to Vietnam. McMichael came into the room, with a tray, some coffee.

"MPs," I said to him, still hanging on the phone. "They arrested Loretta."

"Who?" he said.

"The girl you had checked out."

"Mister Matthew? Are you there?"

"Yeah," I said. "Yes. Thanks, Betty."

"Are you coming back?"

That was all I wanted to do. Put the phone down. Go as fast as I could to the airbase, if only I could see her, if only I could explain, I didn't deliberately knock the trunk off the elephant, it was an accident. I didn't tell the authorities you were hiding in my room.

If she thought that I had, she would be gone for good and I couldn't blame her. If I couldn't get to her, then she would never come back. I looked at Al. He was watching me to see which decision I would make. If I left, McMichael was the main man, the inadequate make-up peeling from the bruise on his chin. Al wouldn't trust him. He trusted me, though, dammit. He trusted me.

"No," I said on the phone. "I'm in the middle of a trial."

42

The judge stormed in to the sound of a full orchestra. We stood. He waved his arms. We sat.

"Did you tell them?" I said to McMichael.

"Tell who what?"

"Loretta."

"Are we ready, gentlemen?" the judge said.

"Hell, I didn't know she was with you," McMichael said.

"You told them?"

"Mr Benson? Shall we proceed?" the judge said.

I stood up.

"Forgive me, Your Honour."

"You have had the whole of the lunch recess to discuss with Captain McMichael whatever it is you're discussing, though I can't see anything that will be of any value at this point."

That sounded to me like he had already made his mind up. And from the phrasing of it, our side wasn't about to win. It's easy to place too much importance on a syllable, to look for emphasis, try and discern a meaning when there isn't one. It can throw out your whole strategy. Short of standing up and asking him if there was any point in us continuing, I would simply have to carry on. I couldn't tell anything either from Soames and Raniero, who were looking at their notes, ready, as I was, for the introduction of their star witness.

"Captain Soames?" the judge said.

"The prosecution calls Private First Class Thomas Saunders, Your Honour."

"Yes," the judge said. "This is the man you have had kept in a jail cell?"

"That's true, Your Honour, but I think it will be apparent when he enters the court room that Private Saunders has suffered no ill effects, it was merely a precaution and I think you will find it was in keeping with allowed procedure."

"Don't tell me what I will find, Captain. I will find what I will find. I don't need your help."

Soames was taken aback at this rebuke, his footing slipped a little. I kept quiet. I decided not to object any further, to wait and see what would happen. McMichael nudged me.

"You going to stand? Object to this witness?" he whispered. I shook my head.

"Why the hell not?"

"Because I don't want to."

"Look, I didn't tell anyone about the girl," McMichael said. "Why would I? I'm no snitch."

"That's fine," I said. At least, I felt better about having him next to me if that was true. "But I'm still going to let them put this man up."

The side door opened. All eyes turned to the MP leading in Tommy Saunders, who came in looking like a scared child, like a kid who had been told off and was trying to be brave. His eyes darted around the room, blinking in the light. His dress uniform hung off him like he had borrowed it from his older brother and although he had been cleaned up he looked like a sick dog, his face thin, grey. The judge watched him carefully as he went to the stand and took the oath from Marty the clerk to tell the truth and took his place seated in the witness box. Soames came out from behind his desk and got straight into the questions, with his big cheesy, soul-capturing grin turned up to full wattage.

"Private Saunders. Thank you for coming."

Saunders sank his head into his shoulders, hunched up. He looked past Soames towards Al. There was a flicker of something on his face, almost a smile. He looked as if he was about to salute. Soames stepped in his way.

"Sir," Saunders said. "Yes, sir."

"You know the Sergeant on trial here, that's correct, isn't it?"

"Sergeant Moreau, yes, sir, we…"

Soames cut him off.

"You were with him at a motor pool weren't you? That was your job, wasn't it? You're a mechanic, that's correct, isn't it?"

"Give him time to answer the questions, Captain."

"Yes, Your Honour," Soames said but it didn't matter, he had got what he wanted, he had switched Saunders back to the questioning. He didn't want any reminiscing about life in the motor pool, not if he could help it at this stage.

"You were a mechanic in the United States?"

"Yes, Sir, I worked in a shop in my home town, back in Greenville, South Carolina, before I was drafted."

"You saw action? In Vietnam?"

Saunders hesitated. It seemed he didn't want to talk about any action he had been involved in. Soames spotted it but he wanted to put Saunders up as a veteran of good standing.

"A little. Sir. Up near the 17th Parallel."

I decided to step in. I wanted Saunders to hear my voice early for one thing and if I could smooth this over, it might work in our favour later.

"Objection, Your Honour. We are prepared to accept that Private Saunders is in the Army. We don't need his record in detail."

"Private Saunders is a soldier who has seen action in a number of battles in Vietnam and by all accounts he has acquitted himself like a good American," Soames said.

"Then that's all we need to know," the judge said. "Let's move on."

Soames had made his point; I had made mine. Nothing to be gained from pursuing that. I sat back down. McMichael was nodding with approval. I was beginning to believe he hadn't tipped off the authorities about Loretta, even inadvertently.

"Are you going to object to that, Mr Benson?" I heard the judge say.

I had drifted away. I hadn't been listening. I didn't have a clue what I was supposed to object to, if anything. McMichael didn't pass me a note so I stood and shook my head.

"No, Your Honour."

The judge raised an eyebrow then gestured to Soames to carry on with whatever line of questioning he was pursuing. I had to hope it was nothing too important. It had got hotter in the afternoon. So much hotter. I was tired. I wanted to call a halt. I tried to listen to Soames. His questioning was designed to get as much as possible out of Saunders without relying on him to fill in any particular gaps; he couldn't, he hadn't been involved in all the transactions and in fact his name didn't appear on the dockets at all. He was there simply to give an overall view of the activities in the camp, to show that Al had been in charge and knew all about it.

Saunders kept his answers short, mostly agreeing and there was nothing to object to. He had worked in the motor pool. Al was in charge. All the evidence had gone to that and it was indefensibly correct. But all the orders Saunders had been given related to mechanical work. Soames wandered casually over to the table to pick up a piece of paper from Raniero, freeing up some space in front of Al. I glanced at him. He was looking straight ahead. He wasn't trying to catch Saunders' eye.

"Do you recognise this?" Soames said, putting a document in front of Saunders. "The defence has a copy, Your Honour."

I had seen this but I didn't recall any special significance. McMichael found it in our papers and handed it to me. It was a document checking in the arrival of a Jeep, one of a number on the charges, this was US1001.4.

"Did you work on this Jeep, Private?" Soames said.

"I guess. I don't know, I worked on a lot of vehicles, Sir."

"This particular one received new paint on the bodywork, see, here, this is written down, right there." Soames pointed to a hand-written scrawl at the bottom of the official docket which had been almost illegible on the photocopy I had been given.

"What does it say, Private?"

"I don't know, Sir. I can't read it."

"Here, let me help you."

"Objection," I stood. "He can't help the witness, Your Honour. Also, I have a faded photocopy of this and I am not surprised the witness can't read it. I can't read it."

"Don't help him too much, Captain. I have a copy of this."

"Can you read it, Your Honour?"

"Doesn't matter. It depends if the witness can read it," the judge said.

Soames pointed to the handwriting and leaned in.

"Can you read it now, Private?"

Saunders was sweating.

"White. It says white," he said.

"And the signature? Next to it?"

"Al. It says. Al."

Soames took the document away. When you knew what it was supposed to say, it became clear. In the dingy light of my apartment – our apartment, mine and Loretta's – I had not seen it. McMichael hadn't spotted it. He jabbed his pen down angrily, hard on the papers on the desk.

"Objection," I said, standing up. "This is the first time I have been told what this document says."

"I can read mine, Mr Benson," the judge said.

"And this is Sergeant Moreau's signature?" Soames said.

"I guess," Saunders said. I showed the document to Al and pointed to the scrawl.

"Did you write this?" I whispered.

"Maybe."

"And this vehicle was painted white and it was later rumoured to be in the Philippines, this same vehicle," Soames was saying. McMichael wrote on his notepad. I stood up.

"Objection, the witness can't answer that question, Your Honour, and the prosecution is leading. We can't allow rumours and hearsay."

"I am well aware of what we can and can't allow, thank you kindly, Mr Benson," the judge said. "Just be careful, Captain."

"You never saw this vehicle again, is that right, Private Saunders? Did you see it leave the motor pool?"

"No. I mean, it was like the others, it was there one day, gone the next."

"The others? The others painted white?"

"Objection. There is no further documentary evidence relating to the painting of vehicles," I said.

"He might have seen some," the judge said. "He was there. He has eyes. He is entitled to give evidence. Carry on."

"Maybe there was a couple more," Saunders said. "But I don't rightly know."

He was trying to peer around the side of Soames to look at Al, who was sitting with his thousand-yard stare focused on the Stars and Stripes behind the judge.

"You saw them?"

"Asked and answered," I said.

"He just told you he wasn't sure, Captain. Move it along," the judge said.

Soames looked at Raniero, who shook his head. They seemed content with the questioning. Soames had done his expert best to cast Al in the role of the villain. He had also put Saunders at the heart of the alleged criminal activity, without directly implicating him. I didn't think any of the men in this motor pool were unaware of how their lives were being made so cushy. Worse, at least one white Jeep had been driven into pole position. There was a signature on a docket. It said Al.

"No further questions, Your Honour," Soames said. He strode back to his desk, pausing only to give me the full glare of his sermonising grin.

"Over to you, Mr Benson," the judge said.

43

The courtroom was completely still. I was on my feet. It was so silent. I have not known silence like it, ever. I was up to bat. The stuffy air had taken my voice away. I thought I had questions before I stood up; now I realised I had none. I could feel Al watching me. McMichael was twisting his pen in his fingers. The judge waited, eyes on the witness. The fan spun. The stenographer waited.

"You have a girlfriend, don't you? Private Saunders?" I said.

Soames was on his feet before Saunders had a chance to reply.

"Objection. Relevance?" Soames said.

"Sustained. What's your point, Mr Benson?"

That was quickly snubbed out. It was the first thing that came into my head. I didn't have much else, apart from Al's continued insistence he was innocent. There was no admission of guilt. It was a thin thread.

"Forgive me, Your Honour, I seem to have got my papers into a bit of a muddle."

I shuffled some papers. They stuck to my fingers. Saunders was swallowing hard, his mouth drying in the clammy air. He flicked at his hair and at his ear, frantically swatting away an insect.

"Let me just get these in some order. She's Vietnamese, isn't she?"

"Again, Your Honour. Relevance." Soames was having none of this. Anything that took the questioning off track would not suit his case. Raniero leaned across to talk to him as he sat down.

"Mr Benson, I told you the court would give you some leeway. Don't take advantage," the judge said.

"Yes, she is, Sir," Saunders said.

"That's nice," I said. "You don't have to call me Sir, as you can see, I'm not in the military, I'm a friend of Al's. Sergeant Moreau."

"Your Honour," Soames said. "This is a court martial. Not a chat over a cup of tea and scones."

"Get into it, Benson. Up your damn game," McMichael whispered.

He moved his legs aside so I could get out. I wasn't sure if I wanted to. I was comfortable behind the desk. Approaching the witness, showboating in the front of the court, it might have suited Soames the preacher. It might not suit me. But in for a penny, I thought. If I decided I wanted to carry on being a lawyer after this – a career move that was becoming increasingly uncertain – I would be back in English court rooms. Nobody moves from their desks. I might never get this chance again. I shuffled out into the well of the court. The judge seemed even bigger as I got a little closer and I could hear the stenographer clicking away, recording everything.

"The Army used your specialist skills, is that right? You're a mechanic? I have a Land Rover you could take a look at. At least, I had, it got sold, just recently."

"Your Honour," Soames said.

"Apologies," I said, picking my notes up from the desk. Saunders was regarding me with a puzzled frown. He was sinking further into his seat. I could ask him some questions but none of them were going to get Al off the hook. I was going in to bat and I had forgotten to shove my protector box down the front of my cricket whites.

"Been a mechanic long?"

"Few years. Since I left high school."

"Enjoy it?"

"Okay, I guess. I like cars."

Soames stayed in his seat, figuring he had already made his point and the judge wouldn't let me chat away amicably for too long. All I could do was hope Saunders would give me something, anything, I could use to cast some doubt on the evidence. I ran through some basic facts, how long he had been in Vietnam. Ten months. He had a month to go. About his work, what he did in the motor pool.

"Better than being in a firefight?" I said.

"Yes, Sir."

"Objection," Soames said.

"On what grounds?" the judge said.

"Relevance."

"Knock it off, Captain."

"So you worked closely with Sergeant Moreau? It was a team?" I said to Saunders.

"I guess. I mean, he was the Sergeant."

"A lot of work, a lot of things going on, very busy camp, so I understand?"

"I guess." Saunders ran a hand across his chapped mouth, licking his lips, trying to get some moisture.

"So things happened pretty quickly, I would imagine? Take, for example, this Jeep, US1001.4. The one painted white."

I had been struck by a sudden thought. A hint of absolute desperation, possibly, but I was going to do it anyway. I picked up the document from my desk and showed it to Saunders.

"The signature," I said. "Are you absolutely certain it says Al? Could it not be a reference to the condition of the vehicle? Could it possibly say A1?"

"You've got to be kidding me," I heard Raniero say. Soames started to rise and then realised he didn't have an objection. It was a perfectly legitimate question. I was quite proud of it, actually.

"I guess," Saunders said. "Yeah. I guess. A1. Yeah, maybe it could."

I tossed the document casually back onto my desk. I glanced towards the judge but I couldn't tell if he had been impressed or not. I decided to forge ahead, just to leave that little bit of doubt hanging there.

"Vehicles coming in, vehicles going out, lot of soldiers coming in, lot of mechanics, drivers, all day long. The government has been shipping over more vehicles than ever for the South Vietnamese Army, we know that. Busy, busy, busy."

"If there's a question there, I cannot detect it," the judge said.

"Apologies, Your Honour. Do you know how many vehicles came through your motor pool?"

Saunders shook his head.

"Probably thousands, I would suggest. Lines of trucks, jeeps. You were working hard in the sheds, you couldn't see what Sergeant Moreau was doing all the time, could you?"

"I guess not. He would come in, he was always watching out for us, you know?"

"Watching out for you?"

"Yeah," Saunders looked across to the prosecution.

"Don't look at them," I said. "Look at me."

I was hoping to give the judge some reason to think the witness had been pump-primed here but beyond that, I had no route to take. The prosecution knew it. I didn't have a line of questioning I could use. Saunders flicked his eyes around the court, anxious for this to be over, probably feeling sorry for me embarrassing myself. I was about to give it up, sit down. I stood there lamely. Then I saw it. His cheek twitched a little. I was close by. Then his head. His arm. He was suffering. The time in the cells had backfired. He had been kept away from the drugs he badly needed.

"Sergeant Moreau watched out for you?" I said.

"He's a good guy," Saunders said, holding onto his arm, clenching himself up, twisting in his seat. Soames could see what was happening. He started to get to his feet.

"A good guy?" I said. "He says he's innocent. Do you say he's innocent?"

"Objection, Your Honour," Soames said but he didn't say why.

"Not guilty," I said. "Is that right?"

Saunders lurched forwards in his seat, a full-scale meltdown churning across his body, twitching and squirming, sweat pouring down his face. He was looking straight at Al.

"They made me say it, Sarge," he said. "I wouldn't have done nothing, nobody would have done nothing."

"Your Honour," Soames said. "The witness is not responding to a question, he's just making a statement."

"Why wouldn't you have done anything?" I got in quickly before the judge. "Because there was nothing to say?"

"Your Honour, counsel is badgering the witness."

"Let it go, Captain, I want to hear this," the judge said.

"They told me to say it," Saunders said.

"Who did? Who told you to say it? Say what?" I said.

"The men who came to the motor pool."

"Who were they? Secret service? Military police?"

"I guess. They asked a load of questions then they told me they knew what had been going on, that all the other guys had made statements. Only they hadn't. See, I didn't know that. It was a trick. They put me in a jail cell, man."

"What else did they do?"

"They made sure I got dope and then they didn't. They took it away. It ain't my fault. They told me I wouldn't never see my girl again."

"Objection, Your Honour. This has nothing to do with the case." Raniero this time on his feet. The judge glared at him.

"On the contrary, counsel. It has everything to do with the case."

"What's your girlfriend called?" I said.

"Lawana."

"Nice name."

"Met her in Saigon. She loves me, she said so. We're going to be married."

"Congratulations."

"Mr Benson, get this back on track or I will be forced to let this witness go," the judge said.

"Forgive me, Your Honour." I had Saunders on my side. Even the MPs were watching the proceedings with interest now. "These men, what did they tell you to say?"

"They told me to write down all these things. They told me what to write."

Saunders was sobbing. He was suffering but the rest, I was hoping, wouldn't take long.

"They dictated your testimony?" the judge said. "They told you what to say?"

Saunders nodded again. His foot was hammering on the floor, a knee-jerk he couldn't control.

"That's right. Sarge is a good guy. He looked out for us."

The judge turned to Soames.

"Were you aware of this, Captain?"

"Your Honour, no, this is the first time I have heard this."

Soames had decided he would rather risk the wrath of God over a falsehood than the wrath of Major Jackson.

"You, Captain Raniero?"

"Absolutely not, Your Honour."

Raniero, on the other hand, had been taught to lie at Harvard.

"I hope not," the judge said.

"So there is no truth in any of these charges?" I said to Saunders. "None of this happened?"

I was pushing it a little far. It was my big shot, a giant hail-Mary swing. I was hoping Saunders would stay with me. We waited while he composed himself.

"Objection," Soames said. "Badgering the witness."

"Over-ruled."

"Private? Do you want me to repeat the question? Is there any truth in your testimony against Sergeant Moreau?"

He shook his head.

"No, Sir," he said. "It ain't true, none of it."

"Take this witness away," the judge signalled to the MPs. "Look after him. Get him the medical attention he needs. Make sure he is taken care of. I will personally expect a report on his progress."

The MPs converged on Saunders, lifted him carefully from the witness box. He took one last look back to our desk.

"Sorry, Sarge. I'm sorry."

I thought I saw a slight smile touch the corner of Al's lips.

"Your Honour, the prosecution contends that the case is still there to answer, it can't be abandoned on the oral testimony of that one witness," Soames said.

"Isn't that the way trials work?" the judge said. "Your star witness just told us everything he said before was a fabrication."

"We have another witness."

"This would be the military policeman. Staff Sergeant Madison? He's the investigating officer, isn't he?"

"He is."

"Given what we've just heard, are you sure you want to put him on the stand?"

Raniero whispered to Soames. I could guess what it was he was up to.

"Your Honour, can we ask for a short recess?" Soames said.

McMichael grabbed the sleeve of my jacket and shook his head but I was already on top of it, stopping Raniero from sneaking out and tipping off Madison.

"Your Honour, there is no need for a recess. The testimony of the last witness was short, there is time for this next witness to be brought in and questioned."

Raniero was up and trying to move away, to get out of the bench on the other side.

"Perhaps Captain Raniero would like to stay and listen?" I said.

Raniero stopped, caught like a rabbit in the headlights as the judge stared him down.

"You want permission to leave the court room, Captain?"

"Yes, Your Honour."

"Forget it. Sit down. Call the next witness."

"Call Staff Sergeant Greg Madison," Marty the clerk said.

44

It was hard not to feel a self-satisfied glow. I had done what every lawyer dreams of. The star witness had been like putty in my hands, he had almost literally melted on the stand. His evidence had been trashed.

"Good work," McMichael said. "Nice, saw the opening, dived in, put some junkie through the mill."

"Thanks," I said, feeling good about approval from a fellow professional, though he had couched it in a way that suggested I had bullied the soldier. I wondered if I had been too hard on the boy. I felt terrible.

"Poor kid," Al said.

I turned to him, the joy of my little triumph subsiding fast.

"He put you in this position," I said. "Without him, we wouldn't be here."

"Makes no difference," Al said. "You think he wanted to be here? Hell, he didn't want to be anywhere near here. He wanted to be home in South Carolina."

"I just took the kid apart on your behalf. He had a breakdown, he capitulated, the case is ours, it's right there," I said, leaning into Al, emphasising the turn-around. We were winning.

"He thinks the girl is gonna marry him. Ain't no way."

I'm sure he was right in his assessment. Not many Americans wanted to be there. They would all rather be in South Carolina.

Or Florida. Or some other state. Anywhere but South East Asia. And as to the marriage prospects of Saunders and his bride, I wouldn't hold my breath for the wedding invitation. Footsteps behind me signalled the arrival of Staff Sergeant Greg Madison. I could see from the corner of my eye Raniero was frantically trying to signal something to the witness. Staff Sergeant Madison merely marched on towards the witness stand, head up, back straight, uniform starched and smart. He sat down and turned to the court.

Marty the clerk swore him in and for the first time I looked up at the new witness. I realised with a jolt I had seen him before. I couldn't think where at first. His face was familiar but the rest of him wasn't. This guy had crewcut hair. He was immaculately turned out, parade ground standard. I peered at him as Soames got to his feet to run him through the questions about his evidence and I had to concentrate because I was looking out for any attempt he might make to tip off Madison that Saunders had driven a great big hole through the prosecution case.

Madison answered without emotion. Yes, he had conducted the investigation following a Senate inquiry into the number of vehicles that had been going missing, many still unaccounted for. Soames was trying to get this to seem like it was a serious conspiracy. There was nothing I could object to.

"That is correct, Sir," Madison said. His voice was familiar, too. "Following initial investigations by the Central Intelligence Agency, the task of gathering the evidence fell to the Military Police, Sir."

The Senate inquiry was indeed top level, into the cost of the war, which was running at something approaching 80 billion dollars by that point. It had been unlucky for Al. The US Government had been shipping over trucks and jeeps as fast as they could be made, hoping that sheer weight of equipment would turn the tide, that the South Vietnamese Army would be so pleased with their shiny new vehicles, they would be inspired to take some of the burden off the US troops. It hadn't happened.

But while they had been sending crateloads of material into ports across South East Asia, across on cargo planes, some of the more unscrupulous had seen their chance to make a few bucks. Like Al. He had been caught by some flying shrapnel from a far bigger investigation. He was collateral damage. But the prosecution couldn't prove anything against him in a court room. I knew they couldn't prove it, not now. Soames knew they couldn't prove it. Madison didn't. It was my turn. I looked at Madison. He was smirking on the witness stand and I realised where I had seen him before. I hadn't recognised him at first because now there was one big difference.

45

I was certain that the last time I had seen him, he had leaned on my shoulder and told me he was on his way back to Montana and suggested that a lot of people didn't want me on this case and they were bad people and I should be running scared, probably looking for a way out. The big difference was that now he had two arms.

"What the hell are you doing?" McMichael said. I was rooted to my chair and I had been for some time while I ran through my previous encounter with Madison, or Stan Bronsky as he had called himself then. Ridiculous, I said to myself. This can't be the same chap. Good as the US medical services were, they couldn't have given him a limb transplant. Certainly not that fast. It must be a different man. But he was looking at me as if he knew who I was. As if he had read my abridged copy of *Moby Dick*. As if he had slept on my bed! He looked at me as if he thought I should have taken his advice.

"Staff Sergeant Madison," I said, rising. "This won't take long."

He looked around. He spread his arms. He had just given a comprehensive run-through of the evidence and he must have been certain it would stick. Soames and Raniero couldn't meet his eye. They looked down at their notes. I walked to the front.

"The previous witness," I said. "You've seen him before, haven't you? Private Saunders?"

"Of course," Madison said. "I took his testimony."

"I'm sorry," I said. This was going to be very satisfying and there was nothing Soames or Raniero could do to stop me. "You said you took his testimony?"

"That's what I said."

"Surely you mean you wrote his testimony?"

"What the hell are you talking about?"

The smirk fell from Madison's face. If I could have delivered the next few questions while dancing, I would have done. On Madison's head, preferably, accompanied by Major Bill Jackson's marching band. I ran him through the witness testimony of Private Saunders, I dug holes in everything Madison said. I was merciless. Soames and Raniero, seconds in his corner, looked around for a towel they could throw in. It didn't take long. I battered him to a knockout in Round One.

"No further questions," I said, returning to my seat past a clearly startled McMichael, who hadn't been expecting the level of vitriol I had poured onto Madison, I had shown the bastard. I wasn't finished, though. I did have another question. I had several questions. They were questions that would continue to disturb me if I didn't ask them. I stopped at the desk. McMichael moved aside. Soames was already on his feet, declining the opportunity to re-examine his witness. He had heard enough. Madison had tried but he was sliding down that slippery slope all on his own and my chance was slipping away with him. Staff Sergeant Madison, is your other name Stan Bronsky?

"Sit down," McMichael said. "It's over."

Until recently, did you only have one arm?

"Benson, get back to your seat," McMichael hissed.

Were you on your way back to Montana without any luggage?

"Mr Benson?" the judge said. "Is there anything we can help you with?"

I took one last look at Madison, who was already on his way off the stand.

"No, thank you, Your Honour," I said but I stood my ground and Madison had to go right past me in the centre aisle and I looked at him carefully but he didn't catch my eye and by the time we left court, he was gone. I still don't know if it was the same guy.

"I take it that concludes your case?" the judge said to Soames. It was getting towards the middle of the afternoon. The prosecution had no further evidence. If I had to put Al on the stand, I wanted him to be fresh and that could mean a recess until the morning. Too late. Loretta would be gone.

"Should I say anything?" I whispered to McMichael.

"Do what you want." he said. "You've done pretty well so far."

"Your Honour," I said. "The defence contends there is no case to answer. The documentary evidence is inconclusive. The conduct of the investigation has been called into question. The primary witness has recanted."

"The evidence is overwhelming, Your Honour," Soames said. "The sheer scale of this criminal activity is astounding and worse, it is robbing the US government."

"Your Honour, Captain Soames is attempting to try his case again, this time without any witnesses," I said. I was on fire. I was hitting everything to the boundary. We waited for the judge to consider. He leaned forward.

"I am not going to have any more of this," he said. "I have been concerned about the prosecution handling of this case for a long time."

Looking good.

"I have also been concerned about the defence."

Not so good. He was blaming everyone and I knew that Al was there to be made an example of. If he was going down, he was going down for a long time. They would give him a deterrent sentence. They would make sure everybody knew about it and while Al was rotting in jail, his Army career over, others would be dissuaded from ripping off the government.

"However," the judge said. "On the strength of the evidence presented to this court, I have reached this decision."

This was it. The verdict. Even Al had directed his attention to the judge. Soames and Raniero waited to hear if their pleasant sojourn in Bangkok trying general court martials was over. They could be on their way back to doing summary misdemeanours in tents in Vietnam if it didn't go their way. It didn't pay to let down the CIA.

"We have had a number of documents that cast doubt on the legitimacy of the operations in this motor pool," the judge said. "I am aware that there were thousands of vehicles arriving in Vietnam at this time. There still are. It is our government's policy to ensure the ARVN can win this war without guidance from the US. Should anything happen to put this approach in jeopardy, such as the vehicles being misappropriated, it would be a matter of very grave concern."

I knew it. Al was to be made a scapegoat. He was being hung out to dry to prop up the Vietnamisation programme.

"In this case, there are a number of matters of concern," the judge said. "In particular, the item on which the prosecution sets so much weight, the Jeep. Painted white. However, as the witness told this court, there is doubt over the signature."

I couldn't believe he had fallen for that one. It worked better than I could have hoped. A1. Out of the blue.

"Sergeant Moreau was in charge of the operation but was he in charge of its day to day dealings? Has it been possible to decide this without reasonable doubt? I do not regard the evidence of Staff Sergeant Madison as wholly reliable. The testimony of Private Saunders is without foundation. The US government policy is to be applauded and upheld. But above that, there has to be a belief in the rule of law. That is the cornerstone of any civilisation. Each case should be tried in a courtroom on its own merits. The US will always uphold the rule of law."

The judge paused after delivering his last line with a flourish. He looked around the room.

"On the basis of the evidence," he said. "I cannot conclude that Sergeant Moreau is guilty."

Major Jackson got to his feet. Marty the clerk and the stenographer got to their feet.

"What did he say? Did he say guilty?" I said to my companions.

"For Chrissake, asshole," I heard from Al.

"All rise," Marty said and the invisible band struck up *The Battle Hymn Of the Republic* as Major Jackson swept from the room leaving in his tumultuous wake a stunned silence. Marty and the stenographer followed him out.

"Not guilty," McMichael said, slapping me on the shoulder. "Good work, Benson. Congratulations. Now where's Raniero?"

McMichael leapt to his feet. Clearly, there were to be no words of consolation for the prosecution.

"Hey, loser," McMichael called across to Raniero, as he tried to leave along the side aisle. "I want my fifty bucks before they put you on the chopper back to Nam."

"Stow it, Travis, let it ride onto the next case. Double or quits."

"Double or quits my ass, you welcher. Pay up."

McMichael pursued Raniero to the doors of the court, holding out his hand for the money. I watched them go. It was just another case to them. They would be back in their office, preparing for the next one and the next one until their tour was over and they could go back home. Maybe their roles would be reversed next time, the trial of Sergeant Al Moreau soon forgotten. Soames approached. I thought he was going to congratulate me. I was ready to look humble.

"May the Good Lord forgive you," he said and marched out. The MPs had gone, no longer needed. Al and I were left alone in the court room. I didn't expect much. Maybe a handshake. I couldn't wait for him to let down his guard, it was too exciting.

"We won, we won, Sergeant."

I grabbed him by the shoulders. I wanted to hug him. I didn't.

"I know," he said. "Not guilty. Like I told you."

He turned smartly without a word and left me on my own. I watched him march out, the bugger. He hadn't even congratulated me. But even that wasn't going to stop me enjoying the moment. I wanted to be a lawyer again. Hell, I was already a lawyer. The fan spun. I savoured the courtroom air. It tasted just a little bit sweet.

46

The streets were usually full of cabs. I had dived out of the court after my brief moment of triumph, dashed along the corridor, the Lieutenant had thrown me a paper ball, I caught it, lobbed it back over my shoulder in the direction of the bin. No, it missed. But he hollered anyway.

Now I needed a driver to take me out to the airbase, to look for Loretta. I put my hand up to shield my eyes before I stepped out from the shade of the Justice Centre one last time. I scanned the jagged rooftops scratching the deep blue sky with its trails of wispy white cloud and grey factory smoke. I had a thought that a sniper might be lurking there. A shot would ring out and the man who had taken on the US military judicial system and beaten it – me – would slump to the floor.

But there was nothing. A few birds. Some washing hanging from windows. There was no-one else in the whole wide world who cared and that's the thing, we were small cogs in the war machine, it would churn on without us, made up of each little life and death as if they didn't matter. And while I was musing on this and the nature of everything, the one person who might give it some meaning was a few miles away. Handcuffed and sobbing quietly on the floor of a dirty cell to the background noise of bombers and fighters. A few hours ago, I would have swum the seven seas to find her but now I couldn't even get a cab. McMichael stood next to me and lit a cigarette. I didn't give up my search for elusive transportation to look round at him. I still wasn't sure if it was down to him that Loretta was gone.

"Got your fifty bucks?" I said.

"Sure."

"Half of it's mine. You can keep it."

"Your girl's at the airbase where they kept Moreau."

"That's where I'm headed."

"Soames called in the MPs."

That bastard. I knew it. He had to shout pretty loud over the gunfire for God to hear him in Vietnam. So he had struck a blow against a modern day Gomorrah. Rickshaws and tuk-tuks slowed down, I waved them on, they wouldn't take me that far out of the city. Certainly not quickly enough.

"Madison and the guys he works for sure as hell going to be a little bit unhappy about the outcome of the case," McMichael said. "Soames and Raniero are already thinking up their excuses."

I could see a coach and wondered if it was heading for the airbase. I stepped out into the street, waving frantically, but it went past me.

"So, I'd be a little careful stepping out into the street like that for a while."

I laughed.

"If I'd taken any notice of all the warnings, I'd have been long gone."

"Instead, you hung around to clear a crook. That's the law. That's what it's there for. Anyhow, I just came out to say cheerio, old chap, and one last thing…"

He ground the cigarette with his heel and closed one eye and clenched his hand into a fist with one finger out like a gun and pointed it at me, grinning.

"No more the FNG."

He went back inside. I heard an engine growling and coughing. Around the corner came a familiar radiator grille and headlights, the old cracked windscreen. There she was. Large as life. Mary Jane, appearing like *The Lone Ranger's* horse. At first, I thought she was driving herself, like a bigger version of *Herbie The Love Bug* but as she slewed to a halt beside me, I saw Al at the wheel.

"Get in," he said, already switching the indicator to pull out onto the main road. Without thinking, I swung gratefully into the passenger seat. Shotgun. It embraced me like my favourite armchair.

"Going my way?" I said. Al concentrated on weaving in and out of the traffic, blasting the horn, missing pedestrians by inches.

"Airbase," Al said. "You want to go get your girl, right? Even if she just tells you what a sad sack you are and get the hell out of her life?"

"You put it so sweetly," I said. "Home, James, and don't spare the horses."

"I don't know what the hell you're saying, asshole."

We set off on one of the main roads out of town. Al had the radio playing, the rock music station. *White Bird* by It's A Beautiful Day. Great song, I had the album at home. Al had the windows open.

"Where did you find her? Mary Jane. You sold her."

"Hell, no, I couldn't sell this piece of shit."

"You gave me the money."

"Call it an investment."

He had paid me a fee but for some reason he didn't want me to know that. In his weird world of bungs and kickbacks and bribes, that wasn't the appropriate thing to do. So he pretended to sell the Land Rover instead. I wish I'd known, however. I had put three quarters of the money aside to give to Pete, Alfie and Mike, it was hidden under the mattress in my rooms, I could have lived it up. Jesus.

"You told me you sold her."

"I lied."

"You lied? Surely not."

"Hey, I ain't no liar."

"You just said you were."

"Only this one time."

"Okay. So couldn't you just say you were employing me?"

"No, man, I couldn't."

We were stuck. The car was heating up to an unbearable degree and all the time, we were getting no closer to Loretta. I watched Al as he sat with his hands gripping the wheel. I thought I had seen the last of him in the courtroom when he just walked off yet here I was, with him in this oven. He had shown up. I think I hated myself a little bit because I was glad to see him.

"This is getting us nowhere," I said, as we sat in the stationary traffic.

"Be cool."

"I'm not going to be cool. We're still miles away and you're telling me to be cool when any minute she's in the skies gone goodness knows where and she thinks I broke the elephant and I didn't. Not deliberately. I have to tell her."

I yanked open the door and jumped out.

"What the hell?" Al said.

I started to run, stepping over the traders with their goods on the pavement. The traffic started up again, moved a couple of yards. Al cruised alongside me.

"Get back in the vehicle," he said, actually 've-hicle' like it was two words.

"And that's another thing, it's not ve-hicle. It's vehicle, it's one word. What's wrong with you?"

I jogged. It was way too hot to run fast. Al passed me in first gear in the Land Rover. I caught him up when the traffic stopped again. He got out. Horns blared as he ran around the front of the

Land Rover towards me. I stood my ground. I wouldn't be in this position if it weren't for him. At that second, I was ready for him if he wanted to fight. I had seen him in action. He would beat me but I didn't care, I was sweating, I was panicking, all the tension was boiling up in me, we were miles from the airbase, the plane was probably on the runway and I had just won a court case for this ungrateful bastard. He stood in front of me.

"You crazy? You're not going to run all the way."

"I don't want to be in the car with you."

"Why the hell not?"

I was hopping from foot to foot. He squinted at me against the sun over my shoulder.

"I didn't want you to take off. Okay?" he said.

"What? Take off?"

"In the Land Rover. I heard you talking. I didn't want you to take off."

"You thought I was going to leave before the case?"

"I'm only going to say this the one time, asshole. I know I would have lost if you hadn't been there, okay? I don't know much but I know guys, I know what guys is like, I know what guys can do, if I didn't, I wouldn't be alive. I knew you was a good guy minute I saw you."

That must have been so hard for him to say. I wiped away the sweat that was running into my eyes.

"You didn't want me to go?"

I don't know if I would have driven off with Loretta instead of continuing with the case. He had taken the decision away from me. I couldn't be angry about that. He had done it for a good reason. Kind of. A selfish reason, maybe, but a good reason.

"I said I would say it one time. Now get in the goddam ve-hicle."

He walked past me to go around the back to shout and make gestures at the angry drivers in a queue behind. I got back in. We had been blocking the traffic. The road was clear ahead of us. Al got in and gunned the engine.

*   *   *

We reached the outskirts of the city. A spread-out stream of traffic flowed both ways, mostly trucks, some coaches carrying the servicemen to and from the airbase.

"Get my smokes, willya?" Al said.

I dragged my attention away from the rolling vista of brown and green damp fields.

"Sure thing," I said. Sure thing? This had to stop. I was no longer speaking English. It would stop when I didn't see Al again. The thought pulled me up sharply as if he had hit the brakes and I had been halted by the seatbelt. Only there weren't any. Mary Jane was a free-living machine.

"In the back," he said, jerking a thumb towards the rear seats. I turned and fished the soft packet of Lucky Strikes and a Zippo lighter from the side pocket of a bulging sausage of a kitbag, olive drab canvas. I didn't think much about it at that moment. I handed him the cigarettes, he shook one from the pack and lit it, steering with his elbows. The blue smoke streamed out through the open window.

"We was in Na Trang or some such Dang, Nang, Trang place, I don't rightly recall," Al said, looking straight ahead at an agricultural pick-up truck containing a goat. "It was hot as hell. You ever hear of Jerry Mulholland?"

"Should I have?"

"He was my buddy."

The likelihood of my knowing this fellow was slight but I didn't disabuse Al of the notion. I felt I was in for one of his war stories. I didn't mind now. I had nothing else to do but watch the road, look ahead, see the planes in the sky, wonder if Loretta was on one of them. Or still in the same airless cell Al had inhabited, being tortured by listening to Clyde playing Miles Davis and slyly comparing her to the models in his magazines.

"He got hurt real bad. We walked straight into an ambush, I had been with Jerry for six months at this time, he was my point man. Real good eyes. X Ray eyes, he could see right through the elephant grass."

Al saw a gap and slung the Land Rover across to the other side of the road and back in front of the pick-up, causing the driver, naturally, to blow his horn.

"Jerry lost both his legs, they was shredded like raw meat, he stepped on a mine. Dust-off took him to a field hospital, he's back home now, wife, kids."

"That's terribly bad luck."

"You want to know why I sold the ve-hicles?"

"I'm your lawyer. I don't have to know."

"Gonna tell you anyway. It wasn't easy. I'm kinda proud of it, truth be told. Had to pay off a load of guys, my own men due a cut, fine, they deserved it. Paid off these guys in customs, Vietnamese government officials, middlemen, those guys from Hong Kong or wherever Kong they come from, hell, I don't know. Russian, that guy you saw in Betty's?"

"The fellow who's afraid of me?"

"That's the one. Maybe wouldn't test that, if I was you, he's the moody kind."

Al laughed. I think it was the first time I had heard him laugh out loud, like he had found something funny. He was, for him, in a loquacious mood. A free man. Against all the odds.

"Quite an operation," I said, watching the palm trees and the jacaranda undergrowth blur past. A noise in the sky. A stick – they called them sticks, flights of three B52 bombers – took off. We were close. I could see them, great giant things, eight engines, staggering gracelessly into the sky. Uncle Sam's aerial doom. Loaded with bombs, headed for North Vietnam, to unleash them on a people that took the hits and carried on fighting. No matter how high the body count rose, throwing their sons up against the cannons. Bomb after bomb after bomb, no quarter given on either side and no way to win.

"Yeah, I figured there was so much stuff, all for the ARVN, I figured they wouldn't miss some. Gave me a rear job. Said I couldn't lead my company no more, hell, they owed me. They owed all of us."

The sprawling buildings of the airbase simmered in the heat. We were close.

"Money I made, I sent it back to Jerry. I know he would be a hero, all guys who get back from war are heroes, right? I ain't been back for a long time but I know the American people, man."

He was telling me he was guilty. A confession. An admission of guilt. He had carried out the crimes he had been acquitted of, whatever the noble reason.

"I know they're right behind us, the majority," he said. "But that don't give you money."

He had been in Vietnam so long, he didn't know what was happening back in the US and in other countries, he didn't know about the protests and the demonstrations and the flag-waving opposition to the war. He didn't know about the fighting in the streets, about San Francisco, the hippies. Or maybe he did. Maybe he just thought they were a few radicals, an isolated pocket of pinko liberal namby-pambies.

"You stole the Jeep? And the earth-moving machine?"

Al burst out laughing again.

"Man, that was good, that was my best. I still don't know how I got that machine out, crazy. Thing was the size of one of them little houses over there."

He pointed to a farm building set in the middle of one of the paddy fields.

"No, it was bigger! It was way bigger than a house. More like one of the hotels in Bangkok. It was bigger than Betty's place."

He threw his cigarette end through the window and hammered his palms on the steering wheel.

"Crazy, goddam it to hell, it was crazy!"

His laughter was infectious. The relief of the trial washed over us. We both dissolved in laughter.

"And the deuce-and-a-half truck, man, let me tell you about that some day."

The traffic formed into a queue as we approached the guards at the airbase, operating their barrier pole. There wasn't going to be a some day for him to tell me the story. I had that feeling. There was no reason for us to be together any more.

"I guess Jerry never knew where the money was coming from," Al said.

The Land Rover stopped and we queued for our turn. In the compound, Loretta would be waiting, a field court martial for her, a reprimand, back to the war. Somewhere in Vietnam where I couldn't find her. It occurred to me I didn't know how long her tour had to go either. It was a lost cause unless I could see her now and I wanted to explain so badly that it wasn't me who had turned her in. That was important to me, even if it made no difference to us.

"You believe me, huh?" Al said.

I believed him. He had taken the money and sent it back home in a good cause. While he was doing that, he had looked after his men, a hundred guys, kept them safe, fed and watered and returned back in good condition. That's why he believed he was not guilty. He had kept some money for necessary expenses but he had used the rest for others. He had committed the crime for the right reasons so, in his eyes, he can't have done anything wrong.

"I believe you, buddy," I said.

The traffic crawled agonisingly slowly towards the barrier where the two MPs diligently checked legitimacy on a clipboard. We didn't have an official reason for being there.

"How are we getting in?" I said. "They're not going to just let in a couple of jokers in an old Land Rover, are they?"

Al seemed unconcerned. From the road, through the plumes of exhaust smoke mingled with the heat-hazed dust, I could see acres of metalled runways lined with row upon row of fighters and bombers, a hulking predatory mass. Air force personnel rushed around between the barracks and office blocks in overalls and uniforms, service vehicles busied back and forth, kicking up dust.

"Jesus, I mean, what am I even doing here? I can't possibly find her. What's the reason?"

"You don't need me to explain that. Even you ain't that much of a numb nut."

Al eased us forwards as our turn finally arrived. The truck ahead pulled through the barrier and it dropped down. An MP checked our registration against his list and, finding it lacking, approached the driver's window.

"State your business," he said.

"Sergeant Al Moreau."

The MP tapped his pen against the clipboard, then waved to his colleague to open the barrier. Somehow, the mere mention of Al's name had unlocked another door. Extraordinary. There must be more to it than that, it couldn't just be that he was a personal friend of every single serviceman in South East Asia.

"Hold on, who's this guy?" the MP said, indicating me.

"You got a dame here," Al said. "MPs brought her in this morning. Nurse."

"Nurse, huh?" the MP said, grinning salaciously. "Rocky, MPs bring in a broad?"

His companion wandered over. Another plane took off with a whoosh. The queue of traffic built up behind us.

"Yeah, I remember. Real cute cookie."

"Yeah, that's right. Real cute."

There was a pause while they reflected on the cuteness of my cookie. I felt a little uncomfortable with them discussing Loretta in such a fashion but at least they were being appreciative.

"This guy's her lawyer," Al said. The MPs considered this. Al turned a little in his seat so the MPs could see the rows of ribbons indicating his medal history attached to the left of his jacket. I don't know if they believed us but Al's credentials spoke loudly in a conversation like this. They thought about it a moment longer then Rocky shrugged and strolled over to raise the barrier.

"Go get her, buddy," Rocky said, grinning, as we passed by and I breathed a sigh of relief as we entered the main compound. I leapt out before Al had switched off the engine. Crowds of people, men and women, bustled all around me. The admin block was ahead, the obvious place to start. Al got out of the Land Rover, his eagle eyes looking around.

I was walking at pace towards the admin block when I heard a piercing whistle. As I turned, he pointed to a gap between the buildings, out towards the runways. The control tower built up on wooden stilts was to one side and at first I could see nothing, then I spotted a trio of figures marching in single file towards a big-bodied aircraft. A cargo plane or something similar was parked nearest to the buildings on the other side of the six foot high chain link fence. The propellers on its wings started to whirr. I could just make out the helmeted pilot in the cockpit. Two men in overalls pushed a staircase on wheels towards the plane. She was in the middle of the three walking towards it, her hands behind her back.

The men in front and behind were wearing uniform and carrying rifles. They were moving in shimmering light, in slow motion but still too quickly for me.

"Loretta!" She couldn't hear me. A truck blocked my view, a petrol tanker almost drove into me. There was a constant noise, like being at a rock concert in a wind tunnel. I started to run, dodged a Jeep, the driver braked sharply, yelled something at me.

"Watch where you're goin'!"

"Sorry," I said, nipping around the back. The driver's shout had caused others to turn around to see what the commotion was about. I saw Al out of the corner of my eye running up alongside me.

"Matthew," he said, grabbing my arm, pulling me to a stop. He had called me Matthew. I looked down at his hand.

"She's gone, buddy," Al said. I shrugged his hand away and shook my head. I could feel tears pricking the back of my eyes. Loretta was almost at the steps of the plane. I was maybe a hundred yards away. I started to run towards the fence.

"Hold it right there," someone shouted nearby, aware only that a man not in uniform was heading towards the airstrip looking as if he planned to vault over the fence to the area where the bombers were sitting. MPs emerged from the crowds, unhooking their rifles from their shoulders. I carried on running.

"Loretta!"

She was climbing the steps. She had something around her wrists. The bracelet I had bought her. No, it wasn't. Handcuffs, holding her hands behind her, glinting in the sun. She didn't look around, she was halfway up the stairs.

"Halt!" One of the MPs shouted, coming up from my side, his rifle now pointing at me.

"Stop or I'll shoot," another one yelled. I kept running. I thought if I hit the fence hard I could get a handhold on the top and lever myself over it. Loretta was at the top of the steps. If she just turned and saw me, she would know I had been trying to get to her, she would know it wasn't me that told the police because I was there and somebody was about to shoot me but I didn't care about the guns. I could see from the corner of my eye one of the MPs raise his rifle to his shoulder and then a body weight hit me from behind the way I had been tackled in the only game of rugby I had ever played and I crashed to the ground, hit the dirt, breath knocked out of me, skidding along to crash up against the foot of the fence.

"I got this," I heard Al say nearby but he wasn't talking to me, he was talking to the MPs, to keep them away as he let go of my legs and rolled over to sit on his haunches beside me. He was holding up his hands to show the MPs he wasn't armed. I turned onto my back. I could see the steps being wheeled away from the cargo plane. It started to move, to taxi along the runway. I had missed the last few moments of Loretta's ascent. I didn't know if she had seen me or not.

*   *   *

The plane rolled down the runway and disappeared out of sight, turning into a speck as it took off then nothing more than a trail of white vapour across the blue. I brushed the dirt from my trousers. The crowd that had gathered began to disperse. Al was talking to the MPs, standing them down. They could have shot me. It occurred to me that Al had probably saved my life.

"Told them I'd take care of it," Al said as he strolled back. "Told them you was a crazy man. Liked to jump fences. Said I'd get you back to the hospital."

"Thanks."

"They don't need the paperwork. They let it go."

"You could talk your way out of anything, couldn't you?" I said. "Ever think of being a lawyer?"

We walked back towards the Land Rover, people looking at us, our escapade having broken up the monotony of the day, the grind of working on this airbase, toiling to put another squadron of planes in the air, seeing them going, seeing some of them not come back. Short of commandeering another plane, which I had no doubt Al was perfectly capable of, and getting someone to fly us in pursuit, there was no more that could be done. Loretta was in the air, in the wind, gone to wherever it was she had gone. Mary Jane was my only girl. She was waiting faithfully for me. I saw Al's kitbag by her side, his cap on top of it.

"Back to Betty's?" I said but I think I already knew the answer. He picked up his cap and put it on. Despite hurling himself at me and landing in the dirt, he still looked smart, the way he had all through the court case. He took the car keys from his pocket and threw them to me. I caught them, a sharp chance, snatched them one handed from the air. Howzat. He picked up his kitbag.

"I ain't going back," he said. "I got someplace else I got to be."

"Vietnam?"

"War needs me. I'm a soldier. It's what I've always done. Maybe you don't like it, that don't bother me none. World needs soldiers. And in Vietnam, they got kids there, need my help. And I nearly forgot, they sure as hell can't win this war without me."

"Betty needs you more. She told me."

"Yeah. She said. I told her I'd think about it. I thought about it. I can't look after no woman. Hell, I ain't never done that. You think that's me? Running a bar? I couldn't do that to her. I been at war all my life, ain't gonna stop now."

I realised that was how we had got past the guards. He had signed up again, he had relinquished his post as a liaison officer. His name was on the list at the gate because he was booked on a flight out. He was an active soldier once more.

"When I get back to the States," he said. "Gonna be a hero."

"How come?"

"Soldiers back from war, ain't they always heroes? Yeah, that's for sure. They gonna throw me a ticker tape parade because I won them this war."

He held the kitbag in his left hand and stepped away from the Land Rover, out from the shadows into the sun. I considered trying to change his mind, to produce an argument that would persuade him to stay with Betty. I didn't have one. He snapped out a sharp salute. His speared hand touched the peak of his cap, quivered a little and then descended straight down to his side. It looked like the finest salute he had ever given. I think it was.

"Wait," I said. He stopped and looked back but I didn't have anything else to say. He turned briskly on his heels and walked across the compound until he was swallowed up in the crowds, to book in, to find his flight. He was going back to a war everyone knew couldn't be won. Everyone except Al.

47

The sun was setting as I drove back. It would be dark very soon. I had no appetite for the drive. Hendrix came on the radio station. *Voodoo Chile*. The trees were briefly in silhouetted relief against the red sky, the road was quieter, the business of the day almost done. One of Mary Jane's headlights worked, the other one was just a sidelight. It had broken in another part of Thailand, not far from Bangkok. I think that's why the others went home, it was just one more thing to sort out, one more thing to go wrong, we had dealt with enough just to get here.

I wondered what they were doing now, Pete and Alfie and Mike. I wished at that moment I had gone back with them. Because then I wouldn't have felt like my stomach had been ripped out and my heart set on fire. But, hey, I wouldn't have had all this fun, right? I wouldn't have had the adventure.

"Dear Mom and Dad," ran the letter in my head. "You know you said when I left university and I got my qualification and I could work and I should just get on with my life and start doing that and get a girlfriend and settle down? I've been thinking about that. I've been thinking about that a lot."

A farmer making his way home ushered a goat from the road, encouraging it with a stick. The glow from the setting sun lit up the fields. I turned a corner in the road and there was a gap in the trees. I pulled over to the side, onto a flat piece of land and looked. In the distance, mountains shone. In the foreground, the water in the rice fields burnt with the reflection, light greens turned to dark, a palette of magic, of beautiful magic. The tarmac stretched ahead of me back to Bangkok. And beyond Bangkok. I had the wheel in my hands.

"Let's just drive, Scooter, let's just drive and not stop, ever."

I had turned her down when she asked me. The engine ticked over. I looked at the fuel gauge. It was half full. I had enough petrol to get me a hundred miles maybe but I knew I couldn't. I had a choice to make. There was something I needed that I had left behind.

*　　*　　*

The crowds were gathering for the evening as I pushed the double doors open to Betty's. The two security guys greeted me like old chums. It was a warm night, they were sitting outside with a couple of the girls.

"Mister Matthew, hi," they said. One of them was Kannika. Number Seven. She gave me her pretty smile. I thought back to the way Loretta had felt sorry for these girls and she was right but it's where they were, it's what they did. Finding a way to survive, however they can. Liberty. It comes with all kinds of costs.

"Evening, gentlemen," I said. "Ladies."

The band was playing, I could just make them out through the dingy smoke-fogged room. I couldn't see Betty. I didn't know if Al had told her his plans or whether she was expecting him to come in with me. We had left for the airbase straight after the trial. He had his kitbag already packed. I don't know whether he had it because he thought he was going to jail or because he knew he was leaving. Either way, he knew he wasn't going back to Betty and he wouldn't have had time to tell her.

The band had learned a new song. One of Loretta's favourites, Roger the singer must have got them working on it. *Stand By Your*

Man. Roger hadn't quite got the Tammy Wynette vocals but he was working on it. The guitarist was strumming the chords overtime, apparently on an entirely different song. I gave a quick nod to Preed as he stood behind the bar wiping glasses and dived out through the back door before Roger could stop me to ask about Loretta and I would have to tell him she wasn't with me. I couldn't face his look of disappointment. I headed up to my rooms and slumped down on the sofa. Outside, the signs were flashing. I could hear the music from below. I didn't switch on the light but I knew Loretta's suitcase and kitbag were gone. There he was on the coffee table. Her headscarf was draped across his back.

"Fixed it yet, Scooter?"

I could hear her in the room but she wasn't there. The eyes either side of his absent trunk stared at me accusingly, the trunk itself on the table beneath. It had fallen off again or maybe she hadn't put it back on after I had dislodged it the night before. Maybe she hadn't had time. The MPs had grabbed her, pulled her out. There didn't seem to be any signs of a disturbance and the only witness was the elephant so I tried to convince myself it had all been as peaceful as possible.

"What do you say?" I asked the elephant. "What would you do?"

I don't know how long I sat there with him, just the two of us, communicating silently, reminiscing on the short time we had all been a family. A family! Pull yourself together, boy. It had never been that, it had been a brief fling, no more. A postcard, not a love letter.

We considered the options a while longer, we discussed them at length, the elephant and me. I finally made up my mind. I knew what I had to do. I got up and went back out.

There was a figure standing in the darkness on the turn in the stairs. I peered ahead and approached slowly. It could have been any number of people I didn't want to see, most particularly Stan

Bronsky or Greg Madison or whoever he was, the Russian chap or the stockbroker from Hong Kong. Soames. Raniero. I saw the swirl of the smoke from her cigarette and smelt the blend of Martini and Chanel that always announced her presence.

"Mister Matthew," she said and it was as if a celestial lantern suddenly lit up the stairway.

"We won."

She took a deep draw on her cigarette and held out a hand to me. "Moreau?"

I took her hand and squeezed it, the only thing I could think of to do. She knew the answer anyway. He hadn't told her but she had guessed. He hadn't said goodbye. She didn't expect him to.

"Said he was going back to war."

Every table was full. Preed was rushed off his feet alone behind the bar, handing out bottles of beer and glasses of spirits to a three-deep crush. There was an empty stool at the far end, on the corner. Betty led me onto the dancefloor in front of the stage and waved her free hand to the band. The few girls remaining sat around watching. Betty never danced with anyone. The band struck up *We Gotta Get Out Of This Place*. It wasn't a slow number but they played it slow and she held me close.

The waltz steps I had learned at school tripped me up but I kept going and we swayed to the music for what seemed like forever. She was singing along so softly only I could hear and I thought she was sobbing a little. The noise in the bar got louder and as the song ended, she straightened up and smiled and clicked her fingers. Ignoring the crowd at the bar, Preed dashed over with a Martini for her.

"I say, it looks like you need a little help," I said to him. He bowed and smiled and hurried back to his place. Betty cruised away to play the room, swinging in between the tables, smiling and chatting. Al wasn't there but she wasn't going to let that stand in her way, I was sure of it. I was left alone on the dance floor. The singer looked at me as if I had lost something he had loaned me, something very precious. The song he had written had been denied its muse. I gave him a thumbs-up and a smile and he launched into *Born To Be Wild* – on his own, the drummer was playing jazz – and I went over to the bar and picked up a Souvenir of Bangkok tea towel. I stood next to Preed and looked out from the other side at the faces crowding around towards me, closing in, these young men, these children, eager to make the most of their time off. The same faces that would crowd around a village in Vietnam, waving their rifles.

"Okay, gentlemen," I said. "Who's up next?"

For an instant, I could see them in camouflage helmets, in uniform, black-striped faces contorted in rage and hate and anger and fear because that's what they had been told to do, that's what they had been trained for. I took a step back from the bar. All I could see were these young faces intent on destruction and then I blinked. They weren't death machines. Commie killers. They never wanted to do this. They were just, as Al had said to me once, fighting and killing because they wanted to get back home.

I grabbed some glasses. All the time, I was wondering just how long I could wait. I didn't know if she would be coming back at all. She had no reason to. Starting right at that second, every time the door opened, I wondered who would be coming through it and I kept on doing that, every day. If it was the dangerous men, I was ready to dive behind the bar. If it was Loretta, I would be ready to vault over it, to sweep her up in my arms.

There were things to do at home, people I wanted to see. But in the meantime, I could stay at Betty's, living upstairs, serving drinks, and every night when the band had played that final song, go to sleep. And get up the next day and do the same. Dad, I got a job. No, not as a lawyer. Working in a bar.

"What'll it be?" I said to the next man in line. "Whisky? Coming right up."

48

Epilogue

The US government sent me his medals with a short letter. It didn't explain much. It didn't say where exactly. It just had the date of his death.

Two months and twenty days after he left me at the airbase to go back to war. KIA. Killed In Action. The letter said he had named me as the recipient of his medals and they had tracked me down, good of them, I have always thought, considering all they had to go on was Matthew Benson, lawyer, United Kingdom.

I am standing in front of the fireplace holding the picture frame. It's a cold day in the Midlands, the fire is burning in the grate, yellow flames. I like to light the fire early now that I'm retired, I like to look into it as I sit in my armchair with a cup of tea, maybe a glass of Scotch, finest. I have a liking for good whisky now. The elephant sits next to me on a coffee table. His trunk lies on the table beneath him. No-one is allowed to touch it. The grandchildren are admonished in my best courtroom voice if they go near it, tempted as they are. It's the voice I have used in what I like to think has been a successful career, taking over my father's firm, building it up, gaining a reputation as an international jurist, specialising in human rights issues. My area of expertise, if I can call it that, has been in issues relating to war. That's been my life, Matthew Benson, I'm a lawyer, pleased to meet you.

My first case, that's what these medals are all about. I won it. The burden of responsibility. If I hadn't won it, Al would have gone to jail. That's the nature of the law. Four maybe five years in Fort Leavenworth. He would have found it tough, losing his freedom. But he would have done it and he would have left the Army and he would have worked at what, I don't know, been a bus driver? Salesman? Gone back to Betty's? He didn't get the chance to find out. Was he killed by a sniper's bullet? Stepped on a landmine? It's strange but the older I get, the more I wonder.

What it comes down to is this – if I hadn't won it, he would have lived. Every time, every single time I have stepped into a courtroom since those early days and weeks, I have thought of Al and I have thought of the weight I carry.

I hear the kitchen door open and close but I don't turn around because I am still looking at the medals, at my own aged reflection in the glass. She has been out, seeing to the arrangements. There is to be a family party. For our wedding anniversary. I know which song will be played last. I hear her footsteps through the doorway behind me. She stops, she sees me looking at the medals, lit by the glow from the fire in the grate on this cold day. She knows how I feel. We have been married for 48 years after all.

I hear her approach and feel her arms around me, her head nestling sideways in between my shoulder blades. And the beautiful soft voice.

"Whatcha doin', Scooter?"

ENDS

Acknowledgement
by David Hallmark

In early February, 1970, with four travelling companions, I set off driving our Land Rover from my home town of Worcester eastwards to Asia.

By the end of April we had crossed the snowy ranges of Europe and negotiated with fierce traffic on the newly opened three lane highway between Istanbul and Ankara. We navigated the desert roads of Southern Persia to Pakistan and then crossed into India before taking a ship from Madras to Singapore and then the drive up to Bangkok.

I found a job with a kindly lawyer family of Mom Freda and Pop Albert and Son David Lyman and their Thai colleagues – new laws, new language, new customs and new challenges and new clients. One such client is represented by this fictionalised version.

I very much hope you enjoy this imaginary interpretation of the case in a military Court Martial during the Vietnam War in which I was involved as a 25-year-old English solicitor attorney acting for the American soldier on trial. He pleaded not guilty to the evidence assembled against him by a determined military policeman and a confident military prosecutor before a tribunal of three military judges. I was the only one in the court room not in uniform.

It is a story of many parts. The real personalities and facts have been given the unique makeover by the imagination of the Worcester UK journalist Paul Francis.

He has created his own version of this unusual story based on my unique experience.